D

WAR OF THE
NOCTURNE'S WIDOW

**A Novel
by
David
Trawinski**

outskirts
press

Outskirts Press, Inc.
http://www.outskirtspress.com

Paperback ISBN: 978-1-4787-9724-1
Hardback ISBN: 978-1-4787-9766-1

Cover Image © 2018 Matthew Wisniewski. All rights reserved - used with permission.

Brandenburg Gate and Berlin Wall images used under Shutterstock license. "Death of Marat" image from en.wikipedia.org.

Chopin Trilogy Storyline co-developed with Elizabeth Marie Trawinski
Edited by Deborah Chapman

Outskirts Press and the "OP" logo are trademarks belonging to Outskirts Press, Inc.

PRINTED IN THE UNITED STATES OF AMERICA

Dedicated to

Mildred and Lee Trawinski,

*The parents who gave their seven children
everything they needed,*

*For whatsoever they had to give,
it was always given with love.*

War of The Nocturne's Widow
(Love Demands Sacrifice)

Duty and guilt through time intertwined,
Flowers of the tree strangled by the vine,
Only to find its pointed barb shred
Open the wound so recently bled.

Hidden they heal, their flesh slowly mends,
Their scars bear the stain of sacrificial ends,
Concealed from sight, preparing their defense,
To wash clean the blood of mortal men.

A soul sacrificed for the greater need,
In all of life be there no greater deed,
Be those saved forever lost in shadowed guilt,
May their lives instead be duty filled.

Filled of remembrance for the perished soul,
Filled of remorse for actions uncontrolled,
Filled for compassion for the dreams of those wrest,
Filled with desire to complete the vanquished's quest.

No greater love than sacrifice exists,
Surrender to God so another persists,
May they realize throughout their prolonged lives,
That the deepest of loves demands the greatest sacrifice.

Figure 1: The Brandenburg Gate, Berlin Germany

"...and men loved the darkness rather than the Light, for their deeds were evil" (John 3:19)

(Photo Credit: Elizabeth Marie Trawinski)

1

THE MESSENGER

*D*uty is the providence of survival. It spreads through those who are saved through the heroic acts of others sacrificed in great betrayal. The survivor's heart is at first obliterated, then slowly recovers, and soon strongly beats a yearnful rhythm of remorse.This sorrow is seeded at a depth of being which makes its call inseparable from one's very existence. Every attempt to suppress the resulting guilt fuels only a greater need for taking definitive action. The mind can only be cleansed by the winds of justice. Justice can only be served through the act of revenge.

The hush of Christmas Eve lays like a thick blanket over the chilled waters of Annapolis, Maryland. Just over the shallows of the Severn River stands a darkened but expansive boathouse, connected to a massive colonial mansion by only a thin stone walkway that resembled a flowing ribbon as it cascaded down the seaside hill.

Within the boathouse itself were simply three shadowy forms, discernable only from the full moon reflecting up from the waters below. The first was of the graceful flowing lines of a hull of a very sizeable sailing vessel, suspended over the lapping waters. It represented the promise of escape, literally able to sail to anywhere on this world graced with a coastline. All it needed was to be lowered and released, its moorings shed free.

The second form was the smallest of the three, but its lines were also graceful in their own regard. Lines whose allure of symmetry could not be denied, nor the fragrant nectar held captive within them. The beautifully simple decanter of single-malt Scotch whisky could also be said to be representative of escape – but of a much shorter duration. The dark glass of the decanter rippled with an occasional reflection of the moonlight from the tides below.

The third form quieted in the darkness was that of a man, hunched in tension without the least grace in form. He sat in the chilled darkness awaiting news from half a world away. The news he hoped would be that of the escape he most coveted.

In the darkness, aboard the suspended hull, grasping at the decanter of whisky, he sat in uncertainty. All the possessions that he loved were about him - the massive wealth of the waterfront home upon the Severn, the sprawling grounds draping down to the water's edge, and his prized hull upon which he sat suspended. Yet, they weighed on him, like the drowning man being pulled under by the treasures he refuses to release from his grip.

Here sat Jack Trellis in the darkness. The Deputy Director of Operations, or DDO, for the Central Intelligence Agency. He awaited his deputy, awaited the news of his destiny.

He soon heard footsteps upon the path coming down from the house. They did not reverberate in any way, just hollow thuds that seemed to be instantly and simultaneously absorbed into both the dreariness of the stones and the silence of the night. He knew these would be from Ellison Redmond, his most trusted staffer. One of the few with which he shared his true intentions. In a profession of secrets and misdirections, Ellison Redmond had the truest view of the man that was Jack Trellis. And even then, it was not complete.

As the door handle to the boathouse opened, Trellis deftly leapt from the sailboat onto the partial decking surrounding its hull. The backlit moon silhouetted Redmond in the doorway, who tentatively called out the name of his boss.

"Jack?" Ellison half called, half whispered into the darkness. "Jack, Evelynn told me you were down here. I have the latest update for you."

Why I couldn't have texted or called you on an encrypted line is beyond me, Redmond thought to himself, *so I had to drive from my downtown DC loft for almost an hour to come to your majestic palace in Annapolis. All because you are so paranoid of the boys up the road in Fort Meade – The NSA.*

"What's the news?" Trellis asked, as he flipped on the fluorescent lighting of the boathouse. He was now standing on the partial decking of the structure, leaning against a beautifully lacquered teak table used to sprawl out navigational charts. It reminded Ellison of a drafting table, as it was angled to assist in the viewing of the maps of the sea and its dangerous shallows.

"The op in Paris is over. Stanley Wisniewski is dead. We have recovered his body," stated Redmond very simply.

"When?" asked Trellis nervously, although the word escaped on the exhaled breath of a deep sigh.

"A few hours ago, Jack."

Redmond had long before created a duality in his addressing Trellis. In the office or other professional settings, it was always "Sir", "Deputy Director" or often more simply "Director Trellis". But in social or informal settings, Redmond always resorted to "Jack".

Redmond opened the large manila folder in his gloved hands. From it, Ellison withdrew and then placed an 8" x 11" glossy color image on the teak map table. It was the photo of a corpse laying in a tortured position upon a blanket of fresh snow. The tall gaunt figure of seventy-year-old Stanley Wisniewski was recognizable, but not the face. Half of the skull had been fragmented away by the sniper's round. Also, the left hand was visibly mangled as it lay upon the snow. Very noticeable in the image was a Rorschach pattern of crimson around the mangled head and torso of the corpse. The blood had flowed in massive quantities and soaked into the crystalline blanket of snow that covered the ground.

"Where?" snapped Trellis, still gazing at the photo.

"Pere Lachaise Cemetery in the east end of Paris. As you might expect from Stanley, at the gravesite of Frédéric Chopin. Very predictable. He laid lilies on the grave…"

"The lilies were not for Chopin..." mumbled Trellis, still staring at the photo of the corpse. Not expecting a response, he snapped another question. "Jean Paul?"

"Dead also," replied Redmond. Trellis had asked of Stanley's accomplice, who assisted him in both the killing of an Aerospace Executive in Warsaw, as well as Stanley's escape from Poland, and his weeks long fugitive journey across Europe. "Carlyle used Jean Paul to locate Stanley, then disposed of him. We also recovered his remains."

"Where is Carlyle now?" Trellis could not afford to have his sniper apprehended in Paris in the immediate follow-up to this operation.

"*En route* to a safe location in Europe, outside France. Better you not know the details, but he is being moved by our people as we speak," Redmond replied. Redmond was relieved when Trellis did not ask for details.

Jack Trellis' mind was racing now. His two biggest threats, ex-CIA Operative Stanley Wisniewski and his accomplice and former agent, Jean Paul, were now silenced forever.

"We have a team accessing Jean Paul's computers and apartment to assure they are no 'delayed distributions' scheduled to go off," said Redmond.

Trellis understood this to be pre-configured tell-all messages to the press or authorities that would send automatically unless Jean Paul was there to stop them. He was confident his team of cyber-sleuths would find and disarm them if they existed.

Trellis lifted his gaze for the first time from the photograph laid over his navigational charts, arching his eye at Redmond.

"What about Diane?" he asked, bracing himself for the answer that she also was dead.

"This is where things get a little sticky..." said Redmond, awaiting an explosion from Trellis that did not come.

Instead, Trellis simply said, "Out with it."

"Jack, she is missing, but presumably mortally wounded. Carlyle arrived at the cemetery late, and Diane had been conversing with Stanley for some time. So, by the orders of engagement we had given to Carlyle, he tried to neutralize her also."

"Why the *f**k* wasn't he successful?" asked the angering Trellis.

"Carlyle got one shot into her torso. The blood trail suggests she will bleed out without some major medical attention. We have all the hospitals and morgues in Paris and its surrounding areas covered. She'll show up one way or the other."

"So, Ellie, how the *f**k* does a woman with a mortal bullet wound escape from such an accomplished special-ops agent as Carlyle? What the hell are you not telling me?"

Redmond knew it was time to come clean with his boss, who he assessed was about to go into an unsuppressed ballistic rage.

"Carlyle had them both pinned down behind some headstones. It appears Stanley sacrificed himself to provide Diane a chance to escape. Carlyle took out Stanley, his primary target, and attempted to hit Diane as she was escaping the cemetery."

"What a *f**king* screw-up!" Trellis erupted. Secrets he hoped to be protected forever were now potentially still at risk. "How long did they talk?"

Ellison was shorter on the response now. "Well, Jack, assuming Diane met Stanley at midnight, it would have been some forty-five minutes before Carlyle was in position."

"*Shit*! Stanley could have filled her head with all kinds of bogus conspiracies in that time," Trellis exploded, knowing just how painfully real these bogus conspiracies were. "Who else was there with her?"

"Only the kids," blurted Redmond.

"What *f**king* kids are you talking about?" screamed Trellis, almost out of control.

"Sorry, Jack. Diane was apparently being elusive to the field team. We suspect she had determined the role that Carlyle was brought in for. She only took two of our junior operatives with her – Sophie Czystowska, the team's Polish Cultural expert and Emory Hauptmann, a young operative from Berlin Station. They apparently helped her escape."

"What about the *f**king* Brits, Ellison?" Trellis was fuming now.

"I don't follow, Jack," said Redmond. "They know better than to get involved in our ops…"

"Damn it, Ellison, this is critical. You told me at our last briefing that George Chartwell's team was trailing Diane across Europe as she pursued Stanley. Are they providing her shelter and aid? Are they nursing her back to *f**king* health? I want every asset we have on this. Get a story out to the boys at the NSA. We have got to find her!"

Redmond thought for a second. Chartwell was British Secret Service, MI6, and somewhere along the way had become Trellis' personal nemesis. Ellison knew whatever he came up with had to be simple enough to leave no threads for Chartwell to unravel.

"I can float the narrative that Stanley turned on Diane during their meeting and shot her, so our back-up support, Carlyle, that is, took Stanley out. Diane was in shock, panicked and ran. We are trying to find her for her own health and safety. That's a nice tidy tale."

"Get your little bi-sexual ass in gear. I want no stone left unturned. Got it?" Trellis was now livid. The secrets he wished to forever suppress were still at risk of being exposed so long as Diane remained at bay.

"Jack, there is one other thing I need to share with you before I go."

"WHAT?" screamed Trellis, exasperated that there could possibly be more.

"When we recovered Stanley's body, there was a slip of paper in each pocket of his trousers with Biblical verses called out," Redmond said cautiously.

"Ellison, are you going to keep me in suspense all *f**king* night? Tell me what they are..." Trellis' eyes were enraged, dancing like daggers above a flame.

"In his left pocket, Stanley had a slip of paper marked **Isiah 1:18**. I looked it up. The passage reads:

"Come now, and let us reason together",
Says the Lord,
"Though your sins are scarlet,
They will be as white as snow;
Though they are red like crimson,
They will be like wool."

Trellis gazed back to the photograph of Stanley's body in the snow, which was stained scarlet with his blood. A shiver ran through Trellis, an ominous foreboding he refused to acknowledge, but could not ignore.

"A soothsayer's trick," quipped Trellis. "He fears us, so he constantly fills his pockets with verses that might seem relevant, in case he is caught. Tonight, it snowed in Paris, so he picks this verse."

Redmond begins to ask, *"Jack, do you know how rare it is for snow to fall in Paris in December? How did Stanley know he would come to harm? That his blood would stain the snow crimson?"* Instead, he did not. He simply continued.

"In his right pocket, he has a slip of paper marked *John 3:19*"

Trellis interrupts him *"For God so loved the world, that He gave His only begotten Son ..."*

Redmond corrected him. "That's *John 3:16*. This passage is a few lines later."

"This is the judgement, that the Light has come into the world, and men loved the darkness rather than the Light, for their deeds were evil. For everyone who does evil hates the Light, and does not come to the Light for fear that his deeds will be exposed."

Trellis listened to the posthumous message sent from Stanley himself. He became angry. His gaze bored into Redmond, its intensity growing.

Yet, surprisingly, Trellis said nothing. He merely poured another Scotch into his crystal rock glass. Not bothering to offer a drink to Redmond, Trellis raised it in a mock salute.

"Here's to Stanley," he said, raising his glass. "The late Mr. *Vish-NEV-ski* won't be shining any light on anyone or anything any longer."

2

A BORDER SKIRMISH

The rain in London fell stingingly cold on New Year's Day. The driver of the black cab lifted his head through the rolled down window and looked up at the doorman of the posh Mayfair hotel. Not directly in the eye, mind you, but in a disaffected way, just past, into the elegantly crystal chandelier-lit and burnished rosewood lobby of the hotel.

"Remember, driver, Mr. Andrews needs to pick his wife up at Trafalgar Square before heading on to Heathrow," growled the doorman at the hack.

The driver watched as the impeccably dressed gentleman lifted his singular, large kid leather suitcase into the back of the London taxi, refusing the assistance of the doorman. He worked his mirror to nonchalantly watch Mr. Andrews palm a five-pound note to the doorman. As the gentleman settled into the back seat, the driver relished the thought of yet another over-tipping American and a large Heathrow fare from city center.

Aloud, he said to his fare, "So, onto Trafalgar to collect the missus, Guvnor, then, afterward, on to Heathrow – which terminal, Sir?"

"Three, driver," snapped the gentlemen in the back, a slight tension in his voice. The answer came nervously and quickly, with the distinct feel of the question having been anticipated and the response previously practiced.

Slightly tight, thought the driver, but perhaps the bloke was nervous for finding his wife at the square and still making his international flight.

The drive to Trafalgar was quick, with much of the traffic thinned out by the holiday. The usually ubiquitous pedestrian flow was further thinned out by the cold rain.

Soon the driver pulled over to the curb just before the Church of St. Martin-in-the-Fields, across from the National Portrait Gallery. The cab came to a stop, allowing them an unobstructed view into the massive square across the street. It appeared all the larger given the small number of people scattered through its enormous space. In the back seat, his fare searched through the scant crowds peppered through the vast openness of Trafalgar Square.

"Driver – I see her, just there in the crowd." The American pointed, and the driver scanned the unusually sparse crowd for this time of day, but he could not determine to whom his fare had pointed.

Then he heard the American exclaim, "Damn it, she must have her phone off, or its dead." The driver looked in his rear-view mirror, as the fare held the phone up to his ear, a frustrated look on his face.

"That was terribly fast for a call to go through," the cabbie thought, as a wave of slight concern passed through him.

"Driver, I'll just jump out here, grab her and be right back. Go around the square, if you must. I have my umbrella. We will wait for you back here."

The man in the back seat reached down into his bag for his compact American umbrella. The driver thought it somewhat odd not to have had it out from the onset with the rain having been off and on all throughout the morning. What else could he be doing in that bag?

Then he realized he was just being skittish, having read too many terror alerts from the Metropolitan Police. This man was not Arab, nor Middle Eastern or in any manner radical in appearance. This fare had not been picked up from the area of London north of Hyde Park, where the Middle Eastern populations tended to congregate. This fare came from a posh Mayfair hotel, and was traveling to Heathrow. It just doesn't get more standard than this.

As the driver watched the man, umbrella in hand, cross the street and walk into Trafalgar Square, he was unable to set his mind at ease. There was enough traffic to force him to drive around the square, but as he began to do so, he adjusted his rear-view mirror to keep his eye on the man walking across, and ever deeper into the sparse Trafalgar crowd.

He then rolled forward to the light for the turn to Westminster, when from his glance back into the square, he saw the man raise his arms in recognition as he approached a woman in the crowd. The driver's tension eased. He stopped as the light ahead turned red, and the cars slowly crested to stop from their lethargic momentum. As he waited at the light, with only the zebra crossing before him, he again checked his mirror for his fare, assured that his suspicions were merely the work of an overly sensitized imagination.

What he then saw immediately catapulted the driver's tension into full flighted terror. The woman his fare approached looked over her shoulder, as if this man must be addressing someone behind her. As she did so, the posh gentlemen, Mr. Andrews, burst past her, breaking into a full run, ripping across the square. Not in a jogging casual romp, but rather in an excited, athletic full-flight escaping gait. As he turned up his heels, the driver, even at this distance, reflected through the reverse image in the mirror, could see the soft-soled shoes the gentlemen wore. While looking like proper dress shoes, they were nonetheless seemingly selected in advance for just this escaping run across Trafalgar Square.

The driver's every nerve screamed at him, as he sat before one of the busiest signal locations in central London. He was now conscious of every single pedestrian in the zebra crossing inches from the grill of his black top. While the crowd was thin by workday's standards, the driver had now assured himself this was a pre-selected target for collateral impact. The driver, sweat beading across his wrinkled forehead, knew now, no longer a suspicion, but a reality, that his own taxi had been converted into a weapon of terror.

He resisted the urge to abandon the cab and run. Even with warning those about him, chances are they would all become victims of his exploding cab's carnage. He decided to follow his instincts, those telling him to drive away, and quickly. Even if he took the parcel in the back seat with him, he could put some distance between his cab and these innocent pedestrians.

The light had not yet turned from red as the driver cut his wheel hard and accelerated through a narrow gap in the crosswalk's pedestrian traffic, knocking one gent to the ground as the cab brushed him with its sideboard. The startled crowd parted in terror, well clear of the taxi, which shot through at a startling pace.

The driver cleared the pedestrians and then veered through the relatively sparse vehicle traffic, before jumping the curb and driving across the empty traffic roundabout containing the equestrian statue of George IV. After he had driven across its pedestrian paving stones surrounding the statue's plinth, he veered back onto the street and then accelerated through the Admiralty Arch onto the sweet, empty red roadway that was the Pall Mall.

The driver pulled up aside St. James Park after several hundred meters. His heart was racing, his breathing labored. He shot from behind the wheel of the cab, running hard toward the safety of the crushed cinders of Horse Guards Parade. He ran to regain his own personal safety, with each step he waited for his vehicle to violently explode.

He now stood some one hundred meters away, in a silence that after a few seconds of calm solitude turned into heavily thickening embarrassment. There was nothing but the dripping of the New Year's rain from the overhanging trees along the promenade.

Had his imagination, overly heightened by the city's weeks of elevated terror alerts, spurred him into dangerous and unnecessary actions? My God, he had thought, he had struck at least one pedestrian to the ground in his panic. He then heard sirens begin to wail in the distance.

An anxious couple was running up to the cab from the direction of the Admiralty Arch, perhaps thinking the driver's inexcusable behavior had been the result of a stroke or heart attack, or some other incapacitating malady. He watched from his distance as they came close to his vehicle. He instinctively began walking back to the cab, wondering how he could possibly explain his panicked flight. Certainly, the Metropolitan Police would soon be asking.

He had panicked. Was this not excusable? Surely the authorities would see that his hack license was revoked. How would he then earn a living?

As he returned to the taxi, the couple were asking him if he were "all right, was he OK?" More damned American Yanks.

As he pondered his response to the American pedestrians, the calming staccato of the rain draining from the trees was ripped by a violent, fiery explosion, fragmenting first the soft leather bag in the back seat, then near instantaneously the taxi, before consuming the driver, and the two approaching American souls who had only the best of intentions.

3

A LAST MINUTE DIPLOMATIC FAILURE

Brompton Cross is an unofficial but widely used moniker among Londoners. It is here where the Sloan and Brompton confluences converge into Fulham Road, deep in Chelsea. At 81 Fulham Road, in the Cross itself, lies the most unique of London Restaurants – Bibendum.

This Friday evening among the white-tiled Art Nouveau structure's interior, two of the highest-ranking security heads of Western Intelligence sat for an off-the-record conversation over dinner. It was a meeting demanded by Jack Trellis, Deputy Director for Operations of the American CIA. However, the location was selected by George Chartwell, Head of Interagency Liaisons for Britain's MI6 Organization. Their security details dined aside them, but far enough out of earshot to allow for uninhibited discussion.

As he sat, Trellis looked about the immaculate interior, complete with table settings, stylized posters, and remarkable stained-glass windows, all featuring Bibendum – better known throughout the world as the Michelin Man.

The building had been the British Headquarters of the French tire, or more correctly in the British vernacular as "tyre", concern from 1916 until the mid-nineteen eighties. Shortly afterwards, the building was bought and converted into the highly ranked French restaurant it is today.

Figure 2: The restaurant Bibendum in Brompton Cross, London

(Photo Credit Wikipedia Commons)

"Now, this is really something," said Trellis, consciously omitting his usual profanities as not to offend George Chartwell.

"Yes, very elegantly said, John," responded Chartwell in his attempt to set the tone for the evening. Chartwell smirked inwardly as he had hoped he had offended Trellis on three levels - first, the obvious pithy insult on both Trellis' restricted vocabulary and his lack of culinary sophistication. Secondly, his failed adherence to the highest Queen's English. Finally, Chartwell intentionally used the form John of Trellis' preferred name Jack, just to aggravate his longtime professional counterpart and personal nemesis.

"I suppose that to the average American, one is unaware entirely that the Michelin Man even has a name..." said Chartwell, intentionally pronouncing the name "Michelin" in his best French nasalization – "*Mee Chay Lahn*" - just to further antagonize Jack Trellis.

"Don't be so damned pompous, George," said Trellis, now staring directly at Chartwell. He continued in a voice no higher than a whisper, so as not to offend the other diners, "As we like to say on our uncivilized side of the pond, *'One really doesn't give a f**k'.*"

By Trellis' account, the gloves were now off, with Chartwell having fired the first shots. Trellis decided to continue his return barrage.

"But, those of us who have trampled all over Europe - and, by the way, we Americans include your little island empire in the term 'Europe', even if you and your countrymen seem to prefer not to - we know of the vain clinging to miscellany and artifice that you adhere so much importance to..."

Chartwell looked up from the wine list he was intricately inspecting, over his rimless glasses as if he had only just realized that Trellis was even speaking. "Of course, John, no sense in investing one's time in what we like to think as culture, is there now?"

Trellis was familiar with this bric-a-brac with Chartwell, although today it was starting right off the bat. Was Chartwell feeling the pressure of the unsolved Pall Mall bombing from exactly a week before? Certainly, the Queen couldn't be happy with the famous black top taxi's exploding in London, no less on the elegant approach to her own front door at Buckingham Palace.

"Yes, Culture indeed. I am surprised you didn't say historical reverence. *'Nunc est bibendum. À votre santé.'* How's that Georgie, how is my culture now? That is where the name Bibendum comes from right, those old Great War vintage Michelin posters, *'Now is the time to drink! To your health.'* Right George? Bibendum himself holds up a champagne glass of road debris. I think I saw the posters downstairs by the staircase. Hardly cultural enough by your standards, George, but more so historical reverence."

Chartwell looked surprised at the depth of Trellis' French, and ability to muster his historical reference. "Quite well done, John" he said as he signaled over the waiter with an effortless motion of his left hand.

The waiter came to the tableside. "Please bring us a bottle of your best *Châteauneuf-du-Pape*. And as you are here, I will set my meal for you. As an hors d'oeuvre, I will have the *Escargot de Bourgogne*, followed by the Roast Partridge with Bread Pudding and Armagnac gravy."

"Excellent selection," said the waiter, before turning to Trellis. "and your pleasure, Sir?"

Chartwell looked through his rimless spectacles to Trellis, as if to say, "do you need assistance in making your selection?"

"I'll have the Duck Liver Pâté and the *Côte des Bœuf*," Trellis said plainly.

"Excellent, Sir, but the *Côte des Bœuf* is a meal we traditionally prepare for two ..." said the waiter, wanting to clarify in order to avoid any confusion.

"It is what I want," said Trellis coldly. "Did you not ask me what I wanted? So, this is what I want," Trellis said adamantly.

Chartwell jumped in to save the waiter. In French, he said without hesitation, "My American friend is quite used to taking the best portions and leaving what is left over for others. It is somewhat of a tradition in their land."

Trellis understood Chartwell's French, and thus his critique, but preferred not to interject. After all, there was an element of truth to Chartwell's observation.

The waiter walked away somewhat dismayed, but more so pondering the nature of the relationship between these two patrons.

Soon the wine was presented to Chartwell, who ritualistically approved it to the sommelier. It was poured, the table cleared, and the conversation in earnest began.

"George, you are likely wondering why I asked for this meeting?" started Trellis, raising his glass.

"Cheers, John. Here's to the young but hopeful New Year," said Chartwell, taking a shallow drink, allowing it to playfully wet his palate.

"A New Year that has not started well for either of us," added Jack Trellis.

"Whatever could you mean, John?" asked Chartwell incredibly. Keeping his voice low. He removed his glasses to peer uninterrupted into the eyes of his American counterpart. "Are you referring to the lone wolf attack in the taxi last week. You came all this distance to tell me you harbor both sentiments of sympathy and concern for our ability to handle this event? I can assure you, John, that this event is well in hand."

Trellis allowed the air to hang heavy for a few moments between them. He knew George was under intense pressure to solve this bombing and prevent any others that may follow in its wake.

"George, I have come to personally assure you we are *'all in'* on this. Anything you need from us, you have it. Our entire apparatus is at your disposal."

George Chartwell returned his spectacles to his face. He set his wine glass upon the table, and then pulled his hands into a praying tent upon his chest.

"Well, John," he responded, "I must admit I get slightly concerned when you put your apparatus at our disposal. Usually that means the only thing being disposed of is second grade information for which you want something bartered in return. Usually, something of much more intrinsic value."

"Come now, George. I know you must have your britches in a bind. A terrorist attack intended on Lord Admiral Nelson's column itself – only the quick action of that cabbie saved your having much higher casualties than the three dead. Two of which were innocent Americans, need I remind you. You were very lucky indeed, George. You know they won't stop there. There will be another attack. You can count on it."

The conversation was suspended as the appetizers were served. Chartwell, using the miniscule seafood fork, focused on spearing his first prey of escargot and extracting it from its protective enclosure.

Half raising it to his mouth, he paused, only to say, "John, I am not sure of whom you mean by 'they'. You know our mister Andrews was an American."

Chartwell slipped the garlic delight into his mouth, awaiting a bombastic response from Trellis, something to which he was accustomed. When the response came, it was quite measured.

"Well, George, our unnamed *'they'* indeed intended that Mr. Andrews would be *perceived* as an American. As I am quite sure you are aware by now, the passport he gave to the hotel was a complete hoax. A very good one, mind you, but not registered anywhere in our database. Further, my team assures me there is no record of any Mr. Andrews attempting to enter your country using it, or any other passport. In fact, if my information is valid, you have nothing at all in your records on Mr. Andrews. So, from where I sit, our sympathy be damned, you most definitely need our help."

As usual, George Chartwell thought Trellis was sure he had the best information that money could buy. Despite all the politicians' wrangling over the US National Debt, their most abundant intelligence asset was money.

Chartwell watched aghast as Trellis spread his pâté across a toast point with the panache of preparing a peanut butter sandwich.

"Yes, Jack, as usual, you have condensed a very complex situation down to its basest elements. There is one thing that your listening posts may not have picked up, is that Trafalgar square was not the intended target, dear friend. Likely our driver would have been blown sky high, then and there. No, it appears, the bag of explosives had a timer in the back seat, only for the occasion if the cab did not reach its true intended target. Near the Victoria Monument outside Buckingham Palace, we found a proximity triggering device hidden there. Had our driver not pulled over on the Pall Mall, relatively vacated as it was in the rain, he would have driven on, and the device would have triggered the bomb in front of Buckingham Palace. Immediately after the Changing of the Guard, mind you. One would presume our Mister Andrews selected the drop-off spot, hoping to spook the driver into frantically driving down the Pall Mall, and past the Palace. There, the blacktop would have exploded amidst the tourist crowds. Never fails to amaze me how the world over criticizes our monarchial traditions for having no functionality, yet even in the rain, large groups of tourists assemble for the Changing of the Guard. Admittedly, I digress. Back to our compassionate driver, he did indeed stop along St. James Park, however, and the back-up timer in the bag eventually went off. So, we are very notably indebted, forevermore, to that brave, but alas, deceased driver."

Jack Trellis, swallowing his pâté, paused, all the while listening intently to George Chartwell's ramblings.

"Hardly, a simple lone wolf attack of a home grown radical," Trellis said flatly, making his earlier point.

"Actually, quite sophisticated. I have more details I can share with you in the proper confines, not here certainly. Problem is with your primary liaison officer gone missing, we find our communication channels somewhat hampered."

"Well, George, that may be an area we can discuss further. This may indeed turn itself into the proverbial win-win situation," stated Trellis, noting his dinner companion's confused look.

"Odd," said Chartwell, glancing away from his escargot, "I don't recall a single culture's proverbs that bring to bear the term 'win-win'. No, I believe that concept is almost entirely an American justification for 'I will let you win provisionally, so long as I win outright.' Yes, thoroughly American, I would say."

"Diane, George. We need to find Diane," said Trellis, cutting to the point.

"Good me, I thought you considered her lost in that ghoulish incident in Pere Lachaise Cemetery the night of Christmas Eve. As I read the report, she was shot by that retired agent you were in the process of apprehending. Diane Sterling, dead at the scene – yes, that is precisely what I read. You were rather fortunate to have had that sniper in place. One would rather think with that amount of horsepower, you could have protected Ms. Sterling adequately."

Trellis stared icily at Chartwell. He had just been reciting, verbatim, the preliminary report, approved by Trellis, himself, from the incident in Paris two weeks ago. Diane Sterling, the most accomplished hunter of men in the CIA, was lost apprehending a criminal she had chased across Europe. Yet, both men knew this to be a lie.

"Fact is, we never recovered her body," said Trellis, gesturing with his open palms, as if to say, *"There, it is out in the open."*

"We had evidence of a substantial blood trail, her blood trail, that led to a street adjacent to the cemetery," Trellis added further.

"Therefore, you presume she survived and escaped in a vehicle?" asked Chartwell.

"Knock it off, George. With the amount of blood we followed, there is no way she survived without some significant medical care." Trellis stared hard into Chartwell's eyes. "Transfusions, for sure. She disappeared from Paris, along with her two assistants. Neither the French nor *us* can turn up any trace of her."

"*We...*" said Chartwell, almost reacting by instinct.

"*We* what, George?"

"Neither the French nor *we* could turn up any trace..." Chartwell corrected Trellis' English with a snobbish delight.

"*F**k you*, George. I know you have her stashed away somewhere. I know your man Devereaux was trailing her across Europe, and I know she ran to him one night in Paris. I want to know where Diane is now. Don't make me start playing hardball, George."

"Now, John, what happened to your proverbial *win-win* that you dangled like such a shiny ornament just a few moments ago?"

Chartwell was affecting the facade of an unthreatened innocent, though he knew he himself was neither innocent nor unthreatened. He knew just how dangerous Trellis could be...

"Fact of the matter is that I have information that you could definitely use in catching your Pall Mall Bombers. When you come to your senses, call me. You will give me what is already mine, and I will allow you to go from feckless espiocrat to Sherlock *F**king* Holmes. I am leaving now, enjoy your roast partridge and Armagnac sauce.'

"John, what shall we do with your double portion of *Côte des Boeuf*?" teased Chartwell, having already angered Trellis.

"George, you take the best cut, leave the rest for your minions, and while you're at it, I hope your fat English *arse* chokes on it. It will be a better option for you than what's coming your way."

4

REBIRTH OF A WAYWARD SOUL

She felt the heavily laden sensation of floating through an immiscible oil, dense and warm, yet lethargically immobile. Her arms and legs resisted all attempts by her mind to control them. They were not restrained but bound by an exhaustion pervasive throughout her being. She seemed to both float and sink at the same moment, as if caught in a weak but constant current that swept her along, all the while nurturing her in an unaccustomed comfort. In the slowed motion that was her mind's eye, indiscreet shapes, moving like vapor, seemed to take form as if figures walking out of a dense fog. It was then that she realized she was conscious, but not yet fully awake.

This was Diane Sterling's first realization of existence. Not of a renewal of the existence that she once led, but more so a new consciousness, unburdened by the shadows and weights of the past. In her, a spark was now growing into a flaming desire to interact with the world she sensed around her. Yet the weight of her comfort, her numbness, shrouded her from all that existed outside the bubble of awareness that was her self-being.

Diane fought to move her limbs, but still the heaviness of her arms, her legs denied her a response. Beyond the floating, sinking cocoon of delirium and comfort, the first sensation that she experienced was the tip of her tongue probing at the dry, cemented seal of her mouth's lips. Her tongue, exploring the crusted seam and then returning to the moisture of her mouth, sent amplified ripples with every probe that tore through the sedated state she was emerging from. Through the fog and haze of her consciousness, the nerves of her tongue screamed in their direct intensity, "I am not dreaming, I exist, this is real."

Diane now focused on the task that she feared, but nonetheless knew she had to perform to confirm her very existence. With a very focused effort, Diane Sterling commanded her eyes to open fully, to look upon the world around her. At first there was no notable response. Her eyelids, like the rest of her body, floated with her. She knew they were there, she could feel them, but all attempts to coerce them to move were futile.

Diane was now frustrated, but for the first time felt the remembrance of determination. She focused her thoughts to nothing else but opening her right eye. She sensed the energy drain from every aspect of her being, until the tension in her eyelid was palpable. The eyelid seemed to unfurl one eyelash after the other, as a seamstress would rip the stitches of a pocket sewn shut.

Her eye opened slowly onto the darkened room, soon followed by her other eye, obeying her newly found authority. The first realization that Diane sensed was not that of the person sitting by her bedside, but of the seam of brilliant light at the end of the room. It called her from her lethargic state, its brightness and purity creasing the darkened interiors at the gap between the room's heavy curtains.

As her eyes adjusted from the bright seam of sunshine to search the dim interior of her room, she came to understand that beside her was another person, and that brought an unexpected response of security. Diane eye's looked at the form that sat by her side, stilled blurred in formlessness by her lack of acuity.

Slowly the image came into a darkened but increasingly sharper focus. The beautiful, straight blond hair, the pure milk white skin, the innocence of the young girl's facial countenance. All was familiar to Diane, but she was unable to define the person. The face that she recognized, but could not name, now looked upon her.

Diane could sense the form of the sitter next to her was exhausted. Not through physical exertion, but rather from the prolonged tension and tedium of continually propping her highest hopes against her deepest fears.

The sitter's shimmering hope of a miraculous awakening wore heavily, grinding against her darkest terror – loss. Loss of yet another human life, loss of her friend, and loss of everything accomplished since that human life had entwined in friendship with her own.

Diane could sense the sitter soon realized the dormant eyes she had been praying over for so long had come to life, and were for the first time gazing back, albeit weakly, at the prayerful companion's own face.

Diane innately sensed this all, even as she pulled herself, seemingly one muscle at a time, out of the depths of the medically induced comma that was initiated as a last-ditch effort to prevent her very expiration. Diane watched as the face of her sitter, whose eyes caught her own with the tension of a fingered trigger, suddenly exploded with the broad smile that on any other person would appear understated. The creases in the corner of the sitter's smile were warm and round and sang out through the utter silence of the moment the physical definition of the word "Joy".

Then, like a treasure pulled from a great depth of the sea, the shrouding waters drained from her remembrance, and Diane struggled to parse her first single word, *"Zosia"*.

5

ONSET OF HOSTILITIES

Two weeks had passed since Diane Sterling's re-awakening. George Chartwell sat in front of the fireplace in his London townhome's drawing room. The two high-backed leather wing chairs sat astride the flickering fire, its flames dancing in muted reflection in the beautiful leather bindings of the books gracing the shelves surrounding him. Here he routinely sat, evolving his strategies to protect his country's future from within the comfortable cocoon of its imperial past.

The impressive library sets that surrounded him were what one would expect from any Englishman of his age and position. Churchill's *History of the English-Speaking Peoples* and *Life of Marlborough* complemented by his triumphant history of the Second World War, sat centered on the bookshelf above the fireplace alongside a small bust of the author. Their bindings were matched in a robust reddish-brown Moroccan leather bearing the heraldic lions that Churchill had adopted as his family emblem. Elsewhere in the room were equally impressive bound sets of Hume's *History of England*, Jesse's *England Under the Stuarts*, Carlyle's *The French Revolution* and Gibbon's *History of the Decline and Fall of the Roman Empire*. In this room, among these hundreds of beautiful and valuable books lay the seeds of George Chartwell's strongest convictions – that the world outside his door was tenuously only steps away from collapsing into chaos and disorder.

"So, my friend, it has been a fortnight since your princess has awakened from her slumber. Of what great insights are we now enlightened? Cheers," Chartwell said to his guest in the opposing wing chair. Chartwell raised his cognac as if punctuating the question.

Malcolm Devereaux raised his cognac, carefully beginning his response to his superior, who he knew was very much at personal risk, having authorized the operation to rescue and convalesce the CIA agent Diane Sterling without the knowledge nor consent of his own supervisors.

Malcolm had just returned from Diane's side while she recovered at the Brit's safe location, a Swiss chalet overlooking *Lago Maggiore*. The lake straddled northern Italy and southernmost Switzerland in the recess between both countries' shared border mountains, which then climbed ambitiously to become the Alps.

"Yes, of course. Cheers. Well, Sir, Diane has been through a very traumatic ordeal. To speak without the slightest hesitation, I really did not think that she would pull through that night in Paris, even with the emergency care we provided her. The wound to her torso was severe. The damage surely would have killed one not so strong-willed as herself. Remarkable really that she pulled through at all."

Chartwell's pudgy hands grasped the crystal snifter containing his beloved cognac.

"Yes, Malcolm, we have discussed this before – the remarkable constitution of our dear Diane. However, this was already known to us through her years as serving as the Agency's primary liaison to our little family, was it not? Diane is Diane, plainly said, and no other in their service could have earned our respect as she has. How possibly could they? *'The Huntress – there is not the man alive she could not bring down'*. Isn't that the appellation they had given her?"

"Yes, yes, quite right," chimed in Devereaux, giving free rein to his superior's verbal discourse.

George Chartwell inspected the fire's flame through the tawny orange lens of his cognac. Its flicker licked in tones of maroon, ochre, crimson and amber. His thoughts had deeper, less playful hues.

Chartwell had plenty of time to assess where this endeavor might derail, and how his nemesis, Jack Trellis, might plant his seeds of sabotage.

"Malcolm, one did not have to be a psychic to see that Trellis would use her to track down the criminal, Stanley Wisniewski, only to have his wolves devour them both. Now, however, and thanks very much to the prowess of our homeopathic minders, she has cleared the hurdle and returned to consciousness. All reports have been that her health improves with each sunrise. I believe you have commented no less in your reports to me directly."

"Yes, precisely so, Sir," began Devereaux in response, "if one limits that prognosis to Diane's physical health. Her wounds heal, her systems stabilize in a lovely manner. Where she lacks recovery is in the cognitive functions – most noteworthy her memory. She has difficulty recalling the events of that dreadful night. It is as if her mind is blocking out the fact that the only real family she has ever had – the CIA – attempted to totally eradicate her life. It is as if it is too painful for her to bear, as if her entire career, indeed if not her life to this point, was for nothing. It is too much for her in her weakened state to accept."

Chartwell now cradled his cognac in both hands held close to his chest. His nose sifted through its aromatic vapors as his mind sifted through his protégé's insights.

"Yes, my Malcolm, how very convenient for her not to recall the details of her discussions with her Mr. Wisniewski that night. She is safely hidden by us from those who wish to literally destroy her. In fact, whilst she possibly possesses the secrets that my friend Jack Trellis desires so desperately to die, Diane is very ably protected by ourselves from the most powerful intelligence agency in the world. Perhaps her acuity is not degraded, but she prefers only to prolong her stay under our protection?"

Malcolm had been with her for over a week, having raced back to the chalet upon the news of her regaining consciousness. He sensed the trauma in her. He had long known Diane as a strong, vibrant woman, independent and, on occasion, willfully stubborn in her convictions.

The woman that had awakened from this trauma was but a mere child, needy of attention, coddling and security. He knew Diane well enough to know this was no act. Something inside her was keeping her from regaining those attributes he had always so respected – her inquisitive perception, her balanced analysis, her emotional maturity.

"Yes, I can see that it would be to her benefit to feign these symptoms," began Devereaux, "but Dr. Alec is convinced that her memory loss is real, and likely will not improve until she begins to feel more stable and secure physically. His assessment is that we need to tread very carefully, or we may never get the Diane we know back at all. He fears that the courageous and independent woman we have come to respect for all her brilliance and persistence may remain the emotional wreckage we are seeing today. I suppose we could open the prognosis to our medical team at-large, but I had rather thought it prudent to limit access to Diane to Dr. Alec alone. We both hold him in the highest regard and trust his discretion. It has never been questioned in the past."

Dr. Alec Rushe was the only medical professional within MI6 to have been given access to the chalet. He was as highly praised for his ability to keep a secret as he was for his ability to treat both body and mind. He had been resident at the chalet from Diane's first arrival there in early January. His careful tending to her body's needs stabilized her physical injuries. Now he gently persuaded her to heal her own psychological wounds. Diane had become very dependent on him, and he had become very attached to her emotionally.

Chartwell's brow furrowed with the thought of the possibility of letting additional service medical personnel access to their greatest of secrets.

"Well, I should certainly hope, for Diane's sake, that her memory returns. I need not tell you that this entire exercise in the recovery of Madame Sterling is unsanctioned by our Service. I am, as the Americans say, *'out on a limb'* on this endeavor. If not for the Pall Mall Bomber episode, the government would be wholly consumed with investigating Trellis' complaints of our interference in our cousin's affairs. The Members of Parliament are already inquiring with regards to the American's entreaties. All the whilst, Trellis continues to insist he has something with which to bargain – information on the Pall Mall Bomber, in exchange for our admitting our guilt, and turning over Miss Sterling."

With this last statement, Chartwell smirked and lifted his cognac to his pursed lips.

"All Diane can remember," offered Devereaux, "is that she lay shot in the snow. She has no recollection of that dreadful cemetery. She remembers the blood and pain from her shoulder wound. She doesn't remember Stanley Wisniewski at all, or perhaps effects to not remember. Dr. Alec insists her mind is blocking the memory of Stanley, and his horrific death, in order to protect herself. He says that eventually, something will trigger her conscious self to recall the complete ordeal. It will jar loose the memories of Stanley's death, and of her own near-death, to the surface. This could be a truly traumatic moment for her, he insists."

"Well right she may be to suppress those memories," observed the bespectacled George Chartwell. "Trellis clearly had given the order to kill one of his own, and it can only be for fear of what may have been passed to her by the now departed Mr. Wisniewski. You had better soon help her recall what secrets 'her Stanley' may have shared with her. Or I shall perhaps be forced by my superiors, once they discover our little clandestine enterprise, to trade her for whatever information and insights Jack Trellis purports to have on the bomber that the public and Parliament so direly want caught."

"Trellis has nothing, and we both know that," protested Malcolm abruptly. "The bomber is dead. You yourself sanctioned the operation to track and kill him. I thought it bloody courageous of you to take him on French soil, even without the DGSI being consulted."

George Chartwell found pleasure in recalling the lightning strike of an operation to kill the mysterious "Mr. Andrews". He had left a broad wake in fleeing to Southampton, and then across the Channel to ultimately come to hide along the French Atlantic Coast. MI6 had sent a small para-military team of former SAS commandos to dispose of him within the week. They had to move fast, before "Mr. Andrews" decided to relocate himself once again. Therefore, there was no time for notification or to gain the co-operation, let alone the permission, of the French Intelligence Service *Direction Générale de la Sécurité Intérieure*, or DGSI.

"Yes, of course we both know that Trellis has nothing to offer," stated George Chartwell, "for he is not aware that we have already taken-out the little bugger. However, outside of our little niche, no one can be aware of that fact. Can't be, for the French will become apoplectic. If there is one action that any Western country will not tolerate is another nation's services - even allies, mind you - running headhunting operations on their soil without their approval and co-operation. The DGSI is still railing at the Cousins for that ruckus in Pere Lachaise Cemetery on Christmas Eve. No, the French must not find out we took Mr. Andrews on their soil. Therefore, the public can't know we caught the Pall Mall bomber. Even our Parliament cannot know, given their long-standing status as a leaky ship."

Malcolm Devereaux interrupted him as his superior paused to draw a breath. "Yes, but the PM and the Palace are aware?"

"Only the Prime Minister and Her Majesty. None of the Palace staff. Too risky to let the seam out that far. The Chief of Service personally told Her Majesty we would soon enough devise a manner in which to make it public that the Pall Mall Bomber is dead. I have some ideas on that I will soon share with you. However, before we can take that step, we must deal with Jack Trellis, I fear."

"So, are you are concerned that Jack Trellis will be tempted to reach out directly to the Parliament?" asked Devereaux.

"Oh, heavens, no. No, he would never be so direct. He will bypass our service altogether. Instead, he will continue to work through his DCI, who will attempt to sway their President, who will pressure our PM on the matter. He will attempt to outflank our Chief of Service entirely."

Devereaux could see the concern register on Chartwell's face. "The Cousins have been out to displace our Chief for some time, haven't they?"

"Years, Malcolm. Ever since he refused to - what is it they say? Oh yes – 'go to bat' for the Cousins when their cyber tools were hacked. Their DCI has no love for our Chief of Service. None the less, we will be forced to play their game. Of course, the PM knows we nailed the Bomber, but we can't publicly say so, can we? Not just yet. Instead, we are forced to play act that we need Trellis' assistance. All the whilst, the Americans are in our knickers, searching for any trace of the damsel-in-distress that is Diane. Once the Cousins sniff the trail of our harboring of Miss Sterling, they will force the Chief of Service to direct me to turn her over. Then, not only will Diane be lost to us, but so will the secrets I am sure she harbors, at this point if only in her subconscious. Thus, any leverage they could afford us over Jack Trellis will be permanently compromised."

Devereaux was troubled by the snare in which they had become entrapped. The mere ruse by Trellis of being able to offer information to catch the Pall Mall bomber could eventually force them to turn Diane over to those who would surely finish the job and quiet her forever.

Devereaux could feel the contempt for Trellis that emanated from George Chartwell. It consumed him.

Malcolm's mind then instantaneously drank of a vision of Diane's smiling laugh over tea in the St. Ermin hotel, as Devereaux had just referred to his superior as King George the *fith*.

"*F**ked* in the head, Darling. No typo," he had said to her ages ago. "Remember, that is our little secret. Just you and me. *King George* would not see the humor, I suspect."

Or something to that effect. He wondered if he would ever again enjoy the wit and acumen of the woman who had been brought to him in such a butchered, shattered state below the steps of *Sacré-Cœur*. The woman Malcolm desperately wished to regain her former status as the brightest star in the constellation that was known to them as "the Cousins". The woman that he, Malcolm Devereaux, admired.

Malcolm knew that his *King George* had only allowed the

medical recovery of Diane in the hope of gaining the secrets by which he hoped to take down his inter-agency rival.

"Then, I am compelled to return to the lake, and extract from it the treasures you seek," Devereaux said dramatically to his mentor.

Chartwell sipped his cognac. He seemed lost in his concern over the possible futures that lay before them both.

"Yes, Malcolm, very well. Just be cognizant that both our prospects weigh heavily on the quality of the gems you pry loose."

6

PROBING ENEMY DEFENSES

"**S**o very kind of you to join me here in my office, Deputy Director Trellis," said Paul Renard. He was the congressional investigator assigned to review the entire Stanley Wisniewski affair, which was now codenamed *Operation ALBATROSS.*

The room was a modern mix of etched glass and anodized aluminum, far from the walnut and mahogany that Trellis was expecting. Trellis sat at the beveled glass conference table that seemed like a translucent highway leading to the inspector's desk. The entire office was visually transparent, with the main interior wall separating it from Renard's staff bearing no curtains available to draw. It was designed to send the message, *no place to hide your secrets, so let's get everything out in the open.*

"How could I possibly turn down such an impressive invitation?" Trellis said with appropriate sarcasm. "Have you worked with Senator Malinski in the past, Inspector Renard?"

"Come, now, Jack, let's dispense with the formalities. You don't mind my calling you Jack, do you? Deputy Director Trellis is such a mouthful, isn't it? No, you call me Paul. Besides, Inspector Renard sounds so *Pink Panther-ish, n'est pas*?"

"OK, Paul, have you worked for Senator Malinski in the past?" Trellis asked a second time.

"Jack, you have the capabilities of the entire CIA at your

disposal. Am I to believe you did not research my background before our appointment? Given that you already know the answer to the question you ask, I might suppose you are just attempting to consume our limited time together – a sort of running out the clock? I will only say that Senator Malinski was extremely irate that a voter from her state, let alone from her district when she was a congresswoman, could not be brought in alive to face justice for his *alleged* crimes abroad."

Trellis thought to himself, *alleged my ass*, Paul. In cold blood Stanley shot dead the best contact I have ever had within the Defense Industry. Stanley deserved the bullet he later caught with his forehead, the bastard! He should have stayed in that cozy retirement we allowed him to have. So what if it was Senator Malinski that was once the Maryland congresswoman who gave him his full scholarship to Loyola College? So what if they are both from the same Baltimore neighborhood of Fells Point? So what if they are both Polish-Americans, and they both went to the same Polish-American church and school, *St. Stanislaus*? So, thanks only to the fact that Senator Malinski is now the head of the CIA Oversight Committee, I am hamstrung with an investigation into exactly what happened in that Parisian cemetery. Despite all that, I am confident that I will soon enough survive the spectacle of this inquiry, and return to the more pressing matters needing to be addressed by my office at Langley.

Renard looked at Trellis almost as if he had heard his thoughts clearly spoken. Trellis knew that Renard - this fit young man who sat before him in his crisp tapered blue shirt and ever-so coordinated tie - had quite the reputation of being very cunning, with an ability for knocking those he investigated off their always well-prepared guard. Of course, Renard had worked closely with the Senator for many years, Trellis already knew. He also knew the Senator had sharpened him to the threateningly keen edge he was today. The investigator was her secret weapon, it was said.

"So, *Paul*, where do you want to begin?" asked Trellis, rising to Renard's request for immediate engagement.

"I thought it best to understand your relationship to Mr. Wisniewski," said the investigator. Trellis noted Renard pronounced Stanley's name in the Polish form, "*Vish-NEV-ski*".

"He was a former employee. I was his boss at one point. By the time he retired, I was his boss's boss's boss. Pretty simple, Paul," Trellis said dismissively.

"But this wasn't his first time going rogue, was it?" Renard watched Trellis closely.

"I don't follow your comment?" Trellis said, effecting an air of being confused.

"Back in 1985 – Project INDIGO – the suicide of Bryce Weldon at a CIA safe house on the Eastern Shore. Do you remember now, Jack?"

"That's ancient *f**king* history, Paul," exploded Trellis.

"Good, good. Now that's the Jack Trellis I wanted to speak to!"

Renard was smirking, as if to say, *Now, we are really getting started...*

Trellis calmed himself, and then had to laugh inwardly. Apparently, Renard had done his own research, and was almost comical in his attempts to coax Jack Trellis' legendary temper.

"Stanley was just in the wrong place at the wrong time back then. He wasn't even in the room when Weldon took his own life."

Jack Trellis said this with confidence, in order to stem the tide of inquiry.

Reading from a classified report, Renard said aloud, "In conclusion, the agency has determined the presence of Agent Wisniewski to be a contributing factor in the death of the detainee, Mr. Weldon. His presence clearly agitated the detainee, who previously only knew him as a co-worker at Marshall Analytics. It is probable that this fictitious work relationship, now revealed to the detainee as the genesis of his arrest, was the triggering function of his suicidal action. Furthermore, Agent Wisniewski, in walking the grounds of the safe house, posed a distraction to the staff of the facility, affording Mr. Weldon the opportunity to commit the suicidal act."

Trellis recognized the report - his own creation in the aftermath of a severe *f**k-up*. The FBI leadership was all over the agency during this time. The powers that be had allowed Trellis to co-lead INDIGO as a joint operation. The FBI had successfully arrested both Weldon, and his more senior partner, Dr. Benjamin Palmer. While Palmer was under lock and key by the FBI, Trellis himself had politicked for the interrogation of Weldon by the CIA. The FBI fought vigorously against this. But, Trellis prevailed, and his agency then cocked it up. So, Trellis needed a scapegoat, and that goat was named Stanley.

"Well, as I said in the report, Stanley should not have been there at that time. Wrong place, wrong time..."

"Interesting. So, what was the appropriate recourse for Mr. Wisniewski's - let's forgo the surnames, shall we? – for Stanley's digression?" Renard's face was flush, alive with expectation.

"What *the f**k* does this have to do with *ALBATROSS*?" Trellis re-ignited.

"That's what I fully intend to find out, Jack!" said Renard, his face becoming sharp and serious. "Stanley doesn't get reprimanded, certainly not fired, he just gets immediately assigned to West Berlin?"

The wolfish accusation was dressed not so sheepishly in a question's clothing.

Trellis' mind was racing to determine why Renard might be going back to what he considered ancient history. In the flash of an instant, he decided to play along to allow Renard to expose his train of attack.

"Yes, I needed him in Berlin. I had need for his language and operational skills in Berlin, so I got him *out of Dodge* to let things calm down. To allow the INDIGO fiasco to settle out. I don't think I was the first CIA leader to have done that."

Renard was smiling again. "So noble of you, Jack! But, I don't really think so. You needed a scapegoat, and Stanley was your man. You also needed to get his asset *Syrenka* in Poland running again, so Stanley was again your man. Finally, you desperately needed someone to mind your other top-grade asset, the East German spy that you, yourself, had turned. What was his operational name – ah, here it is, *Erasmus*."

Where the f**k did this guy get access to all this material? Trellis asked himself. *Yeah, in his role he had access to it all, but how did he cobble all this together so quickly?*

Renard caught Trellis looking defensively through the Lucite conference table, intricately inspecting his own suit pants and shoes. The young investigator laughed to himself, *nowhere to hide, Jack. You so much as scratch your balls and I am going to nail you to the wall. Come now, let's get it all out.*

Paul Renard paused before speaking aloud again. He picked up a small electronic remote device, and having pressed it, the transparent glass wall separating them from the outer office instantly became opaque.

"No need to have the vermin peering into the fishbowl, now is there? So, Jack, tell me about Stanley in Berlin. What happened? How did it all work out for you?" Renard grinned, knowing he was striking where Trellis least expected, and was most exposed.

That f**king smile, Trellis thought angrily in his mind, *I'm going to wipe that f**king smile off your elitist f**king face. It may not happen today, but it is certainly going to happen.*

Instead of the theatrics, Trellis regained his composure.

"Stanley did a yeoman's job," Trellis said, suppressing his rage while he answered aloud. "As I am sure you are aware, I personally escorted Stanley to Berlin, specifically West Berlin."

"Wasn't a bad time for you to have a low profile in DC, also? Now, was it?" smirked Renard, "Only a source the quality of *Erasmus* could justify your 'getting out of Dodge', as you say."

"I could no longer continue to handle *Erasmus* personally given my expanded responsibilities in Langley, so I decided to hand him off to Stanley." Trellis was agitated that Paul Renard had delved this far into his past so quickly.

Renard sensed his aggravation. "Our Stanley wasn't even

assigned to Berlin Station, now was he, Jack? He was Warsaw station, or had been up until he came back to the states in '85. Why not give *Erasmus* to the locals?"

"Paul, I realize this is fun for you, playing amateur spymaster, and all that. Can we just get back to *ALBATROSS*? You're wasting my time with all this..." Trellis was attempting to cut off Renard's line of questioning.

"Jack, every time you buck up and push back on me, I know I am hitting a nerve. In your position, you should be only too happy to waste this session with discussion of material that was not germane to *ALBATROSS*. So, I ask again, why wasn't *Erasmus* handed off to Berlin Station?"

Renard's voice had become hard with authority. "Because *Erasmus* was *Stasi*. High-up in the *Stasi* counter-intel organization. I turned him when I caught him in West Berlin attempting a honey trap operation against a member of our team there. With a little persuasion, he agreed to become a double agent. His cover of spying on the West Berlin office had to be protected. An outside handler was needed. Someone who could pass for Polish and German. That made Stanley the perfect candidate."

Renard now felt he was getting somewhere. "OK, OK. I understand the need for his handler to pass for German, but why Polish also?"

Trellis hesitated. He could forestall this, he thought, by claiming need-to-know, and national security concerns. The fact of the matter was most of this was over a decade ago down-classified, and Renard surely already had gained access to it all. From whom, Trellis did not yet know, but intended to find out. Jack decided to no longer stall.

"Because *Erasmus* was a cut-out. He was feeding us material from an even higher quality source. A Polish army officer who had unfettered access to the Soviet Red Army planning council materials. We codenamed him *Osprey*."

"Now, it's making sense." Renard's brain was on-fire. "Who's going to suspect a source like *Osprey* communicating with the *Stasi* leadership? No one. *Osprey* would have had regular trips to East Germany in his military planning functions. So, he passes information onto *Erasmus*, who you personally handled. Very few, if any, need to know about *Osprey*, and he is classified so highly that he is safely concealed from the ever-probing eyes of most of the agency."

"Yeah, you pretty much got it," conceded Trellis.

"But why Stanley?" asked Renard. "What did he specifically bring to all of this?"

Trellis answered, "I needed Stanley to become the new link between *Erasmus* and *Osprey*. I expected *Osprey* could pass information to Stanley, in Warsaw, once we returned him there. Also, Stanley was to be installed as his exfiltration agent. When *Osprey* eventually needed to be pulled out of Poland permanently, he was to contact Stanley in Warsaw."

Renard now looked a little confused. "How was Stanley going to get *Osprey* out of Poland?"

"Come, now, Paul. You figured out most of this on your own. How do you think we would get a defecting Polish double agent out of the Eastern Bloc?"

Renard grabbed his chin, but already knew the answer. Playing dumb, he answered, "I would assume through East Berlin into West Berlin. After all you had *Erasmus* high up in the *Stasi* who could arrange for him to get over the wall when the time came..."

"Screw going over the wall, or through the checkpoints. That would be too risky. *Erasmus* had responsibility for the patrol boats on the *River Spree*. The plan was to float him out of East Berlin, have *Osprey* and Stanley dropped off on the banks of the *Tiergarten* in West Berlin. *Erasmus* would sell it as an operation against the West, so the *Stasi* leadership would play right into his hands."

"What is the *Tiergarten*?" asked Renard naively.

"It's a big ass park in Berlin. Used to be a hunting ground for Frederick the Great, or the Electors of Brandenburg, or some such shit. Back in '85, as now, it started just on the other side of the Brandenburg Gate. The only difference was that back in 1985, the f**king *Berlin Wall* ran between it and the Gate. *The Tiergarten* was in West Berlin, and it ran right up to the banks of the *River Spree*, as it does today. That part of the *Tiergarten* is known as the *Spreebogenpark*. One of *Erasmus's* patrol boats would wander a little too close to the West Berlin riverbanks. Our guards would be briefed to turn a blind eye, so to speak. Then *Erasmus'* boys would drop *Osprey* and Stanley onto the *Spreebogenpark* grass, before returning to their patrols."

"But, again, why Stanley?" Renard asked. "*Osprey* could go to East Berlin and get smuggled out on his own."

Trellis was becoming tired of re-living this old op. Despite this, he decided to explain the need for Stanley's role in the exfiltration to Renard.

"*Osprey* needed travel authorization from his higher-ups to travel outside Poland, even at his level. The last thing we would want to do is alert his communist superiors that *Osprey* would be making a run for Berlin. In fact, we were counting on their not realizing he had fled for a few days, after he had not reported to work. However, he wouldn't need papers, at least not real ones, if *Osprey* had captured an American spy in Warsaw, who was suspected of acting against the East Germans..."

"... Our Stanley?"

"Exactly. Then *Osprey* had cover for urgently dragging Stanley back to *Stasi* headquarters in East Berlin for interrogation. That is how it was to work. *Osprey* would initiate contact through Stanley, who would then notify us the exfiltration was on. We would notify *Erasmus*, who would get his patrol boat lined up. We would prep the *Spreebogenpark* recovery team. All *Osprey* and Stanley had to do was traverse the three hundred fifty or so miles between Warsaw and East Berlin, before the Poles discovered he was missing. They would have to cross the Polish-East German border, and maybe a checkpoint or two inside the GDR."

"GDR?" This time Renard was confused in earnest.

"German Democratic Republic, otherwise known as East Germany." Trellis was surprised Renard did not know this, but then again, he was a young man. Mid-forties? The wall came down over twenty-five years ago. Renard would have been a kid. Probably didn't even remember when there were two German states.

"I see, Jack, Stanley was crucial because he provided the excuse for *Osprey* to hightail to East Germany on a moment's notice, where *Erasmus* waits to float him to the West. All the time the *Stasi* believe *Erasmus* is just doing his counter-intel function running an op against the West. How tidy." Renard was genuinely impressed

"So, Jack, tell me more about how you turned *Erasmus* in the first place. He was an old hand in the *Stasi*, as you said. Just getting caught doing his job, as you said, 'setting up a honey-trap' couldn't have been that much leverage. He surely would have had diplomatic immunity as a visiting dignitary in West Berlin."

"Paul, let me ask you, how familiar are you with post-war Germany? You can't be more than 45 years old yourself. That would have made you a teenager when all this was going on? How much do you really know about what went on in the Cold War days?"

"I am 42 years old, Jack. In 1985, I wasn't even in high school, yet. But there are lots of history books around. I think I have a pretty thorough understanding of what went on."

Trellis leaned back in his chair, and Renard noticed for the first time how relaxed the Deputy Director looked. The smile of an eel slithered across the older man's face.

"F**k the history books, Paul. You only get from them is the sanitized version. Nazi's are bad, the Allies are good. The Allies took Berlin and Hitler puts a round in his head, just after swallowing cyanide for good measure."

Paul Renard, for the first time was feeling agitated. "I guess you are going to tell me the whole truth of what went on in 1945, and how it pertains to your turning *Erasmus* some twenty-five years later?"

"You are damn right I am, Paul. First thing you need to understand, is that the German people, not the Nazi party officials, mind you, just the everyday German populace, were the ones to bear the brunt of the onslaught that was coming to Berlin at the end of World War II from the East."

"Yes, Jack, the Russians killed and raped anyone they thought might be German on the way to Berlin. Stalin and the other leaders of the Allies just looked the other way. I accept that this happened. You must think anyone younger than yourself is so damn naïve."

Trellis scoffed at the idea of this man thinking he was not naïve.

"Yes, you get it, but you do not realize the magnitude to which this happened. The Poles, the Latvians, the Estonians, the Lithuanians were all driving out the civilian Germans that had moved into their lands as the Russians advanced from the East. In many cases, they killed any German civilians the Nazi's left behind as they fled from the onslaught of the Soviets. It was not a pretty scene, given what the Nazi's, and specifically the SS, had inflicted on these peoples over the prior five years."

Trellis looked at Renard's face, which bore a look of "Come on, let's get on with it. I know all this..."

Trellis continued, "Our man *Erasmus* grew up as a child in what was then called East Prussia, in lands that today are Polish, Lithuanian and Russian. His parents were able to get him and his younger sister out of there as the Red Army approached. They managed to pay an enormous bribe to get them transported overland back to Leipzig. Leipzig still wasn't exactly the safest place to ride out the end of the war, mind you, but their parents had gotten their children out from the immediate path of the Soviet Red Army."

Trellis could see he was starting to make a dent upon this investigator. Renard's face creased with anticipation. Trellis went on.

"In January 1945, *Erasmus'* parents escaped to the then still German city of Gotenhafen, which is Gdynia, Poland today. Here they booked passage on a converted German Cruise Liner to get evacuated out of the war zone that was tightening around them. They were not alone. The ship was packed to the gunwales with frantic German citizens fleeing ahead of the Red Army. They departed in the middle of an epic Baltic winter storm."

Jack Trellis looked at the face of Paul Renard. He could see that Renard had no idea as to what was to follow. Trellis continued.

"The ship was the *MV Wilhelm Gustloff*, which was soon spotted by a Soviet submarine. Even though this was clearly an evacuation of German civilians, that sub was cleared to put three torpedoes into the cruise liner. To this day it is the most tragic maritime disaster ever on the high seas. Over nine thousand people, most of them civilians, died that night. Yet, your history books teach us only about the Titanic and the Lusitania. Both of those catastrophes combined were only a little over a third of the lives lost on the *Wilhelm Gustloff*."

"My God," said Renard, truly surprised he had never heard of this disaster, this blatant spilling of civilian life. "So then, *Erasmus* and his sister were orphaned at the end of the war?"

"Very much so, Paul. With no love at all for the Soviets who were soon to rule over what would become East Germany. The same East Germany wherein *Erasmus* and his sister survived, but had become trapped, after the war."

Jack Trellis was now ready to challenge Renard.

"Paul, what do you know of the Berlin Wall?"

Renard was more cautious now. "Went up overnight in '61. Came down nearly overnight in '89. Separated East and West Berlin. *Stasi* bastards kept perfecting it right up to the end. Massive death strips on the East German side. Look at any remaining pieces of the wall, and you will likely see graffiti on the West German side, and perhaps bullet-hole pock marks on the East German side."

Trellis smiled wryly at the man who was a quarter decade his junior.

"What many people today don't realize is that West Berlin was somewhat of an island inside of East Germany. East Germany was blocked off from West Germany by what was called the IGB – The Intra-German Border. What went up across this border was also known as the IGB, or Intra-German Barrier. It was the predecessor of the Berlin Wall. Technically, a series of barb wire fences, the IGB was complete with death-strips, dog-runs and automated machine guns activated by trip wires. All the good stuff that would later adorn the wall's death strips."

"Except the IGB went up much earlier, in May 1952. It ran from the Baltic Sea to the Czechoslovakian border. Roads, autobahns and waterways were severed and became impassable. The actual barrier itself ran through villages, and in some cases through homes and buildings. While it was sold as a defense against the aggressor Western forces, the real purpose was to keep the East Germans from fleeing to the West. It ran for over 1300 kilometers, or well over 800 miles. Oh, yeah, it was also put up encircling the exterior of West Berlin, separating the city from the East German countryside surrounding it. The only place there was no barrier after 1952 was across the streets of the French, British and American sectors from the Russian sector of the city of Berlin itself."

Figure 3 – Death Strip of the Berlin Wall (circa 1977)

(Photo Credit: Wikipedia Commons)

Renard began to understand now. "So once this IGB sealed East from West, the only way to escape East Germany was to cross over from East Berlin into West Berlin. I guess you are telling me that the East Berliners continued to do just that?"

Jack could see his inquisitor was becoming his pupil.

"Yes, the *Ossi's* did just that," whipped Trellis.

"The *Ossi's*?" repeated Renard quizzically.

"*Ost* is the German word for East. After the war, they referred to the East German's as *Ossi's*. They still use it today to refer back to people from that period."

Renard understood. "So then, the *Ossi's*, whether they lived in East Berlin, or anywhere else in East Germany, would migrate first to East Berlin with the sole intention of crossing over into West Berlin. From West Berlin, they moved to West Germany via the corridor that Stalin failed to close in the days of the Berlin Airlift?"

"Exactly, Paul. Stalin had tried earlier to drive the Allies out of West Berlin altogether, by barricading these train, truck and auto corridors that had been allowed to run from West Germany through the countryside of East Germany and into West Berlin. Stalin shut all these down in late June of '48. The Berlin Airlift started by the Allies the very next day. The allies refused to give up West Berlin, and began flying food and other necessities in through the US and British air corridors."

Trellis could now see just how shallow the investigator's knowledge was of the time-period. And yet, the Senator had the nerve to sick her cunning little investigator on him? Asking him detailed questions of a subject of which he had command of almost no details?

"Paul, the West Germans began to refer to these aircraft as *Rosinenbombers*, or 'raisin bombers', because they brought food. American and British pilots began dropping chocolates and other sweets to the children lined up at the edges of Tempelhof airport in West Berlin. Thanks to the Berlin Airlift, and the fact that even the Soviets didn't want to ignite another war by shooting down an Allied cargo plane, the Russians ended the blockade in May of '49 after seeing they had failed to starve out West Berlin. The Allies kept the airlift going until September of that same year."

Renard added what he knew, "So, West Berlin was here to stay. For the next twelve years, the youngest and best educated of the East Germans could simply walk into the freedom of West Berlin.

From here they could travel to anywhere in the West if they had the proper papers."

Jack Trellis could see Renard had gotten the point. Now, he wanted to put its magnitude into perspective.

"Right, Paul. East Germany was losing up to 200,000 citizens a year to the West. Every five years they would lose a million of its citizens. In a country that was only 17 million people to begin with, this rate of attrition could not be allowed to continue. Especially when the brightest and youngest were leaving. The *"Brain Drain"* became so bad that the East Germans in '61 had no recourse but to seal off East Berlin from West Berlin with the wall."

Trellis paused for effect.

*"**Der Mauer**, the Germans soon called it. **The Wall.**"* Trellis had just covered some of the most tenuous history over any couple of decades that Europe had ever dared to regard as peace.

"Remember our man *Erasmus*? By now, he was in his early thirties and an up-and-comer within the *Stasi*. He knew what was coming when the wall began to go up. He decided it was his last chance to get his kid sister into the relative security of West Berlin in '61."

"So, he got her over the wall?" asked Renard?

"Yeah," said Trellis, "but the wall was still mostly barbed wire fencing then, before the cinder blocks and prefabricated concrete wall segments showed up, before the East Germans began tearing down buildings for the death strips. *Erasmus* bribed the border guards to get his sister across. He got her out, and this proved to be his big mistake."

"How so?" asked Renard.

"She refused to leave West Berlin, Paul. Refused to leave her brother. Even if she was separated from him by **der mauer**. She had no family anywhere in West Germany. What little she had, they were all in the East. She was adamant that she would stay. She had decided she could live in destitution here as well as anywhere else in the West, so she remained in West Berlin where at least her brother could visit her."

"She was forced to live a very meager existence in West Berlin.

So, she was trapped in the bubble, the island that was West Berlin. From across **der mauer,** *Erasmus* could see his younger sister as she became increasingly destitute. It broke his heart when she eventually was forced to resort to prostitution to feed and shelter herself."

"You used his sister to turn him to be a double agent, didn't you?" asked Renard. "What a bastard you were!"

Trellis looked blankly at Renard, certainly unashamed.

Renard paused before adding enthusiastically, "What a brilliant bastard!"

Trellis gave his prize student a knowing smirk.

"Paul, by the mid-seventies, *Erasmus* was coming into West Berlin regularly. We were trailing him every time he did, and he would always spend some time with this one particular prostitute. This was unusual, because the *Stasi* often tailed their own when they came into West Berlin. To visit a Western prostitute was strictly *verboten,* but, yet, *Erasmus* did so without fail. About that time, we had a low-level defector who clued us in that the prostitute was actually his sister, so the *Stasi* leadership looked the other way."

"How on earth were you able to get with him one-on-one without the *Stasi* knowing? You said they trailed their own on visits to West Berlin." Renard was now fully absorbed into Trellis' tale of the cold war.

"Simple, Paul. One foggy night in West Berlin, we kidnapped his little sister. Oh, just for a couple hours. One of our guys went in as a john, claims to have never touched her. At least that is what we later told *Erasmus.* We took her to a West Berlin safe house and fed her pretty well, as I recall, then stuffed a load of West Marks in her pocket."

"What did you do, threaten to lock her up? Kill her? Unless he agreed to spy for us?" asked Renard.

"Kill her? Are you kidding? She was already killing her brother with the life she was leading in West Berlin. I simply waited in her ratty little apartment and intercepted *Erasmus* when he arrived to see his sister. He had been setting up a honey trap against our ambassador, so it was ironic that I cornered him in his own sister's love nest, if you will. Made sure I left some men's clothing lying round to keep reminding him of what he hated about the life she had made for herself in West Berlin.

"OK, so what happened? You only had a few hours at best." Renard was fully engrossed in Trellis' tale now.

"What happened? I'll tell you what happened, I gave him the pitch of my life. I told him how well we could take care of her, well enough for her to give up her profession. Told him we could set her up clear on the other side of West Germany. It was pretty obvious even to him at that time that West Germany was developing much faster after the war. The Russians were being punitive, forcing the East Germans to live among the squalor and ruins. When they did allow some development, it was in the gray, concrete Soviet style."

"So obviously he agreed to become a double agent?" Renard asked like a boy awaiting the next chapter of an adventure story.

"Yes, he agreed to become a double agent. We relocated his sister to a small village along the Rhine River where she could scrape off her sordid past. We provided her a nice home there and a monthly allowance so long as her brother continued to work for us. And we paid him very handsomely, too, into a Swiss account while he was in East Berlin. But perhaps his greatest motivation was that *Erasmus*, like so many of the *Ossi's*, had no love at all for the Soviets. Remember they had killed his parents aboard the *Gustloff*. From then on, he was our highest placed officer within the *Stasi*."

Renard was fascinated. "What ever happened to the sister? She lived happily ever after in the Rhineland?"

"Hell, I wish. Despite the nice home we gave her, the generous allowance, she started hooking again after about six months. Seems she had developed a taste for it. We never told *Erasmus* about it, though. Hell, we had to relocate her from village to village every couple of years because everywhere we planted her, she would repeat the same sequence. Believe it or not, our PSYCH guys said she was acting out against the West German women who shunned her because they could tell she was an *Ossi*. Little sister decided to give them something to really shun her for by sleeping with their husbands."

"And what ever became of *Erasmus* after the wall fell?" asked Renard. "Did he come over to live in the West? Did he go to live with his sister?"

"November 9, 1989, the first night the East Germans once again allowed unfettered access for their people to West Berlin, *Erasmus* walked out of East Berlin, never to be seen again. We were able to confirm later that he had drained the Swiss accounts of about six million dollars and some odd change. He never showed at any of his sister's Rhineland homes. We watched them all. He never saw her again, as far as we know. And we never saw hide nor hair of him again. He is likely still living quite comfortably in some remote part of the world, would be my guess."

"Okay, so tell me about the Polish agent *Osprey*..." demanded Renard.

"I would love to, but our time is up..." Trellis was now looking excitedly at his phone, "And, I've got something heavy brewing, and need to get back to Langley immediately. Can we follow-up on this at our next session?"

Renard realized that while this was an investigation on behalf of Senator Malinski, it was not an interrogation. Professional courtesies needed to be respected.

"Of course, Jack. I'll set it up with your office. Thanks for coming into the District today.'

"Of course," said Trellis. Jack laughed inwardly to himself. *You swallowed all of that,* he thought, *even the part that was blatantly untrue.*

⏤⏤⏥⏤⏤

Later, as Trellis was navigating his way across the Key Bridge from DC into Virginia, he remembered his first night in West Berlin with Stanley in '85. They were walking after dinner in *The Kurfürstendamm* district. Anyone who ever spent any time here, shortened it to *Ku'damm*, as it is colloquially known to the locals.

"When do I get to meet Foley?" Stanley asked Trellis.

"Day after tomorrow," muttered Jack. Foley was the public cover name for *Erasmus*.

Trellis remembered the name being Stanley's concoction. The historical *Erasmus* was best known for his book, **In Praise of Folly**. So, Foley was derived from Folly.

"When is Foley going to cross?" Stanley asked.

Trellis remembered looking abruptly at his agent.

"He's not. You are." Trellis had not yet discussed this portion of the op with Stanley.

"What? Where?" Stanley was genuinely surprised.

Trellis thought this was as good a time to shock his Polish agent as any.

"You'll cross in the late afternoon, as you'll be attending a piano recital at the *Konzerthaus of the Berliner Sinfonie-Orchester,* not far from Humboldt University. I thought it lined up nicely with your cover as talent scout to the Canadian record label. It should be interesting. The building goes back to 1817, but not much was left of it after the Russians came through in 1945. But the *Ossi's* did rebuild it, just reopened it a couple of years ago. Supposed to have the best acoustics in all of Europe."

"I don't give a damn about the acoustics," said Stanley. He feared going into East Berlin. Being undercover in Communist Warsaw was one thing. Being alone among the East Germans was another risk altogether.

"You'll cross at *Friedrichstrasse*." said Trellis, sensing his concern.

"*Checkpoint Charlie*?"

"Foley wants a good look at you. His team will allow you to cross unencumbered at *Friedrichstrasse*. It is still only a short walk from there to the *Konzerthaus*. I can go over it with you on a map later tonight."

The message came as a shock to Stanley. He would cross at the iconic checkpoint, where US and Soviet tanks lined up against each other in October 1961, only months after the wall went up. Ironically, this conflict was precipitated by an American Diplomat, Allan Lightner, wishing to transit into East Berlin to attend an opera. This fact alone was an indication of how dangerous a crossing into East Berlin could become. The fact that it was an opera, a musical event like his recital, seemed ominous to Stanley.

Trellis realized that Stanley had not yet prepared himself for the danger of an excursion across the wall. Even in '85, it could be tricky business.

"How will I recognize Foley?" Stanley asked.

Trellis recognized his concern. He decided that shock treatment would sober Stanley to the seriousness of the situation.

"Easy. He'll be the *Stasi* agent arresting you after the recital."

Stanley was clearly shocked. He stopped walking along *The Ku'damm*, standing motionless as Trellis continued to walk past him.

"Arrest me? For what?" Stanley's face was ashen white.

Trellis walked back the few steps to him. He came in close and reached his arm behind Stanley's back. He whispered into his ear.

"Quite simple. For being a Western spy in East Berlin."

7

THE STASI POLICE STATE

To understand how the East German Police State became so repressively powerful, one must go back to War World II. The Nazi's had great hatred for the Communists and had violently attacked and eliminated that element within the German controlled lands. They viewed the far-left Communists as radicals, incompatible with their extreme-right agenda. The chemistry of these two philosophies was the same as mixing strong caustics with strong acids – explosively cataclysmic.

Yet, they had temporarily managed to coexist. The famous Molotov-Ribbentrop Pact had secretly divided Poland before the 1939 invasions. However, the non-aggression elements of that pact were short-lived. Within 21 months, the Nazi's invaded The Soviet Union in *Operation Barbarossa*.

On Sunday, June 22, 1941 the Nazi's invaded The Soviet Union. They had amassed great armies along the German-Soviet border, land that had less than two years earlier been Polish soil until it was wrest away by the agreements of the German-Soviet Non-Aggression Pact. Despite Russian intelligence that warned of an impending invasion, Stalin was confident that Hitler would not attack him, his partner.

When the Nazi's did indeed breach the pact, attacking in massive *Blitzkrieg* formations, Stalin suffered what can only be described as a personal breakdown. He became reclusive, refusing to communicate with his generals. Leadership at the head of the Soviet Union was paralyzed.

No one dared step into the void created by the missing Soviet leader, who had so infamously effected a series of purges of Soviet leadership who he saw as threats throughout the 1930's. The politicos feared becoming fodder for the next round of Stalin's paranoia.

The Nazi's strikes initially had unfettered success, before stalling out in the Russian winters of Leningrad and Moscow in 1941-42. Later the Soviets armies had blunted the Nazi's deepest penetration of the USSR in Stalingrad during the winter of 1942-43. When the Russians regained the initiative in these three critical cities, they pressed back the Nazi armies all the way to Berlin itself. All along the way, the Red Army repaid Nazi atrocities with even greater atrocities of their own. Those peoples caught between these two armies were doubly damned.

After the Red Army had crushed Berlin in the Spring of 1945, the division between the East and West German States had been effectively set. The division of the city of Berlin into four sectors was documented in the 1944 London Protocol, with the American, British and French controlled sectors becoming West Berlin, and with the Soviet Sector becoming East Berlin.

Perhaps the most significant event in the formation of the *Stasi* was not in Berlin at all, and not even in what would become East Germany, but rather in what would become the West German town of Nuremberg. The world-famous Nuremberg Trials were held here, not because of its resplendent medieval history, but rather for the town's more recent and sordid history of hosting massive Nazi rallies throughout the '30's and '40's. After the war, the Allies chose this site to send the message that even the greatest celebrations of the Nazi party were only preludes for the eventual and ignominious weight of moral justice.

Here the future leaders of East Germany, all avowed Communists, watched as the world levied war crime proceedings against their once all-powerful far right enemies. The impressions that surely were formed in the minds of these communist leaders-to-be must have been of the need for their own sovereign East German communist state. In order to preclude themselves from one-day facing charges of their own by the world community, they would need a highly effective bureau of State Security, something akin to the Soviet KGB.

The East German State was "officially" established by the Soviets "ceding" their authority in 1949. Of course, the Soviets had secretly assured that the new communist state was highly subordinated to Moscow.

In February 1950, the Ministry for State Security *(der Staatssicherheitsdienst)*, or simply known as *der Stasi*, was established. Like the KGB in the Soviet Union, the *Stasi* had both internal and external functions. Internally, it was established to defend against activists and suppress rebellion. Externally, it was charged with spreading communism by actively conducting espionage, disinformation and covert operations in foreign countries.

Two of the longest serving *Stasi* leaders, Erich Mielke and Markus Wolf, were both devoted communists and avoided the Nazi reign of Germany by emigrating to Moscow during World War II. Mielke took control of the *Stasi* in 1957 and was only driven from that position shortly after the fall of the *Berlin Wall* in 1989. His hand led the *Stasi* apparatus for over thirty-two of East Germany's forty years of existence. During his leadership, the Berlin Wall, or as the Germans simply called it, *der Mauer*, was erected, continually "improved" and reinforced, before spectacularly falling in late 1989.

Markus Wolf came back to Germany after the war in the role as a news journalist. In this capacity, he covered the entire Nuremberg Trials. The impact that these trials would have on his future as co-founder and later head of the *Stasi's* Foreign Intelligence Service cannot be underestimated. He quickly built one of the most effective Cold War intelligence services, all the while shunning any publicity himself. He became known throughout intelligence circles as "The Man Without a Face" since it was believed that even Wolf's own photo eluded Western Intelligence for many years.

Markus Wolf led the *Stasi's* Foreign Intelligence Service from his co-founding of the service in 1953 when he was only thirty years old, until his retirement in 1986. For thirty-three years, he was the *Ossi* spymaster. After the wall fell and just before the German Reunification of 1990, he fled the country unsuccessfully seeking political asylum in the USSR and in Austria.

Together these two men, Erich Mielke and Markus Wolf, built the most effective social reporting network and foreign clandestine operations of the Cold War. At its peak, the *Stasi* had over 91,000 employees and over 170,000 informers. Some estimate, that including the informers, this represented one *Stasi* for every six and one-half East Berliners. This is a chilling number when compared to the *Gestapo* of Nazi Germany. The *Gestapo's* comparable figure was approximately one for every two thousand citizens.

In addition to the unprecedented spying on its own citizens, the *Stasi* conducted the policy of psychological harassment of perceived enemies known as *Zersetzung*. The *Stasi* would break into its citizens' homes, rearranging furniture or books, so that the citizenry would constantly be aware of the *Stasi's* capability to invade their privacy.

The combination of being spied upon by neighbors, loved ones, even spouses combined with the ability of a police state to permeate every aspect of their personal lives, led many East Germans to have nervous breakdowns. Even suicides were known to have been attributed to the *Stasi's* tactics. Of course, once the *Stasi* zeroed in on any of its citizens suspected of collusion with the West, physical abuse, and even death by torture, often occurred.

Integrated into the powers of this police state were the foreign intelligence service operations under Markus Wolf. It supported the infamous 1970's Red Army Faction terror operations of the *Baader-Meinhof Gang* within West Germany and elsewhere. Wolf's *Stasi* foreign intelligence service had reportedly also provided assistance to the terrorist known as Carlos the Jackal, assisted the establishment of Idi Amin's secret police, as well as provided support to Palestinian terror groups. Reportedly working with the KGB, the *Stasi* spread misinformation to the developing world that the CIA had created and intentionally spread the HIV/AIDS epidemic.

The *Stasi* Service under Wolf also was extremely effective in placing covert agents within Western political operations. The most notable of these was the infiltration of Günter Guillaume, who rose to become the close personal aid and secretary to West German Chancellor Willy Brandt. In 1974, Brandt was forced from power after Guillaume was exposed as an East German agent.

Wolf served for over three decades as the number two man within the *Stasi,* only behind Eric Mielke himself. Within the inner circle of these two men, was the agent known to the Americans simply as *Erasmus.*

Trellis had given his agent this codename, after the historical figure *Desiderius Erasmus Roterodamus*, or more simply *Erasmus of Rotterdam*. This theologian was a contemporary of Martin Luther at the dawning of the Reformation. While the historical *Erasmus* shared many of Luther's concerns about the abuses of the Catholic Church, he believed that the most effective manner in which to remedy those ills was from within the institution.

That is exactly how Jack Trellis had perceived his *Erasmus.* This man had seen the Soviet Union so cruelly take his own parents' lives but had also seen the moral corruption of the West drive his baby sister from a meager, though pious, existence to one dependent upon the debauchery of prostitution. Thus, the *Stasi's Erasmus* would remain within the power elite of this organization, professing adherence to the same ideology as the zealots Mielke and Wolf, but knowing that his future, and that of his sister, would ultimately be wrestled from the decaying and decadent West.

After the fall of the wall, both Mielke and Wolf would face charges from the Reunified German State. Eric Mielke was stripped of his position, and in 1989 was accused of corruption and detained until 1993. In 1994 he was brought on charges of ordering the shooting deaths of those Germans attempting to flee East Germany. At this time, he was found to be mentally incompetent and unable to stand trial. He was, nonetheless, detained until he was 87 years old, when he was released. He died in May 2000.

Markus Wolf was brought up on charges of treason in 1993. He was found guilty and served six years in prison, at which point the German Supreme Court overturned his conviction on the grounds Reunified German law that had no jurisdiction over the activities of the sovereign state of East Germany. He died in his sleep in 2006.

The agent *Erasmus* would have been lucky to suffer either of these fates.

8

AUSPICES OF THE PROTECTORATE

"When will he come?" asked Diane aloud.

She was standing at the window overlooking *Lago Maggiore*, a fifth of *Monte Gambarogno's* mountain sloped before her. The sky was high, the lake was calm. Across its genteel, mirrored, blue surface, she could clearly see the Swiss town of Locarno.

It was late Spring, and the weather could be unpredictable. That day, however, it was delightful, if not idyllic. The ease of transit across the lake heightened her anticipation.

"When will Devereaux come to me?" she asked her shadow.

Her shadow, who was much younger and more concerned than she was, waited a second to answer.

"When will he come, *Zosia?*" Diane asked yet again. She pronounced *"Zosia"* like "Russia" with a Z in lieu of the R, as Sophie had taught her. Like a young girl, she savored the secret name which was used only between them.

Sophie thought Diane's voice had quivered with excitement much like that of a schoolgirl's. She was not the independent Diane which Sophie had come to know, and she wanted that version of her friend back in the worst way.

Sophie said to her, "He is coming today. This we have been told. Come sit away from the window. Dr. Alec has asked you to not spend too much time at the window."

Figure 4 – Lago Maggiore
(Photo Credit: Elizabeth Marie Trawinski)

Sophie remembered the directions from Dr. Alec Rushe, who was the medical officer resident with them. He had been there since shortly after any of them reached the Brit's safe house that was a grand chalet in these southernmost Swiss mountains. They were just beyond the Italian border, above the lake that meandered between the two countries.

"Sophie, Diane listens to you," Dr. Alec had said. "Emotionally, she clings to you. You are the tie to the past that her mind is keeping from her. You and Malcolm Devereaux."

"Yes, Doctor," Sophie responded shyly, but politely.

"I have told you, call me Alec, please." The doctor took the young woman's hands into his own.

"Yes, Doctor Alec," Sophie replied, giving as far as she intended on the way by which she addressed the good doctor.

"OK, Sophie. Don't let Diane stand by the window too long. It is very important, I am sure you understand…"

"Yes, of course, the satellites and long-range cameras from across the lake..." began Sophie with the answer that she had only assumed, and never verified.

The doctor's face broke into a smirk, preceding a half chuckle. "Good Lord, no, my dear. *Heckle & Jeckle* have assured me that her picture window has been treated with a state of the art reflective coating that effectively makes it a one-way mirror. Adaptive Refractive Index Matching, or some such technical jargon."

Heckle & Jeckle were the names the good doctor had given to their only other co-habitants in the Swiss safe-house. Hector and Gerald, which shortened to Jerry, were the names they used to address each other. They were the Swiss Army knives of the group, being caretakers, cooks, cleaners and communication staff. Most certainly, their primary function was protection and security. Any one approaching the safe-house was quickly met at the gate at the end of the long driveway that climbed the mountainside to their building. On one occasion, Sophie had spotted them pulling automatic weapons from an otherwise locked pantry.

Both with their close-cropped dark hair, and their refusing to dress in anything other than black paramilitary gear, they somewhat resembled the cartoon characters, even without the yellow beaks.

No one left the house, even to access the sloping overgrown lawn or covered rear patio without their express permission.

Doctor Alec's kind face became taunt with importance.

"Sophie, allow me to explain. Diane's mind is waiting for a trigger. Something that will make her consciously deal with the horror that she went through in that cemetery. The longer she stares out onto the world that we cannot allow her to access, there is a chance that something she sees will trigger her, and in many cases the realization can be traumatic. So, allow her some time at the window, but then bring her back to rest."

"Doctor Alec, she does not remember the *cementery* at all."

Alec laughed to himself. One amusing affectation of Sophie's Polish language caused her to pronounce the word "cemetery" as "*cementery*" at times.

Sophie continued, "She only seems to remember myself and Mr.

Malcolm Devereaux. She very much wishes to see him, she keeps saying he saved her."

"Well you can tell her that *Heckle & Jeckle* have informed me that Mr. Devereaux is transiting to us as we speak. It is important for her to know that for her own safety, he must take many precautions. We cannot tell her the exact hour that he will arrive, but he may be here as early as this evening."

"Doctor Alec, is she healing? Will she recover?" Sophie's voice trembled with concern.

"Sophie, do not worry. She is well on her way physically. What I am more concerned with is her psyche. She needs to slowly regain her full understanding of what has happened to her. Once she is able to accept it, and to deal with it, we will be on better footing. However, so long as she is suppressing her memories, she is prone to act out in a manner devoid of caution. One mistake, one rash action on her part, and those who still wish to harm her may find her and come here to finish the job. Do you understand, Sophie? So, no discussion about the cemetery or Paris, please!"

"It is acceptable that I have given her the book of Chopin? His music seems to calm her, and we spend much time discussing Chopin's life. This is good, no?"

"It is good, yes, my dear," said Dr. Alec with a gentleman's smile. "I think it may ease the transition. Only the songs that I have approved though, none of those frenetic études. Much too anxious for her. Certainly, the funeral march is completely out of the question. Agreed?"

"Yes, I am agreed with you, Dr. Alec," answered Sophie, her face now radiant with a soft smile that contrasted with the worry deep inside her for her friend.

Later, alone with Diane at the window awaiting Devereaux, Sophie felt it was her duty to distract her wounded, although healing, friend from her deepest fear, that of being rejected by Malcolm Devereaux.

Sophie walked over to the table where she and Diane had spent so much time together. There was nothing electronic in the safe house that was not in the controlling clutches of *Heckle & Jeckle*. No television, no internet, no computers. Certainly, no cell phones. Nothing that could be hacked, or electronically converted into a listening device by the opposition. Only the singular satellite phone in the greedy clutches of the military magpies.

To pass the time, Sophie had been teaching Diane rudimentary Polish language. Diane was struggling with the pronunciations, but her concentration and study consumed the hours. She had mastered the colloquialisms of "How are you?", "Good day", "Please", and "Thank you". More recently, she was beginning to understand the verbs and sentence structure of the language.

Diane had been asking about Chopin, his life, and his music. Dr. Alec had requested approval of a cassette tape recorder, which took six days to get the approval of *Heckle & Jeckle*, although it was known by all this had to be cleared by their superiors back in London.

Once the music became available to Diane, it fed her curiosity of Chopin's life. While Diane was still confined to bed, Sophie read to her each day.

Sophie taught Diane of Chopin's life story. Born in 1810, at the height of Napoleon's reign, Chopin was a Polish child prodigy. His French father had relocated the family to Poland before his birth. At least what had been Poland, at one time, as technically Poland had ceased to exist in 1795, after the final partitions by Austria, Prussia and Russia. Young Frédéric Chopin was raised in an environment of a people fiercely fighting to keep their language, their culture, and their world alive.

Frédéric Chopin left Poland just before the Polish revolt of 1830, which was brutally crushed by the Russians. He was already renown throughout Europe. The young prodigy ended up in Paris and was celebrated as the genius that he was. All the while, he longed for a free Poland to raise itself from the greed of its neighbor states. This longing is heard through Chopin's music, most notably in his mournful nocturnes. It was this music that Diane seemed to come back to again and again. It touched her, possibly soothed her, but from what she still did not know.

In Paris, Chopin had developed a romantic relationship with the authoress George Sand. Her real name was Amantine Dupin, but like several other female writers of the nineteenth century, she published under a male pseudonym. She first consumed Frédéric Chopin, the man, as her lover, then possessed the composer as her partner, only to grow tired of his child-like spirit. All the while, Chopin had become increasingly more gravely ill, most likely suffering from tuberculosis.

After Sand dropped him, having tired of his dramatic mood swings and need for constant medical attention, Chopin was living in near destitution in Paris. This is where Sophie had last left the story of his life with Diane.

"Diane, come sit with me, please," asked Sophie.

"*Zosia*, I am not in the mood for this today. Can we do this later?"

"No, Diane, today I must teach you about the end of Chopin's life. You will find this interesting."

"I want to think about my Malcolm, my English gentleman," said Diane.

"Diane, this is precisely when Chopin, himself, goes to England. He is saved, for a little while, by one of his students. She was a wealthy Scottish woman named Jane Stirling."

"Sterling? Like my name?" The surprise had not only turned Diane's head from her gazing out the window, but she began to come over to the chair where Sophie sat.

Sophie continued. "She spelled her name differently. With an 'I' instead of an 'E'. She was one of Chopin's best students. He dedicated two of his nocturnes to her."

"How did she get him to England? I thought you said he was sick and destitute by this point."

"Madame Stirling paid his expenses and arranged a tour of England and Scotland for the master. He played for Queen Victoria and Prince Albert, even the Duke of Wellington was present. Later, after playing in Scotland and Northern England, he returned to Paris, where Madame Stirling paid his lodging and other expenses as he continued to give way to his disease."

"She was a great woman," said Diane dreamily.

"Yes, she generously also paid the expenses for his sister Ludwika to travel from Poland to be at his bedside as he approached death. Ludwika would later, after his death, smuggle Chopin's heart back to Warsaw, where it remains, to this day, inside a pillar at the Church of the Holy Cross. All this, along with the funeral itself, was arranged for and paid for by Miss Jane Stirling. She cared for her master so much that to this day she is fondly remembered as Chopin's Widow, even though they never were married."

Diane had been listening intently to this sad story of Chopin's demise. Her eyes teared, her voice became strained, as she said aloud, more to herself than to her *Zosia*, "The Nocturne's Widow?"

"Yes," agreed Sophie, her *Zosia*, "She was *The Nocturne's Widow.*"

After a brief silence, a singular tear escaped Diane's moistened eyes and was slowly pulled down her left cheek by a heaviness that had befallen her. She felt her mood sink from the elations of anticipating the arrival of Devereaux, to the despair of an unbearable loss. What she had lost was unknown to her, but she mourned it nonetheless. Her entire being, from the ache of her heart, to the confused clutter of her once highly organized mind, was branded with the specter of an unidentifiable anguish.

Diane said to her *Zosia* feebly, in a most defeated tone, "I am Miss Sterling, and now I have become *The Nocturne's Widow.*"

⸻ ((◉)) ⸻

Malcolm Devereaux had, upon all his visits, spent the preceding night in a hotel in the resort town of Stresa, Italy, on the shores of *Lago Maggiore*. He would assure he was not being trailed within the small lake town, before renting a car and driving into Switzerland, around the mountains for several hours until he reached the chalet. The tortuous winding of the roads made it nearly impossible for the professional not to identify any vehicles that might be following him.

Each trip, he rested on his first night in the same lakeside hotel that had once been a favorite of Ernest Hemingway. On these trips, late the next morning, Devereaux walked the short distance to the village of Stresa's outdoor shopping area. He would have an early lunch at one of the cafés, under a crisscrossing canopy of strings of incandescent lights, which leapt from tree to tree. Their bulbs appeared depressingly weak against the typically sunny, crisp blue skies above the lake. They would, of course, later breathe joyous life into the onyx blackness of the mountain night sky.

After the lunch, Devereaux would then slowly wind his way through the labyrinth of streets filled with shops. These were perfect for spotting a tail. It was easy to work the reflections in the array of windows, each offering a wide-ranging display of local goods as legitimate reasons for him to pause. If necessary, he could double back on his route, or even walk in circles through the maze of narrow streets pretending to be nothing more than a confused tourist. All the while, he employed his training, observing those who might be observing him.

This trip, he was concerned. Devereaux had spotted a small team that he suspected could be tailing him. As he had dined on his lunch of seafood and pasta in the open-air tables, he had noticed a man and woman at a nearby table. They could not keep their hands off each other. Devereaux noted that she appeared too young for him, possibly by a decade and a half, but that certainly was not unheard of in this part of the world. They were speaking Italian, which Devereaux knew only at a survival level, and as such was unable to follow their conversation.

As Devereaux had ambled via a meandering route through the streets and shops, they had intersected with him on three different occasions. Devereaux realized that once compromised, some surveillance teams will intentionally re-contact with the person being trailed, making that person believe that no professional reconnaissance team could possibly be so inept.

Devereaux knew this was nothing to be gambled with. Any team trailing him most likely wished only for him to lead them to the cloistered Diane. Her life may be dependent on the level of his precautions. On this occasion, Devereaux left the shopping area. Instead of renting a car, as he usually did, he walked briskly to the train station, just behind the hotel where he was staying. He caught the first train into Milan.

After the train left the station, he walked its length to determine if his suspicious lunchtime lovers were on-board. He did not see them, but in his scanning of the riders he was alarmed to see a young man he had earlier observed in the shopping area.

He was easy to identify, because his collar was ripped in the back. Devereaux, ever observant, had picked it up as he had walked the shops. The man now had sunglasses and a cap, as well as a V-neck sweater, which he had not been wearing earlier. However, the collar protruded above the neckline of the sweater, and the tear on its back was such that the wearer could not have seen it. This immediately identified him to Devereaux.

Having assured himself he was now being trailed, Devereaux departed the train in Milan. There, he quickly went to the street, circled the train station, and observed the man with the torn collar looking for him in the square. Devereaux then re-entered the station and boarded the next train to Verona. Once again, he walked the train's length, spotting nothing that concerned him. In Verona, he rented a car, and drove along country roads that led him back west until he came to Lake Como.

Lake Como is shaped like an inverted Y. At the base of the western leg of the lake was the town of Como, somewhat of a metropolis where Devereaux had spent the first night. The next day, he drove up the eastern shoreline of the western leg of the lake, which was mountainous. The narrow roads, climbing and diving like swallows along the lake, allowed him to watch for trailing vehicles.

Devereaux stopped for an early lunch at a roadside restaurant that was more of a cliffside perch, suspended over the blue morning lake. He positioned himself under the canvas canopy, under which he sat as to watch the vehicles coming from the direction he had just ascended.

He saw nothing that concerned him, and after completing his meal, continued north until he came to the tourist destination of Bellagio. This town is densely packed onto the tip of land where the two legs of the inverted Y's waters come together.

Here, Devereaux parked his rental car, and walked along the shops once again. A ferry prepared to depart across the lake to the Italian town of Cadenabbia. He bought a ticket and boarded in the last seconds before it launched.

In Cadenabbia, he had rented a second car. Devereaux completed his drive through the Italian and Swiss pre-Alps, across the bridge over Lake Lugano, which was nestled between Lake Como and *Lago Maggiore*. He had driven into Switzerland, pausing in the town of Bellinzona until late that evening. Driving the dark mountain roads, he assured himself he had certainly lost any tail which he might have picked up in Stresa.

He arrived at the chalet two nights after he was expected, but tradecraft demanded he not contact the chalet in any manner that could have been detected by the opposition. The team there would know to continue to expect him unless they received an encoded abort message from London.

Devereaux could, of course, have simply aborted the trip to the chalet, except now that he was sure he had been spotted in Stresa. He needed to plan the travel routes with the security team to relocate Diane. It would now only be a matter of time until the *"competition"* located the chalet, as they would surely now search along the lake, radiating outwardly, from Stresa. They would have drones with camera coverage scanning the skies of the lakefront, tagging every residence that had potential as a safe house. Devereaux knew now that he needed to move Diane as soon as possible. It would take a few days to make safe arrangements. He hoped that he had enough time to do so.

9

PIERCING THE VEIL

Jack Trellis sat in his office with his adjutant, Ellison Redmond. "Pack your bags, Ellie. I am sending your little bisexual ass to London. DCI just approved it." Trellis offered no other details.

Redmond was surprised, first at the news of his impending travel, but more so at the involvement of the Director of Central Intelligence.

"Why did the DCI have to approve it?" he asked.

"Because I am sending you to fill Diane's vacant spot as liaison with our colleagues in England."

"But that's not even your spot to fill. That comes under Carter Norris," argued Redmond. He knew that as the Deputy Director of Analysis, Carter Norris was a peer to Trellis. He also knew these two powerful men were always battling to keep in the DCI's favor. Redmond knew that Trellis nearly always won the day.

"You're right. It is *f**king* Carter's territory. That's why I had to get the DCI to weigh in."

"But, how? Carter must have objected?" inquired Redmond.

Trellis knew it was a stretch, but he had been able to convince the DCI.

"I told the DCI this was merely a cover for an operational probe of the British Service. I convinced him that it would be good to have someone close to Her Majesty's Service to keep tabs of the Pall Mall bomber investigation. I reminded him we still have two American corpses as a result of that attack."

"Do I get a choice in this assignment?" asked Redmond, already knowing the answer.

"No, you do not get a *f**king* choice, Ellison," responded Trellis briskly. "With your stint in London early in your career, you'll know which hedges to peek under, so to speak. And I want you to be the biggest *f**king* burr under my buddy George *f**king* Chartwell's saddle. Even if it is a *wimpy* equestrian saddle. *F**ker* probably rides side-saddle."

Redmond smiled to himself. Trellis was referring to Chartwell's country estate, and his love of horses. Never mind that Trellis had his own estate, the spread in Annapolis, complete with its boathouse and his cherished sailboat. Redmond knew Chartwell came from old money, while Trellis was *nouveau riche*, having inherited his fortune from his wife's father passing after a long battle with Alzheimer's.

"Ellison, with Diane still missing after several months, I am sure those *f**kers* have her stashed away somewhere. Never forget that we are at war with Chartwell."

Ellison said nothing. He thought sarcastically to himself how great it was to be going to war on foreign soil. A war of old money vs. new. A war of who pissed on who's turf. A war of ego's. If there was one thing Ellison never forgot, it was that people died in war. And he was now being sent to the front lines."

The young lieutenant stared at his boss. "Well, I better get moving. I have some things to do if I am going to be gone for an extended period."

"Ellie, I want your ass on a plane to London tomorrow. No 'ifs', no 'ands', just your damn butt skipping across the pond. Got it?"

Ellison left, firmly closing, but not slamming, the door in meager protest.

Trellis sat behind his desk, having a full ten minutes until his next appointment.

He had not told Redmond that this was actually a war on two fronts. Not only was he doing battle with the Brits, but now also with Carter Norris as well. Trellis convinced himself that it was Norris, Diane's superior who he had outmaneuvered with the DCI, who was feeding the deep background information to the congressional investigator, Paul Renard.

Trellis knew he could handle Renard, even with Norris feeding Senator Malinski's pit bull the raw meat that was the history of Trellis, *Osprey* and *Erasmus*. This was unlike Norris, but he had become increasingly belligerent since the DCI signed off on declaring Diane lost in action in the Wisniewski affair.

How else could Renard have gotten to the topic of Stanley being inserted into East Berlin so quickly? What else did Norris know? Where would Renard's questions take him next?

Trellis thought he was sure that Norris held no knowledge that could harm him. Yet, still there was the minute risk that Stanley had passed Trellis' secret onto Diane, who somehow relayed the info to Norris Carter. Trellis needed to proceed with caution until he found Diane.

All this inconvenience because Stanley couldn't be content with enjoying his quiet little retirement. Why couldn't he? What forced him to give that all up?

"Welcome back, Stanley. You've been gone a while."

Trellis' mind had drifted to late 1985 in West Berlin. After having been detained for three weeks in East Berlin, Stanley had just some eight hours ago cleared Checkpoint Charlie. He had gone to the agreed address in the American sector, where he was received, and initially debriefed, before being moved to this secure op center. He had been waiting in this confined, but comfortable, conference room for nearly three hours alone until Trellis entered seconds ago.

Trellis shook his hand, but without any real warmth or gratitude. It was as if the handshake was simply part of the vetting procedure.

"I read the transcript of your debriefing," Trellis began, sitting across the table from Stanley. "Let's just start over at the beginning. Tell me about first contact."

"It wasn't *Erasmus*," started Stanley, knowing the full re-telling of his story would take several hours.

Stanley was exhausted. He had been detained by the east German *Stasi* for three weeks, and then mysteriously released.

"Who, then?" prompted Trellis.

"As I left the *Konzerthaus*, I wanted to see the Brandenburg Gate from the Pariser Platz. You know, really see it, without that damn wall in the way."

"*Shit,* Stanley, this is not a *damn* boondoggle. *F**king* tourist!" Trellis muttered.

"Well, if it makes you feel any better, I never made it there. I was approached by an old man as I walked along the boulevard *Unter den Linden*. He was dressed in rags, and I thought at first he had decided to take the risk of begging alms from a visiting westerner."

"What did he say to you?" Trellis' eyes were focused, looking for even the most microscopic deviation from what Stanley had told his initial debriefers.

Stanley answered, "He called me by my cover name, as he passed by me. '*Herr Krajewski* - yes, he pronounced it as the Polish do, *Kry-YEV-ski* -please be so kind to follow me. Your friend Foley wants to meet with you.' So, I followed him, of course."

Figure 5 – Konzerthaus Berlin

(Photo Credit: Elizabeth Marie Trawinski)

"He said the name 'Foley'?" asked Trellis.

"Are you surprised?" Stanley awaited Trellis' answer.

"Not really, I had passed that codename to *Erasmus*, so when he used it you would know you were safe."

"How did you pass it to him?" asked Stanley, knowing Trellis would never allow Stanley the courtesy of a straight answer.

"Not for you to know, Stanley. What happened next?"

"I followed the man, at a distance, to his flat. An apartment block, very dilapidated. High density, Soviet-style, concrete building."

"Your being there was certainly scandalous. These people get turned in for having western foodstuff packages in their trash. Here you are, a live-blooded westerner in the flesh. Certainly, his neighbors would feel compelled to report this to the *Stasi*." Trellis was matter of fact, indifferent.

Stanley continued. "Once inside, he told me to wait. Foley's people would be there shortly. He surely seemed to know that one of the neighbors would have reported him. He didn't bother to call anyone himself. In fact, in less than an hour, we were both arrested by the *Stasi*."

"So, our *Erasmus*, now had cover for arresting you." Trellis began, piecing together the operation. "He made you look like a Western spy - which, of course, you are - meeting a contact, although we would never be so brazen to meet in such a high-density environment, where it was sure to be seen and reported."

"I was taken to an interrogation center on *Normannenstrasse*," said Stanley, marking the location of *Stasi* headquarters. They gave me the full works. Strapped me in the chair. Got the yellow cushion treatment. I was questioned for two days, alternating to a dank holding cell when I wasn't in the chair. They kept wanting to know who I worked for. I stayed with my cover, just a talent spotter for my small Canadian classical record label. They never got physical with me, but they didn't exactly roll out a red carpet either."

Trellis knew of the yellow cushion treatment. The *Stasi* had the cushion attached to the chair during interrogations, collecting the sweat of those unlucky enough to be interrogated. They were then removed, placed in airtight containers and warehoused. They were linked to the file of the accused and stored for the possible eventual need of giving one's scents to the dogs in trailing an escapee. The *Stasi* had warehouses full of them.

Trellis thought it unusual to give this treatment to a visiting westerner, but realized *Erasmus* had to convince his superiors that Stanley was a threat to the State.

"Go on," Trellis said, "when did you meet *Erasmus*?"

"Only after holding my own for three days. I was in interrogation. I was finishing up after another long questioning session, when the two guards began to transit me back to the cell. I was always questioned in English, as I denied knowing any German. A third guard entered the room, and assuming that I did not speak German, said to the others, 'What are you doing? *Der Direktor* is coming to see him. Hurry, restrain him.' It must have been a shock to them, as they practically threw me back in the chair and assured my restraints were painfully tight."

"How did you know that *Der Direktor* was *Erasmus*? You had never seen him; you had no visual reference," wondered Trellis.

"He entered the interrogation room and said nothing. He circled the table, taking me in from all angles. He gestured the guards out of the room with a motion from his right wrist. Yet he was cautious. The recording of the room was surely still ongoing. He sat in the chair across from me, staring into my eyes. Slowly, with his lips, he parsed a single word – "Folly".

Trellis repeated the word aloud. "Folly?"

"Yes. All I could think of was the historical *Erasmus'* book, **In Praise of Folly**. He was telling me who he was. It was a codeword identifier. Then he continued,"

'What folly that your intelligence service could think they could insert you to meet with your undercover agent. I can only praise our citizen's recognizing this assault upon our national sovereignty.'

"What language?" asked Trellis.

"Still English. He was putting on a show for someone. Threatened me several times with execution. Told me that my undercover agent, the man I had followed to the flat, had confessed and had been shot earlier that morning."

Trellis was listening intently. "Poor bastard. Likely *Erasmus* had goaded the old man into contacting you. Likely *Erasmus* had something on him in his *Stasi* file. Maybe promised him some incentive, like release to West Berlin or West Germany. When the old man came close to breaking under questioning, *Erasmus* had him shot, covering his tracks. Made you appear to be an even bigger catch to his superiors."

"My God," said Stanley, lowering his head out of respect for the East German whose life was nothing more than a prop in this ghoulish theatre.

"Then what?" stabbed Trellis.

He lectured me for the better part of an hour. Kept using the word 'Folly', kept using the word 'Praise'.

'Your country thinks they can penetrate the GDR – what folly.'

'I can only praise the truth and purity of the Soviet Communist ideology. The strength of our doctrine will crush the rotting core of your capitalism, of your country's imperialist goals. What corruption. What folly.'

"And so on," said Stanley.

"Did he ever name your country?" Trellis asked.

"Very much so. The United States. America. USA. He used them all. When I was finally allowed to speak, I restated that I was not American, that I was Canadian."

"How did he react?"

"He laughed out loud. He then said, simply, 'You are an American spy, and you will be tried as one.' He then walked very briskly from the room, slamming the door.

"Then what?"

"Nothing," said Stanley.

"Nothing?" Trellis was confused.

"I sat in the cell for nearly two weeks. Only occasionally I was allowed a brief march outside for air. Rarely even an interrogation. When I asked what was happening, I was told nothing."

Trellis looked him hard in the eye. "*Erasmus* was waiting for the blowback from Moscow. Via *Osprey*. And it must have come back as we all had hoped."

"What was the message?" asked Stanley.

"Convince the American to turn double. If he doesn't, dispose of him," said Trellis coldly. "Most likely. We haven't heard from *Erasmus* just yet. We can only assume."

Trellis lied. He knew this was the message exactly. NSA had intercepted it.

"That explains the boat ride," said Stanley softly.

"What boat ride?" asked Trellis, even though he already knew the answer.

At the beginning of the third week, I was taken from my cell late at night. I was taken to what appeared to be a canal lock, underneath a bridge."

"The *Spreekanal*, in the *Kupfergraben* section, under the railway bridge," said Trellis plainly.

Stanley continued. "There was a patrol boat there. My hands were cuffed. I was presented onboard to *Herr Direktor*, the man we call *Erasmus*. The boat pulled out onto the canal, which joined the *River Spree*. It puttered along the river, until it came to where the river was crossed by the wall. Of course, the wall didn't actually span the river. It came abruptly to the river's bank and picked up again on the opposite banks. It left the *River Spree* open for cargo traffic but was patrolled constantly by these boats."

"Save the f**king geography lesson. I know all that, Stanley. What happened there?"

"*Erasmus* had the guards take me to the bow of the boat. Chained my cuffs to an anchor. Then, he waved them to the back of the boat. It was pitch black, I am guessing maybe 2 AM. It was then that I got my biggest shock."

"Which was what?" barked Trellis.

"*Erasmus* put a pistol to my head, pressed it to my temple, hard," said Stanley. "He leaned forward and whispered to my ear in very rough Polish. I did not know until then that he even spoke my language, but I suppose it was so the other guards would not overhear."

"What did he say?" asked Trellis, with no surprise in his voice.

"He said I was to admit having been an American spy and would soon agree to act as a double agent for East Germany. Then, he would send me back to you. If I did not agree, there and then, he would put a bullet in my head and dump my body in the *Spree*."

"Exactly as he and I had agreed," said Trellis triumphantly.

"Well you could have let me in on that level of detail," snapped Stanley angrily.

"You needed to be frightened, Stanley. I warned you this assignment was dangerous and could go bad..." said Trellis.

"I thought it had indeed already gone bad, very bad," said Stanley, honestly relaying his fear at that moment. "So, anyway, I agreed, and over the next week *Erasmus* 'interrogated' me, but always alone. Always outside of Berlin, in the East German countryside. It was there that we finalized the exfiltration procedures for *Osprey* from Poland. Worked out the emergency contact tradecraft and so on. *Erasmus* knew you were going to re-assign me back to Warsaw."

"What was he telling his superiors?" asked Trellis.

"That I was now an East German source placed among the Americans. That I was to be returned to Warsaw, and my reports would be fed back to *Herr Direktor*, meaning of course *Erasmus*."

Trellis looked pleased. "We will insert you back into Warsaw, all right. The Communists may even give you a little more leeway, if they are even let in on the myth that you have been turned double. More than likely, the *Stasi* won't share this with the Poles, however. They'll keep this little secret for a rainy day. Just another East German State Secret."

"Moscow surely knows already," Stanley said. "Won't they let the Poles in on this? I'll be rounded up in no time once I am back in Warsaw."

Jack Trellis grunted. He appeared to be distracted, reading from his files.

"I sincerely doubt it," said Trellis. "The *Ossi's* and the Soviets will keep this from the Poles. Gives them a source to one-day spy upon the Poles, who they never did trust."

Trellis thought the Soviet's no more trusted the Poles, and *Ossi's* for that matter, than the Americans trusted the Brits. If there is no honor among thieves, then there is certainly no trust among intelligence services.

10

DELAYED GRATIFICATION

Diane lay in her safe-house bed. The second day after Malcolm Devereaux failed to arrive, as promised, Dr. Alec had to medicate her to calm her anxious spirit. The medication caused her to sleep but had the side effect of making her feel continuously cold in her core. She was empty, drained and depressed.

Her only response after the medication, and before crawling once again into the bed she had come to detest, was to pull the heavy curtains to block out the antagonizing view of *Lago Maggiore*, sprawled beneath her perch. It was taunting her, a view of the world she was not allowed to live in. The lake's calm blue mirrored surface evidenced the easy passage Devereaux could take to come for her. But despite this, her *Mad Mal* had failed to show. In defeat, she raised the thermostat, and returned to her refuge of sheets and covers.

Several hours later, while she slept, the rest of the chalet, outside her now stuffy incubator of a room, came alive. They were still anticipating the delayed arrival of Devereaux. The security magpies that were *Heckle & Jeckle* readied their ops debrief. Dr. Alec prepared his combined medical and psychological analyses of the medicated tenant. Sophie knew she would be pressed to reveal everything that Diane had told her in the strictest of confidence.

Then it happened. A blue Toyota pulled up the gate and was allowed entry to the darkened crushed gravel driveway that ascended to the house. *Jeckle* walked outside to greet its driver, still hidden by its heavily tinted glass. All the while, *Heckle* watched the lower driveway and entry gate on his console, assuring that this vehicle was indeed alone. Behind him were two fully loaded and easily accessible AR-15's, converted to be fully automatic, leaning casually against a bookcase.

Devereaux emerged from the car, looking his usual dapper self in his pressed jeans, complemented by dark grayish-green fitted dress shirt with its cuffs rolled under themselves, exposing his wrists. The only parts of his ensemble that one who knew him might find unexpected, were the wide brimmed hat and clear lens glasses that he wore.

Jeckle escorted Devereaux inside the house. Sophie greeted him and then began to walk the corridor leading to Diane's room, before Devereaux called her name, asking her not to disturb Diane just yet. Then, over the next forty-five minutes, he got the situation report, or SITREP in his jargon, from the magpies and Dr. Alec.

Over the last two days from when Devereaux was first expected, Diane had been at first exuberant, then later severely despondent. Carefree, then paranoid. Energetic, then lethargic. All to be expected, said Dr. Alec, until her subconscious could reconcile the threat it had experienced with the suppressed memories of Stanley's sacrificing his own life to protect hers.

She still failed to recall Stanley or even the cemetery, nor Carlyle and his shots that were meant to claim them both. She only remembered that Devereaux had saved her. From what? She could not remember. She knew she had been shot, but on the advice of Dr. Alec, no one was allowed to speak to her of how she obtained the wound. Only that she was found severely wounded in the *Montmartre* section of Paris. Then it was Sophie's turn to speak to Devereaux.

"How is she?" asked Malcolm, skipping the small talk.

"She is not herself," answered Sophie. "She is dependent on you. She lives for your visits, When they are delayed, her spirits are crushed." The young Pole looked at him accusingly.

"Sophie, you know, there are still many people that wish to complete what they attempted to do to her. We were lucky to have been able to stabilize her in Paris. Luckier yet still to get her here undetected. Each day we are here is one more threat to her. I am required to take the greatest of precautions to come here. It is beyond my control."

Sophie could see in his eyes that he cared for her friend, Diane. However, she had only met this man the night of the tragedy, and despite his having saved Diane's life, Sophie wondered to what end?

Was Diane to become a bargaining chip between the British and the American espionage agencies? If so, this constituted a massive threat to Diane's personal security.

Sophie did not know Devereaux well, and despite his apparent concern for Diane's welfare, Sophie did not yet trust him.

Devereaux decided to rest overnight, allowing Diane to do the same.

Early the next morning, Malcolm Devereaux slipped into the incubator room that was Diane's. He was immediately embalmed in the stuffy, close, and heavy heat that seemed to melt the oxygen from the air. The room was dark, until Malcolm found the lamp next to Diane's bed. As he flipped it on, he sat aside Diane on the bed.

The combination of the light and the shifting weight alongside her in the bed awakened her, although she was still groggy.

"Please, Dr. Alec, no more medication, please," she pleaded to the man's form sitting aside her.

"No more medication, Darling. Although just the sight of you is healing me outside-in."

His voice was warm and sweet. He gently brushed Diane's hair from her forehead, assuring the back of his finger was in lingering contact with her warm, sweaty skin.

"Malcolm, you finally came!" Her smile was but a gentle crease of her face, despite the soaring of the medicated spirit within her. "Why do you tease me for days on end, don't you understand how much I need you?"

"Darling, there are still a lot of very bad men looking for you. I needed to be very careful." Devereaux wondered just how much of this truth she understood at this point.

"It doesn't matter, you are here for me," she said, as she rose to a sitting position. "You came for me."

She was caressing his face now with her hand. It soon wandered over his lean, muscular chest.

"You came for me," she repeated. "Now, you are here to protect me."

"Diane, I have to talk to you about something very important."

She reached her hand behind his neck and pulled herself up close to him. Her lips sought his and found them.

Devereaux attempted not to pull back from her, but that was his instinct, and he sensed her recognizing this hesitancy in him.

She pulled him closer. Now both of her arms were draped behind his neck. Diane hungrily sucked his lower lip into her mouth.

"Darling, control yourself, my dear," he said, pulling himself from her embrace. The closeness of her perspiring body, combined with the infernal heat in the room was suffocating him.

Diane grabbed the muscular arm of his that was closest to her. "Mal, Darling. I need you. I need you so."

"Yes, Darling. I am here." Devereaux now tried to overcome his sense of being claustrophobic.

Diane's hands then roamed his well-defined shoulders. Her face again drew close to his. She whispered into his ear in a lush, heavy, yet soft voice saying, "Take me. I'm yours, I want you to take me."

Devereaux pulled back from her a second time.

"You don't know what you are saying, Diane."

Her voice became louder, but no less vulnerable.

"I know exactly what I am saying. I want you to take this, all of this," she said. Then, pulling his hand onto her breast, said, "I want you to consume me, just as I will consume every bit of you."

Devereaux hated what he was about to do but did it nonetheless.

"I would love nothing more ..." he said to her, his hand now not only lying upon her left breast, but gently groping the fullness of her form. He slowly traced it to the lovely vale between the fullness of her figure. His hand then crossed over to her right breast, and slowly worked upwards, to the heavily bandaged wound just below her shoulder. "... but as my American friends would say, for the time being, you are 'damaged goods'. Let's concentrate on getting you completely better, so I cannot be accused of taking advantage of you."

"You bastard," she spat at him. "Why did you save me, just to torture me?"

Her cheeks became crimson. Her eyebrows became aggressively arched.

"Darling, we need to get some light and some air into this room, I am choking on this heat," he said, now rising from the bed. As he walked to the window, he continued, "Bye the bye, Darling, I didn't save you. I merely pulled together the team to patch-up what was left of you."

Diane was uncontrollably excited now, sitting and then bouncing on the side of the bed. "Stop saying that, you saved me. You are the man who saved my life."

Her voice was shouting with ragged peaks tearing through each syllable.

"We need some light in this room," said Devereaux, intentionally ignoring her outburst. He reached to find the seam of the overlapping curtains, so he could draw them open.

It was then that Diane's mood became uncontrolled in its anxiety.

"No, no, don't do that. Please, God, don't do that..." Diane said, as he drew open the curtains, and became instantly immersed in the fullness of the alpine morning light.

The muscles of her face were now distorted. Fear had pulled them inside out, from the calm beauty they had exuded seconds before. She had risen to her feet, and continued to scream at him, "No, No, No. You can't do this, oh my God, no, get down, please..."

It was then that Devereaux turned to look out over the lake. He did not know what exactly had excited her so, what had driven her to such an emotional response. Dr. Alec was now pounding on the door that Devereaux had locked behind him.

"Open the door, Mal. Our guest is overly excited. If you don't open this instantly, then I'll have our lads here break it through," Alec shouted over the screams of Diane.

"No, No, No, don't do it, don't do it…" Diane's emotional voice *warbled into a crescendo. "Please, get down…"*

Devereaux tried to calm himself. With Diane's unrestrained screaming and the pounding upon the door by Alec and his protectors, the room seemed to close in around him. The heat was still unbearable. Beads of sweat had formed on Malcolm's brow. He raised his left arm, wiping the sweat away with the back of his hand.

At this motion, Diane's screams transitioned from uncontrolled razor-sharp pleadings to nearly incoherent, hollowed-out bellows of internalized anguish. She was now sobbing uncontrollably. Diane threw herself at Mal's feet, clutching his legs with the death grip of a drowning woman. It was then that Devereaux finally understood the trauma Diane was reliving.

"OH, MY GOD! DON'T DO IT! GET DOWN! STANLEY, I AM BEGGING YOU, GET DOWN. STANLEY, PLEASE GET DOWN!"

Then the crash of *Heckle & Jeckle* smashing in the door echoed through the room like the rifle shot that Diane had been fearing. She no longer spoke, only sobbed uncontrollably. Dr. Alec rushed in to her side to hold her, to assist her through her cathartic moment. *Heckle* followed behind with the Fentanyl injection that the good doctor would use to sedate the woman from the terror of her recollections.

Fentanyl is a massively powerful opioid. While Dr. Alec used it sparingly, he needed its rapid onset to sedate Diane before she yielded to this moment of crisis. He squeezed the syringe to reduce the amount of the injection that *Heckle* had prepared by half. He felt his sweat beading on his head as the sobbing, rocking woman in his embrace seemingly tore the veil of her own sanity in half. Her body shuttered as the good doctor administered the injection.

Just before the injection, Diane's face had lapsed into a muscular agony as the horror of her subconscious came crashing into her present. Her face then quickly melted from the agitation of her recollections to an anguish and sorrow that seemed to penetrate deep into her core. The sorrow in her eyes haunted them all, and a chill was felt by all, like that of a spirit sweeping through the overheated room. Her last words before the medication silenced her were ***"Oh, my God, Stanley! It was you who saved me! You...saved ...my ... life...you gave your ...life to save ... ... mine"***

Sophie stood in the doorway as the four men lifted the now sedated body of Diane into the confinement of her bed once again. She thought that Diane's last word trailed off on a heroic breath, one that exhaled in defiance of the sedative's effect taking down the tortured wall of her consciousness.

Diane had wrestled with the terror of Pere Lachaise, and her tremendous will fought to acknowledge aloud what she had only now allowed herself to remember – the man she was tasked to capture had died to allow her the freedom of a life restored.

11

RECONNOITER

The next day, a light rain fell upon London. Preston Almesbury had been in weeks of hiding, due to death threats hurled at him anonymously for the exploits of the website of his small newspaper and internet entity – *The Westminster Conservatoire*. His paper had broken the story of Stanley Wisniewski, with materials provided by the fugitive himself while he was on the run. It then began a series of articles based upon material produced by, and often most wholly written by MI6. These articles questioned the veracity of the CIA and asked why it took over a month to locate Mr. Wisniewski.

Then, shortly after the new year, *The Conservatoire* ran a series of articles acknowledging that while Mr. Wisniewski had been killed by the CIA, was this truly necessary? It also broke the story that the lead of the investigation, Ms. Diane Sterling, had been severely wounded during the shoot-out with the spy and was not to be found anywhere. It went on to publicly ask the question, if the CIA suspect was dead, and the woman assigned to track him was missing, was there something more nefarious at play than a simple apprehension?

The stories were followed with great interest in Britain, who long considered their Secret Services to be a source of national pride, more capable than the CIA, Israel's Mossad, or the Soviet KGB, and its Russian successors the FSB and SVR.

Despite the overwhelming British pride, there were those who felt *The Conservatoire* was undermining the relationship of its services to their American counterparts. Discussion programs on the BBC made this point repeatedly, with a small segment of the population becoming somewhat fanatical. This sentiment resulted in numerous death threats to Preston and his family. To escape this environment, Preston and his wife relocated to their family estate in the Scottish lands known familiarly to single malt lovers the world over as *Speyside*.

Having recently left his wife with family in Scotland, Preston Almesbury now had returned to the city he so loved. On this Saturday afternoon, he decided to indulge himself in one of his favorite pleasures – lunching at the oyster bar in the seafood market within Harrod's food hall. As he began to satiate his taste on Irish Rock Oysters on the half shell, and paper-thin Norwegian Smoked Salmon served with capers and dill, an American woman rested her purse upon the seat next to his at the oyster bar.

"Is this seat taken?" she asked, waiting waiting for Almesbury to finish his conquest of the Rock Oyster he held to his lips.

Preston swallowed and then dabbed his mouth with the cloth napkin, stood to acknowledge the young woman, and said softly "No, Madame. Would you care to join me?"

She was stunningly beautiful, Preston thought. Her hair was black as the night, but with subtle violet highlights that were nearly imperceptible. They crested the swells of her hair, separating them from the depths of her voluptuously intriguing midnight tresses. Her face was warm, well defined, featuring a radiant smile that was complemented by dark, wanting eyes.

"I am so sorry, I did not mean to disturb you so," she said to him in a playful manner.

"I am ever so delighted that you did. Forgive me for asking, but your accent sounds like it is from the American South? It is wonderful." Preston smiled warmly at her.

He looked at her impeccable clothing, so finely tailored. Her bag was Hermes and appeared to be dye matched to her skirt suit. She hiked her hem as she ascended the stool next to him, exposing her athletic and shapely legs just enough to light the fire of his attention. Preston estimated she was slightly more than half his age. He could not help being enamored with her appearance.

"Well, I reckon that is from being raised in Charleston. Although, I am living and working out of Atlanta these days. Good gracious, where are my manners? My name is Collette Corbeau, but all my friends call me Coco. And since you were so friendly to allow me to join you, I insist you call me Coco."

She gently presented her hand to him, which he took softly into his own. Her nails were trimmed in the same violet hue that was so subtly reflected from her long silken hair. He noticed no wedding ring on her left hand, as she used it to grasp the marbled bar.

"And you, Sir?" she asked after a lapse of the seconds as he measured her with his eyes.

"Forgive me, Miss Corbeau, how rude of me. I am Preston Almesbury. I am so delighted to meet you. Are you taking a break from some sightseeing in our grand metropolis?"

She rolled her neck ever so gently, breathing life into her shimmering strands of midnight hued hair.

"No, no. I have been to London so many times I could almost give the bus tours. I was here for work and decided to stay through the weekend to do some proper shopping. When in Knightsbridge, I always love to come here and partake of the delicacies. How is that Brut Rosé champagne you are having? It looks delightful."

Preston was measuring her form intently now, almost not hearing the words coming from that lithe body.

"Yes, of course, the Perrier-Jouët. Its taste complements the oysters magnificently. Please have a taste of mine, if you don't mind."

"I was just fixin' to ask if I could. You are such a gentleman."

Coco took the flute from Preston's hand, making sure to brush her hand suggestively across his. She raised it to her mouth, making a soft delicious moan as she first inhaled its subtle fragrance before it washed across her tongue. As she pulled it away from her mouth, she assured the flute was marked with a lipstick impression of her lower lip.

"Now that is so nice. How have I never paired that up with oysters in the past? I just can't imagine having anything else."

Preston was mesmerized by this animated creature sitting next to him, who effused a passion for life he had not experienced in perhaps the last twenty years. He listened intently as she ordered a half-dozen French brined oysters.

"I just love the salt, don't you?" she said to him.

"Those are even a little overpowering for me, I must admit," he said somewhat reluctantly. "You mentioned you are here for business, what line of work are you in, Coco?"

He looked to see if she took offense with his calling her by her first name. He was comforted by her response.

"Well, Preston, I am a buyer for a major retailer in the states. They actually pay for me to come to Europe several times a year for major shows. It pays amazingly well, and most everything is covered by a very generous expense account. A girl could do a lot worse."

"Most certainly," he replied.

Almesbury was enjoying himself immensely in her company. Soon his attention turned to his own appearance. His face was long, his nose was of the typical British angular proportions. His wife often remarked how droll his appearance could be. He must smile, he thought, but that was not difficult in the presence of this enchanting woman.

"What do you do, Preston?" she asked. "I mean, when you aren't feasting from the half shell."

She smiled at him. The warmth of her charm penetrated him.

"Well, yes, I seem to be in publishing, of sorts," he said instantly, not being able to think of a pseudo-profession as he had been advised.

"Now, don't tell me, Sugar, I would bet dollars-to-beignets that you publish Children's Books. You are much too nice a man to be putting anything else out there."

"Yes, perhaps, but I am the editor-in-chief of *The Westminster Conservatoire*," he said proudly, expecting this to impress her somewhat.

"I am so sorry, Preston, but I am not acquainted with that publication. Must be one of those specialty papers. My ex-husband used to get all kind of specialty publications on gold collecting, watch collecting, book collecting, *ad nauseum*..."

She pronounced the word *nauseum* like a contraction of the words Nasal and Museum. One would never know that first 'u' was even in there. He suppressed the urge to correct her, delighting instead in her tailored Dixie vocabulary.

"You seem so young to already have an ex-husband," Preston said, smiling at her, almost laughing as he said this.

She was just ingesting her first French oyster, and apparently enjoying it immensely given the expression of her face. She held up her first finger, the American equivalent of "wait just one minute."

She swallowed and drank again from his flute.

"Now, Preston, honey, you know a girl shouldn't kiss and tell!"

He laughed aloud. "Or, in this case, kiss-off and tell! Forgive me, I shouldn't have pried so."

She laughed at his joke, telling him he had not pressed too far at all.

"Oh, that's all right, Sugar. Ronald was the sweetest man I had ever met. I just have a proclivity to be drawn to older men. They are so much more interesting than those younger cry-baby athletes and *faux-elite* intellectuals, always trying to impress a young girl. I find older men so much more secure with themselves. Ronald's only problem was that he was a little too old. He passed away after nine years of marriage. His heart gave out."

"We'll that is something I certainly can understand," said Preston brashly.

She reached out and touched him on his arm. "Preston, you are such a scoundrel!"

Her laugh filled the ceramic-tiled food hall. Several patrons from the nearby caviar stand turned to wedge their looks of disapproval.

"Is there a Mrs. Preston?" Coco asked.

"Somewhere north of Edinburgh for the foreseeable future," he said as she continued to drink his champagne.

Coco returned the glass to the bar, which Preston quickly re-filled from the bottle. She returned the flute to his lips, taking great care to assure her lipstick on the glass made contact with his lips.

"Well, Preston, she is a very lucky woman. You are such a gen-tleman, sharing your lunch with me today."

"I do have the afternoon free, I could show you around London, places and things you wouldn't necessarily see on a sightseeing bus."

"Oh, I bet you could, Sugar, but today is all about lady-shop-ping, and that would bore you to tears, Honey." Coco was look-ing intently into his eyes at this point. "Perhaps, tomorrow? Why don't you swing by the Ritz and call on me? I would love to see your London."

"Consider it so. Let's say at eleven?"

"Make it one, Preston. I do so like to sleep-in in the mornings. Besides, give a girl a chance to put her face on."

"Coco, your face needs no adorning. It is one of the most radi-ant joys I have had the pleasure to ever experience."

"Like I said, Sugar, you are such a scoundrel. But I like it. I like it a lot."

———)•((❖))•(———

They finished their lunch, flirting and laughing with each other. Preston picked up the check for the dozen and a half oysters, the salmon, and the two bottles of Perrier-Jouët that they consumed. He politely kissed her cheek as they departed, leaving in different directions from the food hall.

As she reached the street, before searching for the taxi queue, Collette Corbeau dialed a number from her cell phone contacts.

When the man answered, she said very matter-of-factly "Contact made. He bit. Hard. Expect contact to be resumed tomorrow afternoon."

All of this was said without the least trace of any American Southern accent.

12

LINGERING SHADOWS

Deputy Director Trellis once again sat before Paul Renard, in the latter's cathedral of chrome and glass.

"Ready to re-engage? Round two?" asked the investigator.

"Certainly," answered Trellis, giving the appearance of a man who had nothing to hide. Or at least, attempting to give that appearance.

"When we last left off, you had sent Stanley into East Berlin, where he was detained by your double agent *Erasmus*. Right?"

"Yes, correct," answered Trellis.

"Then, he came back to West Berlin, under the guise of being an agent working for the *Stasi*. Handled by *Der Direktor*, our man *Erasmus*, right?" asked Renard.

"Again, correct." Trellis was now waiting for the new line of questioning to emerge.

"Where did Stanley go after that. Did you return him to the States?" asked Renard.

"Of course not. I left him in West Berlin for several months. I was playing my role as Head of Eastern Europe Operations. While *Erasmus* knew the truth, the rest of the *Stasi* had to think we were suspect of our agent who had been held for three weeks. They surely would know we wouldn't immediately put him back in service, and definitely not return him to Langley. For the next several months, we would dangle our Stanley just across the wall from the *Stasi*. They thought they had a double agent, and we were going to reinforce that. *Erasmus* would occasionally come out from behind the wall with their blessing, into West Berlin. I supplied low grade intelligence material to Stanley that he could then supply to *Erasmus*. Thus, *Erasmus* had product to take back to his superiors, all the while, *Erasmus* was passing information to us through Stanley."

"What kind of information, or product, as you would say, did *Erasmus* provide?"

"That's classified, Paul," said Trellis, hoping to cut him off.

"Do I need to remind you that I have been read in on all of this? I can have your own people attest to that, if you like." Renard felt that he was drawing close to Trellis' stash of secrets.

"No, you are right. OK. *Erasmus* was feeding us information from *Osprey* in Warsaw. All through '86. In addition to the Warsaw Pact military information, which was itself priceless, he provided the Communist concerns over civil unrest. The Poles were becoming restless with Prime Minister Jaruzelski's continuing crackdown on *Solidarity*. The economy was continuing to go to shit, also. And the Russians, that is the Soviets, were getting impatient with the Polish Communist Government for not taking stronger action."

"Why didn't you put Stanley back into Poland?" asked Renard.

"I did. In early '87. After there was adequate time to make sure the Stanley/*Erasmus* marriage had taken in West Berlin." Trellis seemed to fidget on this last point.

"And did it?"

"All too well," answered Trellis. "Stanley handled *Erasmus*, all the while *Erasmus* fooled the *Stasi* by pretending to handle Stanley. We continued to feed them some low-level material through *Erasmus*, but the *Stasi* allowed *Erasmus* to keep coming to West Berlin in the hope of the big score. Stanley and *Erasmus* became tight, all the while refining their exfiltration plans for the day when *Osprey* would have to be smuggled out of Warsaw."

Renard was following. "So, why did you pull Stanley out of West

Berlin and reintroduce him into Warsaw, if things were going so well?"

Trellis was becoming somewhat tired of this line of questioning.

"Because, given all that was going on in Poland, we needed to re-activate Stanley's agent *Syrenka*. *Syrenka* had been the best source on what was going on inside *Solidarity*. If we had that perspective, along with the Government Info *Osprey* was feeding *Erasmus*, then we had a pretty complete insight as to what was going on in Poland, and by extension, the Communist Bloc."

"And *Osprey* was now feeding information directly to Stanley in Warsaw?" Renard asked what he had assumed.

"No *f**king* way. *Erasmus* wouldn't allow that. Threatened to cave the whole thing if we cut him out of the loop. And we still needed *Erasmus* to get *Osprey* out, if nothing else."

"So, *Erasmus* didn't trust you, did he, Jack?" mused Renard. "He knew if he stopped handling *Osprey*, you could always find another way to get *Osprey* out from behind the Iron Curtain. Suddenly, you wouldn't need him so much. He knew what he was dealing with in you, Jack. He was afraid you would cut him out completely. So, he dangled confessing his sins to the *Stasi* just to get you to keep him in the loop with *Osprey*. One might say handling *Osprey* was his insurance card. He knew it kept you in need of him, and maybe he even thought it just might keep him alive."

Renard was enjoying this probing into Trellis' Cold War secrets. He was not aware, however, of how close he had just come to Jack Trellis' darkest fear, for despite the anxiety of his internal reaction, the CIA's DDO had merely continued to look blankly at him.

Trellis waited. "Stanley re-appeared in Warsaw in early '87, and the *Syrenka* product starts flowing again just in time."

"Just in time for what?" asks Renard.

"For the falling of the Old Guard...." Trellis smiled. "Events began accelerating in Poland over the next couple of years. Poland was in economic crisis. Gorbachev had taken over as head of the USSR in 1985, and was hell bent on reversing the stagnation of the Soviet economy. He began the policies of *'Glasnost'* ('Openness') and *'Perestroika'* ('Restructuring'). One outcome of this, was the USSR was no longer going to pay to get its satellite states out of their own economic crises."

"So, the Polish Communists were left to clean up the mess they themselves had created?" asked Renard.

"Yup," said Trellis. "In '87 in Poland, the communist party tried to increase food and commodity prices over 100%. Overnight, the prices of nearly everything doubled. Near hyper-inflation set-in. *Solidarity* was still outlawed. In 1988, a series of demonstrations led to a succession of massive strikes, shutting down what little life of an economy remained."

Renard listened to Trellis intently.

"Then in 1989, looking for a way to appease the populace, the Polish Communist government agreed to enter into what was to become known as the Round Table Talks. The Government agreed to reinstate *Solidarity* as a trade union. Lech Walesa then negotiated for Solidarity to run candidates in the upcoming elections, where 35% of the seats of the *Sejm* (the existing Polish legislative body), would be competed. The communists were confident they would retain the majority of these seats, as well as the 100 seats of the newly instituted Polish *Senat*, that had also been negotiated in the Round Table Talks."

"So. Jack, you mean these elections weren't fixed in favor of the communists?" asked Renard.

"With the Soviets no longer subsidizing the Polish state, the Polish communists played it straight. After all, the world was watching these elections very closely. The voting took place just after the Tiananmen Square uprising in China. Communism was under pressure across the globe. Besides, the communists never fully understood just how unpopular their regime was with the people of Poland."

Renard shook his head in disbelief, and Trellis continued.

"*Solidarity* went on to shock the world by winning all 161 of the available *Sejm* seats, as well as 99 of the 100 seats in the new Polish *Senat*. By the end of August 1989, a new *Solidarity* led coalition government was formed. While the communist Jaruzelski retained the title as President, the Prime Minister elected was Tadeusz Mazowiecki, a *Solidarity* candidate who became the first non-communist Prime Minister since the end of World War II."

"A year later, in December 1990, Lech Walesa was elected as President of Poland, displacing Jaruzelski. It was however, the election of August 1989 that lit the fuse to the downfall of the USSR. It was also this period that led our agent *Osprey* to conclude that he then needed to contact Stanley. The time had come for him to be exfiltrated to the West."

"Tell me about this *Osprey*, Jack. What motivated him to spy on his own country?" Renard was digging deep.

"He didn't think he was betraying his country, if that's what you're thinking. Just the opposite," said Trellis, "*Osprey* considered himself a patriot."

"Who was he, Jack?"

"He was a Colonel in the Polish General Staff under Jaruzelski. One of the old man's favorite's. *Osprey* worked for Jaruzelski when he was Defense Minister, later when he was Prime Minister, and even as an adviser when he advanced to the Presidency. *Osprey* had survived World War II as a young child. Saw the brutality of the Nazi's first, then the Russians later as they came through on their way to Berlin. He later entered the military as his country rebuilt itself after the fighting stopped, only to find that the Soviets soon took over all leadership decisions for the re-emerging Polish military."

"So, he, like *Erasmus*, had no great love for the Soviets?" asked Renard.

"No, clearly not," answered Trellis, "but that wasn't unusual for the Polish military. They all detested the Russians at some level for denying their country its true autonomy, its freedom. What was different, though, was that *Osprey* had a keen intellect that was especially suited for military planning. His talents were soon spotted by the Kremlin, who utilized his skills for planning the suppression of the Prague Spring in '68. When *Osprey* saw the brutality that the Soviets had used there, and in putting down protests in the Polish

Baltic cities two years later, he knew that the Russians were continuing their ruthless, overbearing ways."

"This was a surprise to him?" asked Renard.

"Perhaps not, but there was a side of him that was young and idealistic still. He assumed after the war was over, the Russians would handle the Communist states with a more even hand. That is, he thought, with some level of sovereignty. His strategic planning functions were soon required by both the Soviets and the East German's, and that's when the reality of the Soviet Bloc war plans alarmed him. One of the scenarios the Soviets had him prepare was for a first strike against NATO. As *Osprey* ran through various scenarios, it became clear to him that if the Red Army attacked the West, the only option the Western nations would have to slow down the onslaught of Soviet conventional weaponry would be to turn to tactical nuclear weapons. At that point, the Warsaw Pact had too much of a lead in conventional weapons in the European theatre over the NATO armies. And where would the West strike at the Red Army with these nukes? *Osprey's* planning said it would be on Polish soil, as the Red Army reinforcements headed west towards East Germany. He was sure that the whole of Poland would become a nuclear battlefield."

"Was he right?" asked Renard.

"The NATO Generals that we consulted said that *Osprey* was right on the button with his analysis. He eventually passed his concerns onto *Erasmus*, enlisting him to contact the Americans. Why he picked *Erasmus* to share his concerns with, I will never know. Perhaps they came to learn of each other's resentment of the Soviets?

Once *Erasmus* came to trust him, the information that followed in the mid-70's and 80's gave us a ringside seat as to what was on-going on the other side of the Iron Curtain, thanks to *Osprey's* access. The only area he had no insight into was inside the *Solidarity* union and social movement. After martial law was declared, *Solidarity* was again outlawed and went back underground. That is where we needed *Syrenka*, which meant we needed Stanley back in Warsaw"

"So, *Osprey* did all this to keep Poland from becoming a

sacrificial nuclear buffer to Russia in the world's first atomic war?" Renard said. "And the agent you used to get him out of Poland eventually was Stanley. Amazing."

————)((●)(————

Trellis had conveniently condensed the period of 1987 – 1989 in his historical lecture to Renard. All the while, his mind was dutifully guarding those events that were not to be shared with the investigator.

Stanley indeed returned to Warsaw in early 1987. Just as in the years before, Stanley was run once again outside the formal US diplomatic corps. Stanley was again under his Canadian cover as Mariusz Krajewski (*Kry-YEV-ski*) as a talent spotter for a small classical record label. He had even arranged for a contract with a pianist to be drawn up in '83, only to have it invalidated when the government refused to allow the artist to perform abroad. Trellis had pulled Stanley out of Poland in early 1985.

When Stanley was reinserted in '87, it was after he had been made known as a CIA agent to the East German *Stasi*. Trellis had been assured by *Erasmus* that the East Germans would not share this information with the Poles. However, to be sure, Trellis directed a tail from the US Embassy be put on Stanley whenever possible. Stanley was not made aware that the embassy would be periodically tailing him. Ultimately, this surveillance proved difficult, as the entire CIA Warsaw Station was less than 10 agents.

During Stanley's first tenure in Warsaw, he had generally successfully evaded the ZOMO paramilitary police. As he was not officially attached to the US Embassy, he was also not on the radar of the SB, the Polish counter-intelligence service for anti-state activities. The SB would routinely follow embassy personnel upon their departure of the embassy.

For the limited staff of the American Embassy CIA Station to trail Stanley, they would first have to shed their SB tails. Typical procedure for this time in Warsaw was to have Surveillance Detection Runs (SDR's) of at least two hours to assure the embassy personnel were not being followed. The difficulty for the CIA agents was that after these lengthy SDR's, they then had to find and tail Stanley. With his counter-surveillance training, this was no easy task.

Stanley found he was rarely surveilled by either the ZOMO or the SB. He assumed he had been vetted as a low priority target, given his near lack of contact with the Canadian and American Embassy personnel. Occasionally, Stanley would identify loitering persons, usually two men in a car. Whenever this occurred, Stanley assumed these to be SB agents, and would not engage his contact – the lovely Agnieszka Danuska, the wife of the Economics minister, and also the mother of Stanley's primary agent *Syrenka* within *Solidarity*.

Over the next year and a half, while Stanley adeptly spotted the ZOMO and SB assets, he had never become aware of his infrequent tails from the US embassy. This was partly because these were not usually the same person, but a rotation of the clandestine staff embedded there.

One day, a female agent from the Embassy had just completed her SDR when she noticed Stanley entering a Warsaw bookstore. The agent had not been tailed by the SB, as they were often chauvinistic in their coverages, and did not believe that women would be entrusted with sensitive espionage operations. She could not believe her luck in spotting Stanley entering the shop, and quickly parked her car and watched the premises.

She waited for approximately thirty minutes for Stanley to emerge. He did, leaving the bookstore by a rear entrance. She decided, at that point, to wait and see if he returned. She feared he might be conducting counter-surveillance himself. Then, only five minutes later, she saw Agnieszka Danuska exit from the same doorway. Agnieszka was well known to the embassy personnel. This was, however, the first time she had been potentially linked to Stanley Wisniewski. Soon the agency had rotating coverage of the bookstore and confirmed the Stanley-Agnieszka connection.

It was not long, before knowledge of Stanley's meetings with his Agnieszka, in the apartment over the communist bookstore, was fed back to Jack Trellis. Once Trellis had this knowledge of Agnieszka, he stood down the Embassy tailing operation, and then methodically purged the CIA records of any reference to Agnieszka Danuska.

Trellis then began slowly rotating the Embassy Staff out of Warsaw. He eventually replaced the Chief of Station there as well. He was sure the information regarding Agnieszka would provide critical leverage at some point in managing Stanley. Trellis wanted this influence over Stanley to be known only by himself.

———————⟫«(●)»⟪———————

Stanley was observed leaving the bookstore on the afternoon of June 14th, 1987. He did not spot the woman in the parked vehicle upon his exit, for his mind was racing. He thought only of the woman he had just left in the parlor above the bookstore.

"I have something urgent to share with you, my Agnieszka" he had said to her in Polish. He had been addressing her as "my Agnieszka" or "my *Sarenka*" ever since his return to Warsaw early that year.

"Yes, my *Stasiu*," she answered, calling him by his affectionate name as it is pronounced in Polish, "but tell me only good news."

"This is the best of news," he said to her. "Are you aware that our President Reagan was in Berlin two days ago?"

"Yes, I saw it on the news telecast. He drew crowds of 50,000 West Germans protesting his visit. Is this your good news?"

There had indeed been protests of that magnitude a few days before Reagan arrived. Through effective editing, the communist news agencies made it appear that they were opposing the American president in real time. Likely, this might have occurred had the West German government of Chancellor Helmut Kohl not shut down sections of West Berlin, including some subway lines, in order to keep these crowds from materializing.

President Reagan, even in 1987, was still viewed in Europe as the war-mongering extremist he had been painted as since his 1980 election. Conversely, the General Secretary of the USSR since 1985, Mikhail Gorbachev, was viewed as an agent of change, given his young age and his openness to restructuring the Soviet Union's extremely bureaucratic government.

When President Reagan did give his speech in Berlin that day, he did so in front of two sheets of bulletproof glass to protect him from the evil that was East Berlin. His speech was given at the edge of the *Tiergarten*, such that the Berlin Wall and the Brandenburg Gate behind it were visible.

"Agnieszka, that is the version the communists wanted you to believe," Stanley continued, "but the truth is so much more beautiful. Let me share his words with you."

Stanley had translated the entire speech by his own hand into written Polish. He sat next to her, showing her three passages that he had highlighted.

The first read:

"*Behind me stands a wall that encircles the free sectors of this city, part of a vast system of barriers that divides the entire continent of Europe. From the Baltic, south, those barriers cut across Germany in a gash of barbed wire, concrete, dog runs, and guard towers. Farther south, there may be no visible, no obvious wall. But there remain armed guards and checkpoints all the same--still a restriction on the right to travel, still an instrument to impose upon ordinary men and women the will of a totalitarian state. Yet it is here in Berlin where the wall emerges most clearly; here, cutting across your city, where the news photo and the television screen have imprinted this brutal division of a continent upon the mind of the world. Standing before the Brandenburg Gate, every man is a German, separated from his fellow men. Every man is a Berliner, forced to look upon a scar.*"

Stanley could feel the words penetrate her. He pointed to the second passage:

"*We welcome change and openness; for we believe that freedom and security go together, that the advance of human liberty can only strengthen the cause of world peace. There is one sign the Soviets can make that would be unmistakable, that would advance dramatically the cause of freedom and peace.*

General Secretary Gorbachev, if you seek peace, if you seek prosperity for the Soviet Union and Eastern Europe, if you seek liberalization, come here to this gate. Mr. Gorbachev, open this gate! **Mr. Gorbachev, tear down this wall!"**

Agnieszka sat next to him quietly as she read the passages. Stanley could then feel her begin to heave. He looked to her face to see tears streaming down her cheeks.

Stanley then pointed out the next passage, that he had translated from just before the end of the speech. It read:

"As I looked out a moment ago from the Reichstag, that embodiment of German unity, I noticed words crudely spray-painted upon the wall, perhaps by a young Berliner, 'This wall will fall. Beliefs become reality.' Yes, across Europe, this wall will fall. For it cannot withstand faith; it cannot withstand truth. The wall cannot withstand freedom."

Fighting back her tears, Agnieszka took his hands in hers. Her face was still damp with her emotions.

"Stasiu, it is so beautiful. When will your president come to Warsaw and do the same for us. We do not have the walls of concrete and barbed wire, but what they have built throughout our lives is just as limiting. Dependency upon these communists, who only give our people long lines and no food, no goods. And yet, they continue to raise the prices for the little that we can buy. We are at the breaking point; the people are already filling the streets. The Polish people fear the Soviet tanks will once again roll into Poland to take control. I fear for us all."

"What does your husband fear?" asked Stanley, in as gentle a manner as he could.

She scoffed at the mention of the man she did not love.

"That bastard. He only fears for himself. He is afraid that the people in the streets will result in his being sacked by the communist leadership. He fears to lose the luxury that we are entitled to in this perverted system. He cares not for the people who already have nothing."

"I thought you would be happy, my *Sarenka*. The President of the United States calls for the Soviets to tear down the Berlin Wall. I will tell you, Agnieszka, that the state of Poland will be free before this comes to pass. The Polish people are too proud, too unified, to not have their freedom restored."

She cried as she hugged him tightly. He could feel her torso heaving against him as she strained to say,

"My *Stasiu*, my *Stasiu*, I thank God every day for sending you to me."

The London Sunday afternoon was sunny and spectacular. Preston Almesbury arrived at the Ritz Carlton towering over Green Park. After a brief Mimosa at the bar, he escorted her to his Austin-Healy Sprite convertible, whose top had been put down nimbly by the valet staff.

"I hope you don't mind the Healy, it's quite vintage, but I thought perfect for a Sunday's drive."

"I absolutely love it, Preston. It is so fun, Sugar," Coco practically squealed.

As they drove through the London streets, crossing over the Thames, Preston said to her "I have somewhat of a confession to make, Coco".

"What's that, Preston, Honey?"

"I have a few friends in the apparel business. They tell me there are no shows in town this month. Also, which company puts their buyers up in the Ritz Carlton?"

"Well, you have blown my cover, Preston. I don't really like to go around town telling everyone I meet that I am an independently wealthy young woman travelling alone. You can understand that, can't you, Sugar?"

He laughed aloud. "Well, that makes more sense than what was going through my mind..."

"Which was what, exactly, Preston?"

"That you were a plant by the CIA..."

Coco allowed the wind to push back her head as she laughed upwards towards the sky. Her ravenesque locks were captured by the Hermes scarf, pinned beneath her chin. She turned her sunglasses toward the driver.

"Now, you must think yourself rather a tad important if the CIA would be interested in your weekend activities," she teased him.

"Asinine, I know. One goes through life second guessing everything, it seems. That's what I love so about you, you are so spontaneous, enjoying life as it comes at you. I am indeed sorry," said Preston regretfully.

"Oh, dear me, don't get so serious, Sugar." Her smile was once again radiant.

"Where exactly are you taking me. I thought you were going to show me *your* London". The city was well behind them at this point.

"I thought I might introduce you to Leeds Castle. Have you been there before?"

"Never! How delightful! And you call me spontaneous, this is perfect!"

"I thought, after touring the castle, we might have an early dinner in Maidstone. There is a lovely pub there on the town green that I thought you might fancy. Very simple, not posh at all, but also very English." Preston was pleased to see the level of her excitement.

"Well, Mr. Almesbury, I promise you one thing. I won't be carrying any concealed weapons after dinner. You'll see."

"This is likely how old Ronald bit the dust," he thought to himself. "Certainly, there are worse ways to go."

13

DÉJÀ VU REVISITED

"**H**e should be here tonight," said her *Zosia*, expecting to light the flame of anticipation in her.

"Who?" asked Diane without expectation. She had been sullen and morose since Devereaux' last visit several weeks ago. She had barely spoken to anyone, including Dr. Alec, and had eaten even less. It was clear that she now remembered the full account of the events of Pere Lachaise Cemetery on the emerging hour of Christmas morning. It was even more clear that she refused to relive her time with Stanley with anyone in the chalet. The team hoped Malcolm Devereaux could pry loose the details upon his return.

"Of course, Diane, there is always the possibility that his operational requirements may delay him a day or two. He wants to assure you are safe." Sophie was trying to keep her from elevating her expectations too high.

"Devereaux will get here when he gets here," responded Diane with a dearth of emotion.

She could read exactly what *Zosia* was trying to do. Her young friend seemed crestfallen with the blasé response, worrying that it signaled a total antipathy in Diane. Could this be the sign of a woman who might do harm to herself?

"I thought you would be happy to see again the man who saved you," said *Zosia*. The tone of her heavily accented English was deflated.

Diane turned from the window, where she had been looking

out over the lake. Today, it was gray, and frothed with whitecaps evidencing the winds that had been howling down the slope of the mountain all morning. Like the weather, her mood had been gray and frothed ever since her breakthrough, when she remembered the fate of her Stanley.

"He did not save me, my *Zosia*. He just prolonged the life I had been imprisoned in. And true to form, I remain imprisoned," Diane said, raising her arms to indicate *within all this*.

"I am sorry, Diane, I am only retelling your own words," said the innocent Polish maiden.

"Can I tell you a story, *Zosia*? It is one I had almost forgotten with all of Dr. Alec's medications pulsing within me. Also, the shock of remembering the night in the cemetery also caused me great confusion."

"Yes, certainly" added Sophie, "Please tell me."

"*Zosia*, when I was a young girl, only eleven years old, my parents told me that they were getting a divorce. It shook my whole being. I remember we were on a trip to London with my father, as he had business there. My mother took me for a walk in St. James Park. There is a path there called the Birdcage Walk, and my mother knew I loved to watch the birds there. It was full of geese, ducks, swans and even pelicans. I suppose she intentionally picked this place I loved to tell me the horrible news."

"She must have loved you so very much. It must have been so very difficult for her to hurt you so," said Sophie.

"I remember it to this day, as if it were a photograph I had to pull from my pocket. We stood in the grass, only inches from the pond. My mother was very nervous. She held my hand, but it felt as if she was trying to break my bones, because she was squeezing it so tightly. As she told me that she and father were getting a divorce, I just stared out into the pond."

Figure 6 – Solitary Swan in St. James Park

(Photo Credit: Elizabeth Marie Trawinski)

"Yes," said Sophie, "I can imagine that."

Diane went on.

"Under a great tree, strings of moss dripping from its boughs, there swam a singular white swan. My mother was clearly devastated by telling me the news. She had broken into tears. She could not accept the divorce that was being forced upon her by my father. Between gasps, she asked me if I was upset, but I said nothing. I just remained fixated on that lone, solitary swan. That was me, I remember thinking. Alone without a mate. That is how I will live. I will never let any man destroy me in the way that my father had destroyed my mother. I vowed that I would always live my life as the beautiful and content solitary swan."

"So, you never had a lover?" asked *Zosia*.

"I have had many, many lovers," she replied in as honest a moment as she had allowed herself in some time. "I just never allowed myself to love any of them. Beauty, pleasure, excitement and satisfaction, just never the commitment of love. I always lived that way, intent to not make myself dependent upon any man."

"Not even the man who saved you?" asked *Zosia*.

"The man who saved me is dead. Taken by that bastard Trellis. Devereaux and his bosses keep me here, only so they can strike back at Trellis. Stanley saved my life. He sacrificed his life, so I could escape. Now that I am nearing full recovery, I owe Stanley a debt that I have never owed to any other man. I have a duty to fulfil to him, and I plan to do exactly that."

"How?" asked Sophie.

"*Zosia*, you will see exactly how, because you will be there with me. I need you, and we both need Emory," Diane said as she continued to gaze upon the windswept Swiss waters of *Lago Maggiore*.

Later that evening, Devereaux did indeed arrive. After his in-briefs with *Heckle & Jeckle* and Dr. Alec, Malcolm spent the rest of

---

the evening with Diane. He continually questioned Diane about the lengthy discussion she had with Stanley before the arrival of the sniper Carlyle.

Diane told him that her memories were not pristine. Some elements she could relate verbatim, they were so clear to her. Other elements seemed to slip her consciousness like elusive, degraded images of a vivid dream one tries so hard to recall. These were like wisps of steam on a cold day that morphed their shape so rapidly, that the harder one tried to grasp them, the more they deformed, dancing and slipping through your fingers.

"So, Stanley was convinced that Trellis was skimming operational funds from his field assets?" Devereaux asked her.

"Yes, he kept referring to Trellis' greed. Kept saying Trellis was in league with Langston Powell."

"How did Stanley know the two were connected?" asked Devereaux.

"Stanley said Powell knew of the charges against him of embezzling five million dollars. Only Trellis could have passed this onto Powell, or so Stanley thought. Stanley had taken less than a million for operational needs. He was sure the other four million plus was siphoned by Jack Trellis."

"What else?" followed-up Devereaux.

"It seems Stanley was sure that Trellis was getting kickbacks from the sale of each drone bought from Powell's company. Although, I can't remember why he thought this..."

"Stanley never could prove this, though, could he?" asked Malcolm. "Even after he was pulled back from Poland to Langley in 1996?"

"I don't know. I just can't remember," Diane explained.

Devereaux looked at her, "We were always suspicious about the drone-maker connection, but we could not find any money trail that supported the kickback theory. Besides, Langley's own money-watchers cleared Trellis. His money was inherited from his wife's father's estate."

"Is it worth another look?" asked Diane.

"Most assuredly," answered Devereaux. "However, we will need to consult with King George."

Their discussions had been professional and free of the usual innuendoes peppering the banter between them. Diane recognized that Malcolm was pulling back to assure his intentions were not misread. Diane, in turn, wanted to make sure Devereaux understood she was healed and no longer dependent upon him. She desperately wanted to believe this herself, but she did not.

"Diane, I think it is time our little hatchling spreads her wings and flies from the nest..." he said, as he reached into his rucksack and produced a portfolio which he handed to her.

Diane looked at the printed information on its sheets. "I won't go alone."

"Of course not, I wouldn't hear of it."

He smiled warmly back at her.

14

SLEEPING WITH THE ENEMY

"**W**here the *f**k* is Carlyle?" screamed Trellis.

"He is in Germany, Sir. Nuremberg, I believe," answered Trellis' new lieutenant, "tracking down the AWOL analyst Emory Hauptmann."

"Get him, now. Right *f**king* now!"

Twenty minutes later, Carlyle was on the secure phone with Trellis.

"I need you in London. Tonight," Trellis told Carlyle.

"I was about to seal the deal with Hauptmann. It's imminent, exceedingly imminent."

"Get yourself to London. Call me when you are on-site at the Embassy. Move. NOW!"

"Are you sure? Do you know how long it has taken me to find this kid? I could finish this and be on a plane tomorrow."

"That's too late. I don't give a rat's ass about Hauptmann when we have an opportunity to close an even bigger deal. One that you managed to let get away from you last time. Now don't let me tell you again, you get your *f**king* skillset to London."

The call ended with Carlyle confirming that he would do just that.

Trellis smiled to himself. This new adjutant wasn't worth a shit compared to Ellison Redmond, but, Trellis needed Redmond in London, replacing Diane.

Redmond was filling in as liaison with MI6. In fact, his closest liaison was with a somewhat junior member of George Chartwell's staff, a young man named Rhys Tarquin.

Rhys Tarquin was a mid-level espiocrat. He was the deputy to Chartwell's staff lead on European immigration. As his boss was often in the field these days, analyzing the flow of Syrian immigrants through central Europe, Rhys often was expected to attend staff and meetings in his stead. It was openly known that Chartwell detested Rhys as incompetent and would often test him in these events.

Ellison Redmond first witnessed this in a joint meeting on American-European surveillance of known Russian agents in London. This was actually less a joint meeting, than a courtesy of MI6 to have the Americans learn from their superior techniques.

During the daylong conference, Rhys Tarquin presented how the Russians were attempting to recruit members of recently immigrated families in Britain to be Russian sleeper cells. Rhys was a man who Ellison viewed in no way to be incompetent. He was however, not a confident public speaker, appearing to always be in fear of his supervisors questioning his material. He developed a soft stammer, as he proceeded through his slides.

Chartwell, who had been openly dismissive of Tarquin throughout the day, decided he had enough of the man's incompetence. He removed his rimless spectacles, and while cleaning them with his handkerchief, expressed his frustrations aloud.

"Fine, Tarquin, that's enough. Stop. Please stop. You're wasting our precious time. I will cover this material privately with Mathers when he is in from the field. You are finished, off with you," said Chartwell rudely in an open attempt to belittle the man.

And belittled he was. Rhys was a frail man, a sensitive man, who Ellison had befriended as soon as he had arrived in London. Ellison watched as the humiliation reddened Tarquin's otherwise pale face.

Ellison felt the depths of Rhys' embarrassment. At this point, Redmond stood and began gathering his papers, obviously preparing to leave the conference.

Chartwell took the opportunity to launch another vitriolic volley at the already disgraced Rhys. "Well, there you have it, Tarquin, you have single-handedly driven off our chief representative of our American collaborators, Mr. Redmond."

Rhys began to stammer in his attempt to apologize, still at the podium, but he was interrupted again.

"Actually, Sir, nothing could be further from the truth," said Ellison, respectfully, yet defiantly. "This presentation by Mr. Tarquin was the highlight of the conference to my agency, and as you are so quick to sack it from the agenda, my day is effectively over."

Tarquin watched as the hush that spread across the large room had a gravity to it, pulling down the heads of the attendees, who only seconds ago were enjoying the degradation of their colleague. Their chatter was vacuumed into a precarious silence. The dense seconds lingered, until Chartwell, who was now quite visibly angered, responded.

"Well, I suppose I am to allow this man to continue then his butchery of the subject material. Very well, Mr. Redmond, I will accommodate your service. Tarquin, please carry on..."

While not a complete victory, Rhys Tarquin's humiliation waned, and his confidence slowly restored itself. He completed his briefing without further interruption.

That evening, during a splendid Chinatown dinner among colleagues, Tarquin sought out Redmond to thank him for his comments.

"I was quite appreciative of your robust confidence in me today," he said.

"It actually was an excellent presentation," said Redmond to his British peer, "but I was determined not to allow that oafish brute to attack you in front of the conference like that. It was a disgusting abuse of power."

"Well, Ellison," said Rhys, "I haven't had someone stand up for me like that in a long, long time. I really appreciated it. Especially against that prehistoric mastodon of a boss. What say I buy you a drink out of gratitude?"

Ellison Redmond looked hard into Rhys' eyes. The spark he saw there he read as desire, not gratitude. It was exactly what he was hoping to see.

"Not a chance," Ellison said sternly. "Not out of gratitude. Now, if you would like to buy me a drink for another reason, I would be delighted to accept."

Rhys warmed as the smile spread across Ellison's face like fire through dry trampled tinder.

The two soon migrated to a nearby seedy Soho nightclub. They went on to consume between them a bottle of vodka, and a few stiff Irish whiskies to boot. The liquor was loosening Tarquin's persona, while speeding the quickness and sharpening the edge of his tongue.

The entertainment played loudly in the club. At one point, Rhys whispered into Ellison's ear, "I truly loved what you did for me today. It was so chivalrous. You rescued me. I was so disgraced. Then, when you called out Georgie on his arrogant behavior, I couldn't believe it! You can never know how much that meant to me."

Ellison then touched Rhys' stubbled cheek with the cupped palm of his hand, then forcibly turned his head. In a heavy voice, hot on Rhys' ear, he said "Well, what say we go back to my hotel suite and make a proper night of it?"

Rhys raised his own hand, and began stroking the strong grip of Redmond that still cupped his jaw. He then almost apologetically removed Ellison's hand from his face.

"I definitely would love to," said Rhys above the noise of the club, "but tonight is simply not the right night for that, my white knight. I would love nothing more than to loosen your armor, but I have a very exciting day ahead of me tomorrow. Preparations have to be made for Mr. Devereaux's big catch."

"What big catch is that, Rhys?" Redmond asked in as nonchalant a manner as he could.

"Only the biggest. *The Huntress*, herself, returning from the field..." said the Brit.

"*The Huntress* herself, huh! I'll bet George Chartwell is positively licking his chops for that," said Ellison.

"Yes, Georgie, that piglet, he must be salivating. She'll be on his doorstep about thirty hours from now. They are flying her in overnight tomorrow. So important is it that Malcolm Devereaux is keeping her under heavy guard at his flat on the mews just off the Cromwell Road."

Redmond mentally stored the critical information he had just unearthed with the shovel of intimacy and the spade of anticipation.

"Well, Rhys, as significant as that all is, it can't be so important I can't convince you to come over and spend the rest of the night. I can have room service serve up a delightful breakfast," added Ellison.

Rhys looked at his watch. It was just past three AM.

"I am going to have enough trouble explaining to my wife as it is," said Rhys, as he struggled to pull on his suit jacket. "Out drinking with a Russian embassy worker doesn't usually include breakfast, does it now?"

And so, Rhys Tarquin had become the source of Jack Trellis' most cherished information. It demanded that he pull Carlyle out of Nuremberg, even as the assassin was in final preparations to silence Emory Hauptmann.

Trellis could not pass up the chance to silence Diane before she had the opportunity to inflict any further damage to his plans.

15

MOMENT OF IMPACT

Carlyle had obediently dropped everything, including his near final pursuit of Emory Hauptmann, and transited to London. He checked in at the Grosvenor Square Embassy, where he obtained a sniper's rifle with which he was familiar from CIA stores. He then spent the rest of the remaining daylight hours reconnoitering the streets around Devereaux's home.

Devereaux lived in a flat on a mews, that is, a street that had once been an alley full of coach-houses behind the residences proper. Today it more closely resembled a collection of American rowhouses on a tucked away side-street. At either end of the mews, this narrow street opened onto much wider, more heavily travelled thoroughfares. At the top of the hill where the mews began, there was an abandoned medical facility, complete with a "To Let" sign in the window.

As evening descended, Carlyle forced entry into the unused medical suite. It had been abandoned for some time. Best of all for Carlyle, it had a long hall way that led to the rear of the building. The structure had fire escape ladders, so that after taking out his target - that being Diane - Carlyle could egress through the rear, and soon enough be on the busy Cromwell Road.

Carlyle set-up his rifle and scoped it in. He rested in front of the window that he would use as his firing position. At three-fifteen AM, he was awakened by what appeared to be a government Land

Rover dropping off Devereaux and a female accomplice. Carlyle watched through the rifle's scope as Devereaux escorted the woman, whose face was covered in a veil, into the flat. They were accompanied by two armed male agents.

It was never Carlyle's intention to fire at this point. In the dark, his position would have immediately been given away by his muzzle flash. Even worse, with no one on the streets at this hour with which to blend into, even using the rear escape route he would have soon been picked up easily.

Carlyle watched as the Range Rover departed. He watched the lights in Devereaux's home come alive for the next fifteen minutes, before the entire flat again went dark. Carlyle now only had to wait until the morning pickup. This is when he would take his target with one shot, escape the firing position and head directly for St. Pancras station and the next Eurostar train to Paris.

His cover passport was in his pocket. The sniping rifle, its serial numbers long removed, would be left at the site, as Trellis' own special message to George Chartwell. The British Services would formally speculate on its origin, but Trellis was sure George Chartwell would know it unreservedly to be American CIA issue.

Dawn awakened Carlyle from his lightest fatigue, which certainly could not be confused for sleep. An hour and a half later, two Range Rovers pulled up the mews in front of Devereaux' flat. Four finely suited, very fit young men emerged, each openly bearing weapons in a show of force. The passengers from each Rover had what appeared to be a Heckler MP7A1 automatic compact machine guns, while the drivers appeared to carry standard 9mm semi-automatic handguns.

The door of the mews flat opened. Soon the head of Malcolm Devereaux appeared in Carlyle's scope, first looking up the street into his view, before turning down the street presenting the back of his head. Carlyle's instructions were to avoid any MI6 casualties if possible but assure the target Diane was taken and eliminated.

Thereafter Devereaux soon emerged, his arms around the target. She was wearing a trench-coat, but her head was obstructed by Devereaux. Carlyle followed them both in his sight as they approached the nearest Rover. Carlyle still had not definitively identified his target. He would have to decide whether to shoot without ID before they got into the vehicle.

It was then that the target separated from Devereaux, just as they readied to crouch into the trailing Rover. She looked in the direction of the street which gave Carlyle a clear view of her face.

It was clearly not Diane. The agent wore a blond wig, but Carlyle could see dark flashes around the hairline. The nose and eyes were not Diane's. It was as if the Brits had taken just enough care in making this woman appear to be Diane to cause him to pause, but still leave her, upon closer inspection, identifiable as clearly not being the woman Carlyle and Trellis sought. It was as if all they sought was to capture his attention before causing him to delay. Which would have meant that they knew he was there.

He felt the hair on the back of his neck stiffen in response. It was at this moment that he realized this carefully staged enactment was nothing more than an elaborate trap. He knew it in the logic of his mind, but more instinctively so in the pit of his stomach.

Carlyle's every instinct told him to move from the window. Nonetheless, the professional in him momentarily glanced along the rooftops of the mews when he spotted the Royal Marine sniper's muzzle flash.

The first round shattered the glass of his scope. The impact drove the other end of the scope sharply into Carlyle's orbital socket. The pain was immediate and unbearable, radiating into his sinus cavity. The bone mass of his skull instantly throbbed. His acuity, as sharp and focused as it had been a split second before, was now a blurred and laggard reality. Still, Carlyle knew what was to come next.

The second shot came instantaneously afterwards – it found him as his head had reared upward in reaction to the first impact. The second bullet caught Carlyle in the forehead, at nearly exactly the same location where Carlyle himself had once placed the fatal round that had taken the life of Stanley Wisniewski.

━━●((❶))●━━

Later that day, The Prime Minister of the United Kingdom held a news conference to publicly announce that the Pall Mall Bomber had been killed earlier that morning during an attempt to ambush British Security personnel. He was identified as Sean McManus, a member of a fringe IRA faction. The photo shown was not that of the American assassin Carlyle, but of a man who could pass for him in frame and general appearance.

Indeed, the real Sean McManus had been killed resisting capture by MI6 while hiding in a small farmhouse situated along the Atlantic coast north of the French town of St. Nazaire just four days after the bombing itself.

Stitching together surveillance videos throughout London and throughout the country, the British Security Services had no difficulties in reconstructing his escape on a fishing boat out of Southampton immediately following the bombing. They then were able to trail him to St. Nazaire. Agents dispatched to that town soon traced him to his hiding location.

Fearing that he would escape by yet another sea rendezvous, the Brits sent in a special forces team, launched under the cover of darkness from a British commercial vessel. McManus resisted, and was killed in the attempt to capture him. However, this covert operation had been conducted without the sanction of the French government, and as such, it had needed to be kept classified. The British public could not know the Pall Mall Bomber had been eradicated. That is, not until MI6 could create another narrative as to how he was killed resisting capture.

When Jack Trellis bluffed that he had information that would assist in the immediate capture of the bomber a few days later in the restaurant Bibendum, Chartwell immediately knew he was lying. Nonetheless, it was as Trellis stormed out of the restaurant that George Chartwell conceived the idea of how to both lure the assassin Carlyle to London, with the secondary benefit of having a mechanism to declare the Pall Mall Bomber as having been eliminated. And in doing so, Chartwell would exact revenge upon Trellis' assassin for the severe pain he had inflicted upon Diane.

So, Chartwell and Devereaux had devised the plan to force Trellis' hand. Knowing that Jack Trellis had implanted his adjutant Ellison Redmond into Diane's vacancy to collect information, Chartwell directed the leaking of the "Diane" rendezvous information at the mews. Rhys Tarquin had been instructed to befriend Ellison Redmond, and at the appropriate time to make the casual reference to Diane's return to London.

George Chartwell was less than sure that Trellis would risk bringing his sniper into the UK. Yet, it was apparent that Jack Trellis was prepared to go to great lengths to keep Diane from talking to anyone. Chartwell had hoped he would be offered the opportunity to respond to the egregious actions taken against Diane.

When Carlyle did, indeed, show at the mews, Chartwell realized just how desperate Trellis had become. So, when Jack Trellis sent forth his assassin onto the streets of London, he offered Chartwell not only revenge for the attempt on Diane's life, but also a convenient way in which to publically declare the Pall Mall Bomber had been forever silenced.

Yet, all along, taking out Carlyle had been the primary objective, with Chartwell knowing this last action was an open declaration of war between himself and Jack Trellis.

16

ASCENDING THE ALPS

Two hours before Carlyle was taken by the Brits, Diane and Sophie had departed the chalet per the overall plan devised by Devereaux. They were escorted by *Heckle & Jeckle*, driving the mountain roads of *Monte Gambarogno* until they reached the train station in the Swiss town of Bellinzona.

The morning sky was gray and threateningly close as the sun rose above its clouds which were cast lazily below the mountain peaks. The clouds diffused the Spring morning's light, casting it in eerie peals of greenish-gray. It matched the mood of Diane, who was still slightly sedated from an early morning injection from Dr. Alec. While he stayed behind at the chalet, his bag of sedatives had been entrusted to *Heckle & Jeckle* along with simple dosing instructions.

As they boarded the train in Bellinzona to cross the Swiss Alps, Diane and Sophie, wearing sunglasses and large summer hats that were suspicious given the overcast conditions, took their place in the first-class cabin. Their escorts positioned themselves fore and aft in the same cabin, wishing not to draw any more attention to the two women, but remaining close enough as to provide cover in case any attempt was made on them.

They travelled uneventfully, with Diane taking tourist photos with a cell phone provided by Devereaux. These images were automatically transmitted to MI6, a fact known only to Diane, Devereaux and Chartwell. Each photo file had the location GPS data embedded within it, as well as the timestamp. This was enough information to track their transit as they progressed to reaching their destination of Bregenz, Austria.

"Diane, do you remember much about steganography?" Devereaux had asked her in their last meeting at the chalet.

"Text hidden in photographs," she said, confident she was right.

"Yes. Exactly," he said. "The Russians used it extensively around the turn of the millennium. Hard to break if you don't have the crypto-key. It tells the computer which pixels are encoding the text characters. Since a typical digital photo file today can have over seven million pixels, you can embed quite a lengthy message. Even Tolstoy's *War and Peace* has less than six hundred thousand words, but I suggest limiting your text to a couple of lines. The crypto-key is embedded in your phone, and we have it of course on our end. You merely select the image you like, press these buttons, type in your text, and then hit transmit. It has a satellite transmitter and will keep your images from going out over the internet. It will also allow me to send encrypted images to you."

Diane, even though the medications made here groggy, was exhilarated by the freedom of travel, especially after being confined to the chalet safe house for so lengthy a period. The train began its ascent through the thickening gray of the low-lying clouds. It had the eerie feel of a journey into uncertainty.

Diane's thoughts were anything but clear. For days now, in her mind, she had been having a recurring image of Stanley. His face was drained pale and gaunt, and his eyes had no life in their prisms. Yet, she saw his purplish gray lips round to form the sound "*Oh*". The more she attempted to focus on this image, the more it dissolved like a mist in her mind's eye. It was only when she relaxed her thoughts, focusing on something else altogether, that the image unexpectedly returned.

Diane snapped photos all along their route through the Swiss Alps. She sent a photograph of the high mountain village of Airolo, shrouded still in clouds that seemed to climb the mountain along with their train.

Diane embedded text within one of these mountain scenes to test the steganographic capability.

"This is where I want you to bring me when this is all over," she embedded to Devereaux, fully knowing the commotion it would cause amongst the decrypting team, and even Chartwell himself.

A few minutes later she received an image of the River Thames from Devereaux. She processed the image through the embedded software on the phone to reveal its message, "Yes, when this is all over, Love."

She smiled. As the lightness of the moment evaporated, Diane once again felt the ghostly face of Stanley in her confused mind. The pale lips rounded *"Oh"*, but now stretched a slight bit further to complete the sound *"Ossi"*.

It was then that the train plunged into the St. Gotthard's tunnel, the railway cutting through the once impenetrable Alps. In the tunnel's darkness, Diane had the feeling of a presence imposing itself claustrophobically upon her.

For the third time that morning, she saw the face of her Stanley. While still weary and scarred, it now had somewhat more color, appearing to her as she rememberd it in life, not the previous ghostly apparitions. The face now appeared unburdened as it completed its mouthing of the word it had started earlier. As *"Oh"* had become *"Ossi"*, the latter was now completed as the word *"Osiris"*. It was then that Diane knew this was not a premonition, but a memory from the graveyard coming back to her slowly.

Just as this image came to her, the train exploded out of the tunnel into the bright sunlight of the Alps. The gray skies she and Sophie had endured up to this point were now trapped behind the peaks they had just traversed under.

The high snows now sparkled like gems. The bright mountain sunlight illuminated their carriage, more than fully justifying the women's summer hats and sunglasses.

The magnificence of the Alps, their uppermost elevations still painted white with the remnants of their winter's wardrobe, towered over her train as it traversed the valleys between their peaks. The gray shroud of confusion had been lifted not only from the mountains but cleared from Diane's mind as well. The sharpened ridges of the mountain stabbed ever higher into the spectral blue sky. Diane's mind was now filled with hope and definition.

Sophie and Diane gaped in awe, and unsuccessfully struggled to identify the *Eiger* and *Zermat* summits. What they did discover, was the soaring freedom of the upper altitudes. Their prison that was the chalet, like most of the world, was both behind and below them. It was then that Diane realized, she could never again trade this feeling of freedom for yet another sentence to be served in a new structure of incarceration.

The train soon descended the Alps into the Swiss city of Lucerne. Diane snapped photos of the lake as they approached. Here, they changed trains and soon headed east along a route that took them across the border and into the town of Bregenz, Austria. *Heckle & Jeckle* had made the connection and had passed through their cabin only once so the women would know they were still protected.

In Bregenz, they would depart the train before it continued onto Munich. They would walk the short distance, with *Heckle & Jeckle* trailing, to the address as instructed in the portfolio Diane had received from Devereaux.

Bregenz is situated upon the westward extending tongue of Austria, forcibly wedging itself between the Italian, Swiss and German borders until it licks the lower shores of Lake Constance. The city sits on the edge of this beautiful alpine lake, known to the Austrians and Germans as the *Bodensee*.

The lake is a swollen collection point of the Alpine Rhine River which flows from the melting snows of the Swiss Alps. In late Spring, as it now was, its blue surface is rippled by a bevy of sailboats, enjoying its depths. These very waters would continue on to re-form the Rhine River, whose flow will then snake along the Swiss-German border, past Basel, and then northwards defining the French-German border before plowing deeper into Germany.

As Diane and Sophie walked through the station, Diane had spotted a poster advertising the upcoming Bregenz summer festival.

The poster, written in German, was not understandable to either Diane or Sophie, as neither spoke nor read German. However, the photo showed the massive floating stage that was so very close to them as they departed the train station.

Top: Death of Marat
as painted by
Jacques-Louis David

Bottom: Bregenz Festival
Bodensee Stage for
the Opera
André Chénier

Figure 7: Bregenz Festival Stage on the Bodensee

(Photo Credit: Upper -Wikipedia Commons;
Lower - Kecko/Flickr Photo Sharing)

With its amphitheater seating along the shore of Lake Constance, the stage itself was moored offshore. Every other year it was dramatically reconfigured for the opera that was to be highlighted. This poster included a photo from a past season, when the entire stage was converted into a massive floating three-dimensional sculpture of the French artist Jacques Louis David's painting *The Death of Marat*. The opera was *Andrea Chénier*, based on the life and death of the poet during the French Revolution.

The artist Jacques Louis David was one of France's most celebrated artists through the Revolutionary and the Napoleonic eras. *The Death of Marat* is considered one of his finest works. Marat was himself a leading member of the ultra radical *Montagnards*, a faction of the leftist *Jacobins*, during the French Revolution. He published his revolutionary newspaper, *The Friend of the People,* and was known to brag that if anyone brought him names of counter-revolutionaries then he would have them guillotined within the week. Having an incurable skin disease, he often found comfort working in a warm, medicated bath at his home.

David's painting captured the exact moment of Marat's death, slumped in his medicated tub, his head draped in a white, turban-like bathing cap, after having been stabbed repeatedly by a young woman named Charlotte Corday. She had arrived in Paris after a long journey from the French countryside. She had told Marat's housekeeper she had names of counter-revolutionaries from her province.

Marat asked her to bring the list of names into the room where he bathed and worked. Charlotte Corday did so. Corday then drew a hidden knife and stabbed the revolutionary to death as he attempted to defend himself from within his bath. She would go on to take the life of the man who had already decimated her own. Marat had recently had the revolutionary rival group, *The Girondins*, with whom Corday was affiliated, brutally purged.

The stage on the poster was eerily reminiscent of the masterpiece. Marat's head, complete with the white flowing bathing cap, was slumped to one side upon the chest that disappeared into the waters of the *Bodensee*.

Rising out of the lake was Marat's arm, holding the list of conspirator's names. The *Bodensee* had been transformed into the waters of Marat's funereal bath.

Yet, it was the scale of the stage that caught Diane's attention. Marat's head soared above the lake, complete with stairways and landings for the many performers, who were dwarfed by its size. The relative miniaturization of the amphitheater's rows of seats spoke volumes of the scale and perspective of this dramatic undertaking.

Diane could not help but think of the newspaperman who had been so recently such a prominent participant in Stanley's plan – Preston Almesbury. She took a photo of the opera poster and transmitted it to Devereaux. She embedded the text "Please make sure *our* newspaperman is safe and sound. I would hate to find him in this state, within his own bath, or elsewhere."

17

RETALIATION

D r. Alec Rushe had spent the night alone in the chalet over-looking *Lago Maggiore*, as *Heckle & Jeckle* had escorted the two women to the new safehouse in Bregenz.

The chalet was eerily silent, with every creek of the floorboards threatening an impending disaster of invasion. Dr. Alec was concerned for his personal safety, and he knew this angst would deny him the comfort of sleep. While he had packed much of the medications to be taken with the travel team, Alec still possessed some residual sedatives from his treatment of Diane.

Alec was ready to self-administer a small dose of the massively powerful opioid, Fentanyl, but he noticed it was not to be found among the medications he retained. He then feared that he had misplaced it into the medical kit that he had sent along with *Heckle & Jeckle* but was nearly positive he had not. He knew Fentanyl was too powerful for a layman novice to administer. Even if those laymen had rigorous military medic training, which they both had.

Devereaux had been adamant that everyone in the chalet should all clear out earlier that day. *Heckle & Jeckle* refused until they could execute the lockdown sequence. Devereaux, back in London, demanded they leave before dawn. It was left to Dr. Alec to lock down the chalet. He had worked through these procedures throughout the day but would need to finish in the morning.

It was the insistence of Devereaux that had heightened his fear.

Did he know something he had not shared? Was the chalet in danger of being compromised?

It was the night that he feared, like a frightened child. That was when he took an oxycodone tablet to allow him to escape to sleep. After twenty minutes or so, the shadows of darkness melted away, and he slipped into a restful sleep.

He awoke from a deep rest late the next morning. His head was still somewhat groggy from the self-medication, but soon enough he was fully functional. It was his responsibility now to finish shutting down the chalet, and he had completed all the checklist of items the previous day except for deactivating the communication equipment.

This was new for him, but the procedures were easy enough to follow. He completed the activities over his hot breakfast tea as the morning's light illuminated the spare bedroom that doubled as a communications center.

Dr. Alec wondered if the four other inhabitants had reached their new location in Bregenz. He hated knowing this destination, but now having overheard it, it was impossible to cleanse from his mind. It was a dangerous liability if he should be apprehended and questioned.

While predominantly a medical and psychological asset of MI6, Alec had been involved with the espionage community long enough to recognize the recent operational response as being to a safehouse that potentially had been compromised.

He had initially become concerned on the visit by Devereaux that had been postponed for two days, agitating Diane to levels that required Dr. Alec to up her sedatives significantly. The night that Devereaux failed to show, Dr. Alec had detected a heightened level of alert in *Heckle & Jeckle*. For the first time since they had been brought here, the two men had broken out the automatic weapons and began pre-positioning hardware throughout the chalet. They became obsessed with the night vision monitors of the grounds. When Devereaux did arrive two nights later, Dr. Alec overheard the story as Devereaux recalled it to the security magpies. Devereaux feared he had been identified in Stresa, and it was just a matter of time before the chalet would be identified by the CIA.

Dr. Alec, alone in the chalet had completed his checklists. He immediately loaded his few personal belongings into the remaining Land Rover that he would drive through the Alps into Lucerne. From there, he would fly back to London, knowing that he had done what was demanded of him. He had stabilized Diane, brought her back to physical health, and transitioned the woman through her traumatic recollections. He had prepared her mentally to share her secrets with Devereaux.

Dr. Alec felt he had accomplished all this, with the exception of stabilizing her mental status. Yes, her trauma was behind her, but her mental state still was recovering. While she could now remember the events in the cemetery in Paris, the professional in him wondered how efficiently she would be able to deal with those dark recollections.

He was still very concerned about Diane, but his orders were to now return to London, which he fully intended to do. Doctor Alec drove the Rover down the winding driveway from the shuttered chalet. As he came to the electronic gates at the bottom of the drive, he pressed the button to remotely open them. However, instead of swinging open in response, the gates strained against themselves. As they did, Dr. Alec could see in the overcast mountain sunlight that a chain had been wrapped through the two sides of the gate, binding them together in the closed position.

A surge of nervous energy ran through him. The bile in his stomach increased, the sweat on his forehead beaded and ran. He had stopped the Rover in front of the gate, and his only thought was to back up and attempt to ram his way through. As he put the vehicle into reverse, he leaned back throwing his arm across the front seat.

His foot hit the accelerator just as the first bullet exploded through the windshield. The laminated glass frenzied into a spider's web of cracks but remained intact. The shock of the impact forced Alec to stomp harder than he intended on the gas pedal. The Rover reversed up the winding gravel drive for a few hundred feet before the rear window was likewise rendered a web of cracks by gunfire from behind the vehicle.

He had been ambushed at the gate. He now was racing backward at high speed with effectively no visibility. He knew that these men, whoever they were, wanted Diane. In her absence, they would torture him to find her. Dr. Alex damned himself for knowing where she had traveled to.

Alec's nerves calmed. He slowed and stopped the Rover, which was now off the gravel in the grass. They had stopped firing. He knew they had only been trying to immobilize him, for they likely had enough firepower to have killed him by now.

Alec re-engaged the transmission into drive. He drove forward until he felt, more than saw, the gravel driveway beneath him. He had just enough visibility to follow it now, peering through the cracks. He accelerated as fast as he could, heading directly for the gate. He had remembered *Heckle & Jeckle* mentioning how its stone columns had been but a facade over steel beams extending deep into the ground.

The firing restarted anew. Alec realized this vehicle was designed to protect him, so long as these intruders did not resort to the heavy caliber weapons that were surely in their arsenal. Alec also knew from the thickness of the chain tying together the heavy iron gates, that neither it nor they would yield.

He sped faster toward the gate. He slipped his hand down to his safety belt and released it. The belt disconnected and retracted across his body. His speed was nearing forty miles an hour as he approached the gate. At the last second, Dr. Alec intentionally swerved into the left stone gate post.

The momentum of the Rover's impact was reacted through the stone façade into the rigid steel supports that drove deep into the ground. The vehicle decelerated instantly, with the gate post deflecting only minimally. The driver side airbag deployed, but with no safety belt, the doctor's body dynamically thrust forward. The airbag caught his head, like a baseball in a glove. Yet the momentum of his body twisted him, throwing him into the laminated net that was the bullet riddled windshield. The summation of these discrete actions and reactions was that the neck of Dr. Alec snapped, instantly killing him.

18

ESCAPE FROM BREGENZ

"**D**amn it, Dom! I told you I wanted no *f**king* casualties. Your job was to get her, so I could question her. What the *f**k* went wrong?"

Trellis was infuriated as he berated Dominic Reeves across the sat-link.

Reeves had been returned to the field, to find Diane. His team was small, but one of the best para-military teams in Europe. After Devereaux was spotted in Stresa, Dom and his team had surveyed the lakefront properties of *Lago Maggiore* using reconnaissance drones and existing satellite imagery. It took nearly ten days before the Swiss chalet was identified. The nine-foot wall and gate initially identified it as a candidate, but it was the Rovers that gave it away. The Brits loved these vehicles, and while generally, it was not unusual to find Rovers in these Swiss pre-Alps, a drone pass caught sight of the exactly matched pair while the garage door was temporarily opened. Even the most functionally minded Swiss chalet owner would not likely possess two identical vehicles, right down to matching exterior colors.

"Director Trellis, we had identified a possible safe house and were moving to put a surveillance team in place when you accelerated our orders. We had just arrived when we noticed the Rover moving. Our alpha team had just secured the gate at that point. The beta team was by then over the wall and heading to secure the house when all hell broke loose."

Trellis bit his lip. He remembered ordering the chalet secured immediately after getting the news of what the Brits had done to Carlyle. "*F**k* the surveillance," he had screamed at Reeves, "Move in and round up the *f**king* lot of them."

Trellis had been out on a limb. Conducting a raid with live fire on Swiss soil was bad enough, but now he had a dead Brit on his hands to boot.

Reeves was too dumb to stop there.

"We have identified the deceased as Dr. Alec Rushe, a British medical professional affiliated with MI6." Reeves sounded proud of himself.

"We know who the *f**k* he was," barked Trellis. "and so will the Brits in a few hours."

"Perhaps not," offered Reeves. "It appears our good doctor was putting the safe house in cold storage. Nobody else was at the house, and it appeared they weren't coming back. The checklist we found in the good doctor's possessions was to put the house into long-term lockdown. No security systems engaged, no comm links left standing. They weren't coming back here for months, most likely."

"No signs of the princess?" asked Trellis. Dom knew he referred to Diane.

"Oh, she had been here, alright. We found ashes of clothing burned in the outdoor firepit – most likely what they couldn't take on the run with them."

"A pile of ashes that you think not only were woman's clothes, but that also fit the princess. What the *f**k* are you going to tell me next, you read the *f**king* tea leaves they left behind."

Dom was not intimidated by Trellis. "Well, Sir, it appears the doctor was left behind to clean up and shut down. In his Rover, as I said, we found the checklists. Our guys read through it and are sure even for him it could not have been more than 24 hours total activity. Had he left last night, we would have missed them totally."

"Dom, is that supposed to be good *f**king* news?" Trellis was becoming agitated.

"It likely means that the rest of the party is only a day ahead of us. I have the team already accessing the Swiss highway and rail station imagery. We are still hot after them."

"What am I *f**king* supposed to tell the Brits when they come looking for Dr. Rushe?"

"Sir, I wouldn't tell them anything. We have policed the scene. Only thing shot up was the Rover itself. My men are recovering the rounds fired. We have thrown a cover over the Rover, it will be visiting the lake bottom tonight."

"The crash-site?" asked Trellis.

"I recommend you leave it. Rushe had an accident, is missing and may be laid up somewhere. That's all the Brits will know. If they suspect this safe house was compromised, they won't come within a hundred miles of this place for quite some time. All I need to know is what do I do with the doc?"

Trellis was sensing that this could work. "Put him in the Rover. Can your team keep this to themselves?"

"I can vouch for every man, Sir."

Trellis thought to himself, "Well that isn't very reassuring."

Instead he said aloud to Reeves, "I wish we had something tying the Princess to this house."

"You mean besides the infirmary set-up, the medical supplies? How about this. They left behind a book that the doctor had in the Rover. They must have forgotten it in their hurried exit. *The Life of Chopin* - smells like our missing Sophie. And where Sophie is, the Princess is, I guarantee it."

"Process the book for prints," said Trellis angrily, "and then send it to me."

⸻ ⟪◉⟫ ⸻

The safe house in Bregenz, Austria was totally unlike the chalet that they had been confined within. This was a small house a few blocks from the lakeshore. It was hidden from sight by a row of other houses, but still offered quick access to the water, if needed. Diane knew it was a temporary holding location until Devereaux and his team could safely relocate them to a more permanent facility.

Diane also knew that the game was all but up. Once the agency had them on the run, it was just a matter of time before the technical and human assets of the CIA outpowered the experience and deception of the British Secret Service.

They had been here for two days now. Only a single steganographic photo had been received from Devereaux. It was, oddly enough, an image of St. James Park, the same area Diane had just been describing to Sophie. Except no swans. Just a willowy tree upon the water's edge with the London Eye peaking over the row of Westminster's buildings in the background.

The decoded message read simply "The buck snorts no longer. His last ride was from Nuremberg."

The initial reference was clear to her. Carlyle, the assassin who had nearly killed her, the man from Bucksnort, Tennessee, was taken out. Why the reference to Nuremberg?

Then, she worked through it. After laying low following the Christmas melee in Pere Lachaise Cemetery, Carlyle would have been assigned to track down herself, Sophie, and Emory.

Sophie had told her how Emory had walked away that night into the darkness of Paris' *Montmartre* district as she was fighting for her life. He just couldn't handle all that was going on, and Diane certainly could never hold that against him.

She had determined that he knew his own life was on the line, and he needed to get to a safe location. He would never make it out of Europe with the CIA watching, so it was only logical he would go to somewhere he could blend in.

Germany. Eighty million people. How could she find him there without being spotted herself? Near impossible. Yet, the message from Devereaux made it sound like Carlyle had already found Emory there.

Diane feared there might be nothing of Emory left for her to find. Despite her fear, she had to know for sure. If he was still alive, she knew she had to find him.

Sophie walked up to Diane, and quietly said, "It is done. Do not drink the tea."

Diane looked over her shoulder into the kitchen. *Heckle* was sipping from his morning cup of tea. *Jeckle* was not to be found.

Sophie passed the container of Fentanyl to Diane, who had stolen it from Dr. Alec. Diane knew that while Fentanyl was more usually injected, it could also be administered through trans-dermal patches and could even be absorbed through the mucous membranes of the mouth and sinuses. The only problem was she was unsure what size of a dosage to administer in this way. The trans-dermal rate of absorption must be slower, they thought, so they weighed to the high side of the recommended dosage.

A few minutes later, *Heckle* was slumped in the chair in the kitchen, from which he had been watching their movements. There still was no sign of *Jeckle*. Diane moved quickly to the kitchen. His breathing was shallow, and overall, he was non-responsive.

She prayed that they had not overdosed him. There was nothing they could do but call for an ambulance. She put the container of Fentanyl between the teapot and his cup. There, the medical team would be sure to see it.

Diane had watched *Heckle & Jeckle* both closely since they arrived here. She knew where they kept the house funds, all in clean untraceable Euros. This would be the road stake for her and Sophie to escape Austria *post haste*.

Just before leaving they again checked *Heckle's* breathing. Still shallow, but regular. They called the Austrian emergency number and said the English words "Emergency – Overdose. Please hurry".

Then, they slipped out the door onto the streets of Bregenz.

19

DECEPTION IN THE CONFESSIONAL

Jack Trellis returned for a third time to the chrome and glass cathedral that was Paul Renard's offices. He tired of driving into DC, but rather this than be seen with Renard in the halls of Langley.

"Well, Jack. I have to tell you that I have been looking forward to this session with you today," Renard began with an almost boyish enthusiasm. "Today, I would like you to pick up on where we left off – Stanley was reinserted into Warsaw in 1987. The Polish economic crisis afforded *Solidarity* the opportunity to take over the majority of the Polish legislature in 1989. By the records I have from your files, this is approaching the period when *Osprey* was exfiltrated from Poland through East Germany by Stanley."

Trellis relaxed in his chair, trying to look as comfortable as possible. Beneath this façade, his nerves were tightening. Why was Renard wasting so much valuable time covering this ancient history? Where was he heading? How much of Trellis' darkest secret did he already know?

Trellis cleared his throat and carefully began.

"*Osprey* was under suspicion at that point by both the Poles and the Soviets of having leaked information to the West. He had gotten sloppy, sending Baltic military maneuver plans to us that only he and a few others had access to. The Soviets and Polish Communists had to be careful, because if they arrested *Osprey* and they were wrong, they risked tipping off the real spy who would immediately go dormant and still remain among them."

"You said *Osprey* was the real spy. He was your guy," said Renard.

Trellis shot the young investigator an evil look

"Yes, Paul. Okay. Let me finish the *f**king* story! *Shit*, I haven't even really started it yet, for *f**k's* sake."

"I love when you get flustered, Jack!" exclaimed Renard. "What am I getting so close to that has you this agitated?"

"*F**k* you, Paul," Trellis said bluntly, "are you going to let me finish, or should I just go ahead and start back across the Potomac early today?"

Renard smiled at him with an annoying look. "By all means, Jack, please continue..."

"*Osprey* had been trained to initiate the exfiltration procedure by placing a red book in the rear window of his car while it was parked outside his domicile. Not any red book, but Lenin's book, *The State and Revolution*".

"Light reading for *Osprey*?" joked Renard. Trellis ignored him.

"By design, the signal to begin exfiltration was a three-step process. Once Stanley was aware of the initial signal from *Osprey*, he acknowledged by marking a chalk signal at a predetermined location, visible from *Osprey's* home. The final step was for *Osprey* to re-acknowledge by removing the curtains from his apartment's kitchen window."

"Pretty damn elaborate," stated Renard. "Why waste so much time?"

Trellis was becoming annoyed with this lawyer who knew so little of the elegance and simplicity of the tradecraft of his world.

"First of all, this could all be executed in a few hours. Better to take an extra couple of hours than initiate a move that could be a death sentence for both men, should they be caught, Paul."

Trellis glared at Renard.

"Okay, I get it," said Renard. "So, when did this all happen?"

"Wednesday night. November 8th, 1989" said Trellis flatly.

"So, then what happened?" asked Renard.

"What the *f**k* do you think happened, Paul? They rendezvoused on the other side of Warsaw at a pre-arranged location. With time enough for *Osprey* to assure he was not being followed. He wasn't. Stanley had forged *Osprey's* transit paperwork to East Berlin, based upon travel papers that *Osprey* had earlier provided to him. The forged papers for exfiltration were prepared in advance for just this event. All Stanley had to now add was the date. And off they drove to East Berlin."

"No, issues?" asked Renard.

"Not really, they just had to clear the Polish - GDR border before *Osprey* was noticed missing from his office the next morning. They cleared into East Germany around midnight. They arrived in East Berlin in the middle of the night. At a checkpoint going into the city, one of the guards questioned the papers. Apparently, he became suspicious because the ink on the date of *Osprey's* travel documents was smudged.

Osprey showed his Polish military credentials and told the guard that he was escorting a captured Western spy to be delivered to the *Stasi Direktor*. When *Osprey* demanded that the guard call and wake the *Direktor*, that is our *Erasmus*, they were cleared through. The border guard's concerns had miraculously disappeared."

Trellis could see that Renard was listening intently.

"They transited to their pre-assigned location - a vacant apartment in the *Mitte* district where they laid low until the next evening when they were to meet *Erasmus* at the landing to board the *Spree* patrol boat."

"Why didn't they just go straight there?" asked Renard.

"The extraction procedure always had some slack time built into it to assure the entire plan didn't scuttle if Stanley and *Osprey* were delayed in any sense. They had to take this precaution to assure the river patrol boat wasn't compromised. The next day *Osprey* reconnoitered the launch site, and found the go signal – a chalk mark on the bridge support in the form of a hollow star half-filled in."

"So, everything was a go for that evening?" asked Renard.

"Just about everything. *Erasmus* and his team had been notified the extraction was on. I had just reached West Berlin from London, the extraction on the rivercraft was to be affected that evening. Our recovery team was waiting in the *Tiergarten's* *Spreebogenpark* along the river shore just past the *Reichstag*, which was on the West Berlin side of the wall. That was when all hell broke loose. It was November 9, 1989."

"What do you mean, Jack?" Renard was lost at the reference to the date.

"For *F**k's* Sake, Paul, it was the night the damn Berlin Wall was opened up. Don't you remember that?"

"Vaguely. I remember reading about it. Later. Much Later. I was in my teens when it happened. I guess it wasn't that important to me at the time. I was more than likely focused on getting in my girlfriend's pants."

Trellis could only shake his head in response before continuing.

"November 9th, 1989. The East Berliners, in fact the entire population of East Germany, the *Ossi's*, had been getting very rebellious. They were led by the students. They were tired of seeing what was going on in the rest of the Soviet Bloc. They saw Poland and *Solidarity* defy the Soviets and reshape the government into a non-communist institution just a few months before. They saw the Hungarians open a border crossing that led into Austria. They saw the throngs of Hungarians and Czech and other Soviet Bloc citizens line up to walk across to freedom."

"East Germany had been repressed for so long by the communists, which had been brutally enforced by the *Stasi*, but now they were witnessing the crumbling resolve of the Soviets. Gorbachev had made it clear that the Soviet Union would no longer interfere with these satellite states. They could no longer afford to. The East German people, especially the East Berliners, were now staging mass rallies. Something had to give."

"So, they just allowed their citizens to cross the wall that night?" asked Renard.

Trellis grunted. "I got off the plane in West Berlin early that afternoon, but the city was already buzzing. We later found out it was all a mistake. The East German security committee had met earlier that day and had voted to allow an easing of the requirements for the *Ossi's* to visit West Berlin. They still would have to show their papers, and the visits were supposed to be temporary only. That afternoon there was an East German press conference where a spokesman announced all this. Damn bastard wasn't even present at the committee meeting. After he announced a gradual easing of the crossing policy, he was asked when this would go into effect. He clearly didn't know, but instead of saying so and looking foolish, he simply said the policy went into effect immediately."

"My God. There must have been chaos..." Renard said softly.

"Everybody from both sides of the wall instantly migrated to it. The guards had heard the spokesman's announcement and they basically stood down. Soon the masses were jamming all the crossing points. The guards couldn't keep up with the paper checks, and eventually opened up all the crossings to transit in both directions. It was mass hysteria. These people who had been separated by this wall since 1961, 28 years, were now embracing each other. Then, they began to scale it, standing atop the wall, spraying champagne, defiant in a triumphant frenzy. People often forget the wall had a round pipe along the top of it, to make it tougher to get over. So, when you see images of people standing on it, dancing on it, these pipes had been ripped off the top. Once that happened, out came the hammers. The rest was history."

Figure 8: River Spree at the Bode Museum, with Spreekanal at right

(Photo Credit: Wikipedia Commons)

"What did you do?" asked Renard.

"My team was waiting to receive *Osprey* along the banks of the *Spree* in the *Tiergarten*. I thought to myself, this is *f**king* crazy. I took an aide and crossed the wall at the *Sandkrungbrucke Bridge* along the *Invalidenstrasse*. In a few minutes I had walked across some additional bridges and down to the *Kupfergraben* loading platform in the *Spreekanal*. The city streets of East Berlin were deserted, a ghost town. At least once you got away from the wall. Everyone, and I do mean everyone, was at the wall. It was like the biggest *f**king* people magnet in the world that night."

He continued. "*Osprey* and Stanley had just boarded the patrol boat. I couldn't believe it, they were going to go forward with the extraction plan."

"I said to them, 'What the *f**k* are you guys doing? We don't need to take any risks with this. Just walk across – it's all open. Wide *f**king* open.' So, my aide took *Osprey* back the way we had come.

They walked across the bridges until they passed freely into West Berlin. We flew him to London that night. Before you know it, he was relocated to the States, after he rested in London of course. Ironically, he arrived at what was then Andrews AFB on November 11th."

"Ironic because it was veteran's day?" asked Renard.

"Yeah, but more so because it was Poland's Independence Day," snorted Trellis.

"So, back to the night of the 9th, that left you, Stanley and *Erasmus* on the patrol boat alone. Why didn't you all walk out together?"

Trellis shuddered. Had Renard set this all up, just to get Trellis to entrap himself.

"I had some final business to conduct with *Erasmus*. I had brought him a gift from our government for services rendered. I had planned to present this to him in the *Tiergarten* after the op, but this might be the last opportunity to do so aboard the moored patrol boat. Even before this, we knew Berlin was breaking down fast, and it was likely we might never see *Erasmus* again after this visit. He was likely to flee to the West himself."

"What was the gift, Jack?" pried Renard. "I mean besides the Swiss bank account that by this point had millions of dollars deposited into it."

"The gift was gold," said Trellis, "in the form of a massive belt. Beautiful, negotiable untraceable gold. Best gift for a man on the run."

"You're *shitting* me, Jack," exclaimed Renard.

Trellis continued. "The belt was not your typical accessory. It was oversized and was segmented. It could be worn under the clothes. The individual segments could be sold off for cash. It was meant for *Erasmus*, so he had negotiable currency as he fled the GDR. Back then, gold was around $400 an ounce, so this thing was massive. I presented it to him as a gift from our nation for risking his life for us."

"Just you, he and Stanley, huh?" Renard pried further.

"Yeah, just us three. After my man had walked *Osprey* across,

Erasmus released the two guards who were to pilot the vessel. Told them to go to the wall. I guess he didn't want any witnesses to his meeting with the Deputy Director of Operations for the CIA."

"So, what happened next?" asked Renard.

"Just like I told you, Paul. I presented the belt to *Erasmus*. He disappeared off into the deserted streets of the *Kupfergraben* district along the canal."

"And Stanley?"

"He and I walked out of East Berlin and headed directly for the plane on which *Osprey* was waiting to start his new life in the West."

Trellis looked hard into Renard's eyes. He thought to himself, *it was almost all true. Did this young punk lawyer have any idea which part was not?*

"I have to travel overseas next week, Paul," said Trellis. "Can we pick this up again when I get back."

"Sure, can I ask where you are heading?" asked Renard.

"Just to London. Nothing exciting."

20

REALIGNMENT OF COMBATANTS

The next morning found Jack Trellis at the Marriott Hotel on Grosvenor Square in London. He had flown over on the agency's executive jet, arriving early enough to check into the room that had been booked for him the night before. Though he had eaten breakfast on the plane, Trellis still had a light continental breakfast at the hotel's executive lounge, then washed, changed his clothes and walked across Grosvenor Square to the American Embassy.

Soon, Trellis was secure in the CIA Head of Station's office within the embassy. The Head of Station, himself, was on travel back to the states, and Trellis was treated with reverence by the CIA staff resident there.

"It is so delightful to have you here, Sir," said the staff admin, Melissa. Her New England intonation was overlaid with an effected British accent she had adopted in her fifteen years in London. It made for a rather strange overall enunciation, but Trellis had been coming to Grosvenor Square for years, and his ears had become accustomed to Melissa's amalgamated accent.

"Perhaps this is your last visit to the square, Sir, as Nine Elms will be opening soon," she said excitedly.

Trellis knew her comment was to the impending move of the American Embassy from its traditional Grosvenor Square location to the trendy new Wandsworth redevelopment zone along the

River Thames. The new embassy had now surpassed one billion dollars in construction costs and had several delays but was now soon to open.

"Of course, one knew all along they would never hold to their original schedule," she added. Trellis despised that she went out of her way to pronounce the last word as *"shedule"* as the British, of course, do.

"Coffee, please, Melissa," was all the niceties that Trellis could offer.

"How about a lovely breakfast tea, Sir?" she countered.

"Lissa, can I ask you a personal question?" Trellis answered her question with his own.

"So long as it doesn't shred my privacy," Melissa answered playfully with a smile. Again, her last word was the British pronunciation, where "priv" rhymed with "shiv". Trellis winced as if he had been stabbed with the latter.

"Are you looking forward to moving to Nine Elms?" Trellis asked her.

"Oh, Sir, I treasure the thought. It's said to be the greenest building in London. And quite lovely, too, if not a bit modern for my personal taste. It even has a water feature surrounding one side of it, which the Londoners are calling a moat..."

Trellis was raging inside himself at her gushing about the new embassy, even though he had asked her thoughts on it.

"Well, Melissa, if you wish to stay employed with us long enough to make it to Nine Elms, I suggest you drop the fake British accent and get me my damn coffee. And for future reference, I do know the difference between tea and coffee. If I ask for a coffee, I don't need a list of alternative beverages. OK?"

Melissa, who always thought herself to have an insider's relationship with Jack Trellis, shrunk away, realizing for the first time that it was not a privilege, but a burden, to be so close to this man.

"Of course, Sir," she said meagerly. "Your coffee, straightaway, Sir."

Minutes later she re-entered with a silver tray, with a steaming cup of coffee and sides of fresh cream and sugar. Laying it down in front of him, she uttered, "Mister Redmond is here to see you, Sir, for your scheduled appointment."

She pronounced "scheduled" as "*sked-uled*".

"Show him in," said Trellis, arrogantly fidgeting with his coffee.

"Shall I bring him a coffee as well, Sir?" Melissa asked.

"Don't bother," clipped Trellis as he sipped from the coffee for which he had not thanked her.

Ellison Redmond entered the office, closing the door behind him, taking the seat opposite the desk Trellis held court over. There was no handshake, no small-talk.

"Ellison, you've really cocked things up over here. Allowing your-self to be fed disinformation so these Brits could take out Carlyle. Do they understand what a flagrant violation of our relationship that was?"

"Sir, they, in this case, is George Chartwell. It appears he and Devereaux cooked this whole thing up. I doubt the rest of their leadership was even aware of what was going on. As you know, we have very strict rules of engagement in the UK. By agreement, we don't even meet with sources on UK soil unless we have one of the Brits with us. Therefore, they saw our sending Carlyle to snipe on them as a severe provocation."

"Aw, quit the *f**king* bellyaching for them, Redmond. They knew he was just here to take out Diane..."

"Who was in their custody..." added Redmond.

"Who is our *f**king* renegade agent that they have been har-boring from us," Trellis fumed. "They set us up, Redmond, and used you to do it."

"Sir, it now appears they had neutralized the Pall Mall bomber a few days after the bombing." responded Redmond. "If you ask to view his body, it will surely show he has been deceased for quite some time."

"Too *f**king* late for that," said Trellis, cutting Redmond off. "They claim to have already cremated his remains. Besides, I have another message for you to personally carry back to Chartwell."

"Yes, Sir, of course," said Redmond, knowing from his years with Trellis when to press and when to comply.

"Carry this message back to George. The President is going to protest directly to the Prime Minister over this. He is going to ask for the Chief of Her Majesty's Secret Service to be replaced. The President will not allow the taking of a CIA operative's life on UK soil to occur without consequences, even if the public is unaware of this transgression."

"Really," reflected Ellison, his eyebrows arched.

"I told the DCI that Carlyle was only there for surveillance of our agent Diane when they took him out. The rifle was a plant. He convinced the President to elevate this aggression to the PM."

"Interesting," murmured Redmond. "Anything else I should relay, Sir?"

"Yeah. Tell him either he can go out with the Chief, or he can profit from his own mistake. If he wants to be signing his directives with letter 'C' in green ink, he needs to play ball with me."

Ellison Redmond knew the reference that Trellis had just espoused. By tradition, ever since the British Secret Service was created in 1909, the Chief of The Service had always signed his memoranda with the letter C in green ink. The green ink was a British naval tradition, and the first Chief, Mansfield Cumming had indeed been an Admiral from Her Majesty's Navy. Even today, the traditional signature of the Chief is a singular 'C' in green ink.

"Sir, do you really think we can convince the Brits to appoint Chartwell as Chief of Service?" asked Redmond, incredulous at the thought.

"Doesn't matter if I believe it, Ellison. Just matters if you can make Chartwell believe it," said Trellis, a faint smile creasing his lips. "It shouldn't be too hard, as he has been coveting that position for years."

"He will expect that you'll want something in return..."

"And I do," said Trellis, "I want Diane and her two flunkies delivered to me by George Chartwell. I promise no harm will come to them, but they must be returned to the United States to answer for what went on after Stanley was brought to justice."

Brought to justice? Thought Redmond, *Trellis considers himself judge, jury and executioner, it seems.*

"I think I can make that play," said Redmond. "George Chartwell will salivate at the chance to have a shot at the Chief's chair. If he believes no harm will come to Diane, then he may just play along."

"Let him believe what he wants to believe," added Trellis. "Where is Diane, now?""

"We know that she and Sophie slipped out of their custody. We assume she is looking for Emory – the Hauptmann kid from the Berlin Embassy." Redmond looked pensively at Trellis.

"Then get a team to Nuremberg right away. That was where Carlyle was before I MANDATORIED his ass to London. He said he was closing in on Hauptmann's trail. Chartwell's people likely traced him back there as well. I can only hope those dumb bastards shared that tidbit with Diane."

"Sir, what do we do if Chartwell refuses to play ball?" asked Redmond.

"Then, we get Diane and the others ourselves and come after him and Devereaux later. I am sure that goes unsaid. George and Malcolm know exactly what they have gotten themselves into."

————)(●)(————

Two days later, Devereaux sent an encrypted message to Diane's satellite linked cell phone. The message read "CAUTION: There has been a realignment of combatants. Those who went to war over you are now joined in war against you. Recommend you come in at once."

From the phone's GPS coordinates, Devereaux could see they were in the Moselle River Valley, having branched off from the Rhine, and would likely continue heading west into France. What he did not know is that Diane had abandoned the phone aboard the **Pfänderbahn**, the cable car that took her and Sophie from Bregenz up to the **Pfänder**, the mountain summit which overlooks **Der Bodensee**, or Lake Constance.

Diane had intended all along that someone would pick it up and keep it, sending Malcolm on a false track. The Alsatian woman and her partner had decided not to turn it in to lost and found, instead taking it on their lovely river cruise that left Basel the next day.

Devereaux could tell from his link that the message had not been decrypted.

Instead, aboard their riverboat, the young French woman turned to her partner and said, "*Ma Cherie*, look, someone has sent us a photo of the Tower of London. You have been there, *oui*?

Her travelling companion, a British woman, looked at the image on their newly acquired phone. "My dear, you are quite right, that is a photo of the Tower, but more specifically of its section known as *'The Traitors' Gate'*. How strange. How very strange indeed."

21

NUREMBERG

The sky over Nuremberg, Germany was threateningly gray, heavy with the rain that would soon fall. A weary young man in an athletically cut slicker waited in the old town for his client to meet him at the square outside the *Albrecht Dürer* house. Out of his need for currency, he sold himself online to American tourists willing to pay for guided walking tours of Nuremberg. Out of his need for self-preservation, he always asked them to meet in this sloping cobblestoned square where he could size up his prospective clients before engaging them, assuring they were not those whom he suspected were still searching for him.

Emory Hauptmann had been on the run since the preceding Christmas day. He had walked away from witnessing the death of the woman he had come to admire. Knowing his employer would be hunting him next, he knew he would soon not be able to access his electronic funds, his credit cards, his bank account (meager as it was). He had walked off into the darkness of the *Montmartre* night, wandered through the streets of Paris before making one last withdrawal of his funds via an ATM. Soon, he had made his way by train to the German border. Once inside Germany, he had wandered from town to town, hostel to hostel, until he had ended his wandering in Nuremberg.

Emory was isolated and devastated. The CIA career that had initially seemed so adventurous and promising with his posting to

Berlin had, over the past few years, morphed into an unbearable tedium under which youth is so often penalized by the entrenched bureaucracy. What had become a boring German immersion assignment had ignited aflame when Diane had entered his life, leading the search for the fugitive Stanley Wisniewski.

During this chase, this incredible woman had not only recognized his skills and talents but had allowed them to materialize into many significant contributions. She had shunned the agency legacy resources and trusted him to conduct her most critical research. For once, he felt important, vital and above all else, useful.

Then, as the Parisian Christmas Eve fell in a muted silence of an early December snow, it happened. The veil of solitude around Pere Lachaise Cemetery was pierced by multiple shots that ripped through the night.

He and the Polish girl, Sophie, had been stationed in the rear gate to the cemetery. His first reaction was to rush into the grounds of the dead to assist Diane, but Sophie had grabbed his arm and told him to start the car. Even then, Emory hesitated, until Diane emerged from the cemetery, bleeding profusely and apparently on the verge of collapse.

The guiding star that Emory had been following had exploded like a supernova right before his eyes. By the time they reached the steps of *Sacré-Cœur*, Emory's crestfallen heart would not allow him to witness Diane Sterling's last few struggling moments on this earth.

Alone and afraid, he relied on his instincts and the only negotiable currency he had – his knowledge of the German language. He had first thought of hiding within the confines of a small Rhineland village, but thought the better of it. Anonymity dissolves rapidly in small towns, where outsiders are watched with scrutiny, whether those towns be in Midwest America, the Middle East or the middle of Baden-Baden. He needed somewhere he could earn monies to support his daily existence while attempting to remain undetected.

Berlin was out, as he would eventually be recognized by agency personnel. He thought of Frankfurt or Hamburg, before he settled on Nuremberg. Here were many American tourists traveling with river-cruises along the Main River Canal connecting the Rhine River with the Blue Danube. Applying his skills in the local internet café, he was able to set-up a website for local guided tours of the *Altstadt*, or Old Town. It paid enough to keep him fed.

Shelter was another matter. After he had arrived here months ago, he lived briefly at a youth hostel. Then, Emory had met a young local woman in the local bars, and soon moved in with her. The months had worn the luster from her American lover, and Emory feared it was now only a matter of weeks before she asked him to leave.

This day, he sat on the bench watching for the young woman who had secured his services via the internet. He hoped the threatening skies would not allow her the excuse to change her mind, as he desperately needed the sixty euros he was charging for the tour.

Emory scanned the crowds, always looking for telltale signals of agency surveillance. Passively loitering personnel, disguised as lost tourists always made him nervous. Seeing the same faces in different combinations, or wearing alternate clothing in successive passes, would cause him to abandon his potential client. Today, only the skies concerned him.

Then he saw her, walking back and forth in front of the *Dürer* house, awaiting him. As she had said, she wore a yellow raincoat with a knitted scarf and a large brim hat to protect her from the sun that today was not a threat.

She looked somewhat familiar to him. Her face was shrouded by the long, blonde hair cascading from underneath the hat's brim. Despite this, it was her walk, the manner with which she held herself, modest and unassuming, that caused his nerves to ripple. He sensed this could be a trap, just as the first drops of rain escaped from the clouds.

Emory's fear was now in full flight. He still had not seen her face, but he knew her by form, by frame, by her fragility. His tongue thickened in his throat, his pulse raced. He stood to escape the square, away from the *Dürer* house and the mysteriously familiar figure that threatened him so. He walked down slope away from her, and almost fell, tripping on a cobblestone standing unexpectantly proud.

He caught himself, but that was when he saw the second figure moving toward him, with purpose. It had been hiding in the shadows of the massive stone archway that was carved into the wall behind him. The figure moved swiftly to intercept him from his escape route through the *Altstadt* streets. His fear rose from his gut to his head and matured into full blown panic just as the rains began to congeal.

The figure neared him. It was also a woman, again hiding behind a large hat and sunglasses. She was more mature than the first, not only in years, but in confidence and the total absence of indecision. She neared him and placed her hands on the arms of his slicker. He meant to run but was somehow frozen by her touch.

She spoke softly to him as she held his forearm.

"Emory," she said, so only he could hear, "it's me, Diane"

Holding him as tightly as she could with her right arm, she then reached with her left arm to remove her sunglasses. She had not needed to do this, as her voice swept through him like a wave of unbridled joy. However, the wave crashed instantly against the rocky coast of fear within his head, transforming it into something less threatening but even more debilitating – shame.

The rain came down now in sheets. The square emptied except for these three figures. The first girl, Sophie, had now closed ranks to Emory and Diane.

His shame shuddered through him like an echo of far off thunder. He hoped the shower streaming down his face hid his tears, but the tremble in his voice betrayed him.

"Diane, Oh, God, Diane. I thought you were dead..."

"Everyone thought I was dead, Emory..."

"I betrayed you, I walked away, I couldn't watch you die..."

"Emory, I fully understand. The mind can only take so much..."

"No, No," he sighed, not able to control himself. "It was breaking my heart, seeing you like that, watching the life drain out of you."

He began to shake involuntarily. She pulled him close to her. Sophie came along them and touched Emory lovingly on the back. In her heavily tainted accent, she said aloud to them, "Now, we are whole."

"Yes," Diane responded, still holding Emory close to her, "indeed, now, we are whole."

The rain came down more heavily, cascading in torrents that soaked through the three of them, as if washing them clean of their pasts, absolving them of sins of yore.

"I need you now, Emory," Diane said, "more than ever. Come with us. You are not safe here. They know you are in Nuremberg. Come with Sophie and me. We both need you!"

He continued to cry in front of her in his shame.

Then Sophie said matter-of-factly, "There comes a time that even the ewes must fight the wolves to protect their lambs. They know the end they face, but they still fight."

Diane squeezed him tightly to her, "Come with us."

The three figures walked to egress the square. The waters of the rain chased down the slope after them, flowing angrily over the cobblestones. A few minutes later, as they left the *Altstadt*, the clouds parted, and a warming sun pierced the residual haze.

———◈———

Later that afternoon, asset teams from both the CIA and MI6 moved into Nuremberg. They would search for Emory Hauptmann, and before too long find only traces of his time there. It was two days later when they interviewed his German lover, under whose roof he had been sheltered. They presented themselves as American FBI, assuring her it was his family who was concerned for his safety.

She had told them only of what she knew of her American lover. She told them of when he had first come to her, and how he had left two days before without a trace. He left nothing behind save a few changes of clothes, because he had nothing else to leave. She described the outfit he had been wearing the day he disappeared. She told them of the internet café where he used the computers. No, she herself did not have a computer or a smart phone. She told them how he had been fun at first but became more silent and morose with each passing week. He had become a drag on her, and she was glad that he was now gone.

The joint CIA/MI6 team knew at that point they had missed their chance. They also knew that Diane must have needed him. They assumed that Emory had been picked up by the fugitives Diane Sterling and Sophie Czystowska.

Jack Trellis, still in London, knew why Diane needed Hauptmann. He was an expert in the *Stasi*, or so his file suggested. Diane was following a trail that Stanley Wisniewski had passed on to her in the 45 minutes while they met in the French cemetery the past Christmas morning.

⸺⋙‹‹‹◉›››⋘⸺

Diane, Sophie and Emory had escaped Nuremberg, and unknown to them, just in time.

Diane had taken a page from Stanley's playbook, hiring local drivers to escape the cameras of the train routes. They had adequate cash to keep them moving for another month, thanks only to the theft of the Bregenz safe house provisioning funds.

They sat now at a roadside restaurant, the driver impatiently pacing in front of his car. The three ate of necessity for nourishment, not comradery. Diane thought of how Stanley had been on the run alone, save the intermittent meetings with Jean Paul. How difficult that must have been. She watched while Emory and Sophie ate heartily. They had not stopped to eat since leaving Nuremberg.

As she herself ate, the thoughts of Stanley drifted like a haze through Diane's head. Then, in an unexpected instant, its mists solidified into a vivid image of Stanley standing before her in the cemetery. The last piece of their conversation, that had eluded her mind for so long snapped into place. In that instant, her last missing piece of dialogue became clear to her as a memory restored.

She could now hear Stanley saying to her, "Diane, what I know, but cannot prove, is that Trellis enriches himself with each drone the CIA bought from Powell. The profits to both men were great - great enough that their greed could only see one future. Expand the Global War on Terror, perpetuate it, until no man, woman or child was safe, as our freedoms were being extinguished in the name of safety and security."

Diane could just then recall Devereaux telling her of the corruption that George Chartwell had accused Trellis of perpetuating.

Stanley had finished his discourse. "This is the tangled knot of greed tying together these two corrupt men. This is why Powell had to be taken. This is why Trellis does not want my story told."

"Stanley," Diane started, "you yourself said you could not prove this. Perhaps there is nothing to prove. Perhaps you took Langston Powell's life for no reason."

She remembered thinking, of course, there was no valid reason for Stanley to have executed Powell, but she was testing his logic, as flawed as it was. She expected the decay of his own sanity to show itself.

Stanley then paused in the night, as the crystalline music of Chopin salted the frigid air between them.

"*Osiris*," he said simply.

"What?" Diane gasped. Was he totally deranged? The word "*Osiris*" struck her as proof of such. "You mean the Egyptian goddess of rebirth?"

"It is not what I meant, it is what *Erasmus* meant…"

"Stanley, I am totally lost," Diane said, "Please, help me understand."

The old man looked at her and stood silent, as if gaining the strength to explain himself.

"After the death of Bryce Weldon in Project INDIGO, Trellis took me to West Berlin…" Stanley began cautiously.

"Yes, I remember," Diane said softly, encouraging him to continue.

"I was given to the East Germans, to *Erasmus* himself, under the guise of becoming a spy against the West. It was ridiculous, of course. My real mission was to exfiltrate an even higher-level asset from Poland code named *Osprey and* deliver him to *Erasmus* in East Berlin. It was *Erasmus'* task to get him over to West Berlin."

"Oh, my God," gasped Diane. She had known of *Osprey* from her role during the search for the mole Aldrich Ames. *Osprey* was a high-level asset who had been delivering Soviet and Warsaw Pact information to the Americans. Yet, this was the first time that she heard *Osprey's* name associated with *Erasmus*. She knew *Osprey's* cover had been compromised by one of the moles in American Intelligence in 1989, and that he was emergency extracted from Poland before the communists could find and execute him.

"I remember *Osprey* was delivered back to the states just after the wall was opened." Diane said. "About the same time *Erasmus* went missing."

Stanley continued, "The four of us, including Trellis, were aboard a moored vessel in the *Spreekanal*, which was prepared to carry *Osprey* to freedom down the *River Spree*. It turned out that it was not needed, as the wall had just fallen that evening. *Osprey* was able to walk to freedom, leaving *Erasmus*, Trellis and myself aboard the moored craft. I had prepared to escort *Osprey* to the West, when *Erasmus* forcibly grasped me to stay. He was terrified to be with Trellis alone. No one else was around. Everyone was at the wall. I suspect that with the wall opened, he thought Trellis no longer needed him. In fact, *Erasmus* feared he had become a liability to Trellis."

"I am not understanding what all of this has to do with your concerns of corruption." Diane wondered if Stanley was still sane at all.

"Trellis had a belt made of links of gold for *Erasmus*. It was for him to use to make his own escape to the West. Gold was readily negotiable, easily turned into cash, and most untraceable. Trellis presented it to *Erasmus* in front of me. Said it came with the gratitude of our country for his services over the years. Trellis then walked up to *Erasmus*, opened his heavy overcoat, and secured the weighty belt around the East German's waist, making sure to hear its clasp click. Then, Trellis embraced him in a squeezing hug."

"Yes," said Diane, "still how does this..."

"At this point they were a few feet from me in the stern of the vessel. *Erasmus'* face was in sheer terror," said Stanley, not allowing himself to be interrupted. "Trellis released his embrace, and while still inches from the *Stasi's* face, said to *Erasmus*, 'You have earned this!' Then, suddenly, Trellis with all his might, thrust *Erasmus* backwards with a great push, into the *Spreekanal.*"

"Oh, my God," gasped Diane.

"I rushed to the edge of the boat. It was dark, but I could see his face about a foot beneath the water. He was in terror, fighting for his life, but the weight of the belt, which he could not remove, and the weight of his wet clothes, was keeping him from coming to the surface.

He made a last frantic effort to swim to the surface, breaking its waters in his thrashings, he yelled out the word '*Osiris*' repeatedly between gasps for air. I reached for him, to help him, but he was beyond my reach. This is when I heard Trellis' cold voice say 'Stanley, don't. Let him drown. Let him die.'"

"I ignored him, I found a long rescue rod attached on the boat. I grabbed it and began to reach to the drowning man. *Erasmus* was now ripping erratically at the surface of the water, but the weight of his uniform, his boots, his overcoat, his newly acquired gold kept pulling him under."

Diane then realized the only defect of Stanley's sanity was from the burden of having carried this memory for so long.

"I extended the pole to him to grasp, when Trellis stopped me," admitted Stanley feebly.

Diane remembered a sadness, a weight of guilt came over Stanley at this point.

"He grabbed you? Forcibly stopped you from assisting *Erasmus*?" asked Diane.

"No. Not at all," responded Stanley, his head now hanging low, his chin on his chest. "He froze me with a terror, worse than my own death. Trellis spoke softly into my ear, from behind, as I reached the pole to *Erasmus*," Stanley said painfully, "Trellis had said to me, 'Stanley, put that down, right *f**king* now. I know all about your little Agnieszka. Either *Erasmus* dies, or your Agnieszka dies instead.' I was stunned."

Diane could not believe what she was hearing. "You are telling me that Trellis murdered his own agent, in front of you, and then threatened to kill your source Agnieszka?"

Stanley raised his head slowly to look directly into her eyes.

She remembered there being a hollowness that seemed to cavitate through him. As if his shame had swept away every fiber of his integrity. It left him a man without any trace of self-respect.

"It is exactly what I am telling you. I had already come to love my *Sarenka* at this point, although we had denied giving ourselves to each other for a few more years. She had captured my heart. I could not allow her to be taken away by Trellis' greed," Stanley was now more mournful than at any point within the cemetery.

"I put down the rescue device I had used to try to reach *Erasmus*, and I watched the man drown in the canal. I am haunted to this day with the look of betrayal on his face as the last of his life's spirit left him under the surface of those waters. I will never forget those last bubbles cracking the surface, leaving only his dead, accusing eyes staring up at me."

Stanley shuttered involuntarily.

"My God, Stanley," Diane said softly. "You didn't kill *Erasmus*, Trellis did. He put you in an untenable position. How did Trellis justify this to you?"

Her absolution meant nothing to him. Stanley could still see the body of *Erasmus*, staring up at him, from the waters of the *Spreekanal*.

"He did not. He was brazened. He merely told me I was now his to control. If I told anyone, even cryptically, he would have Agnieszka killed. He had me trapped, and he knew there was nothing I could do."

"You could have turned him in…" Diane suggested.

"Who would believe me? The *Stasi* scattered soon after that, it was all too believable that *Erasmus* had disappeared to collect his Swiss monies and retire anonymously into the West."

"He couldn't collect his monies if he was dead…" Diane countered.

"Which is why no one missed them when Trellis emptied his account. The DCI was told *Erasmus* had walked off into the night, and the emptying of his Swiss account was proof."

Diane found all this to be unbelievable. "Stanley, now you are speculating wildly."

"Am I, Diane?" he said to his former student. "Do you know what a *Nagra* recorder is?"

"Yes, sure. Small East German battery powered reel-to-reel recorders, about the size of a cigarette case. They are electronic now," she added.

"Technically, they are Swiss. Created by the Polish inventor Stefan Kudelski. The name means 'will record' in Polish. The East Germans loved them for their reliability and small size. I later discovered that *Erasmus*, when he grasped me to stay with him on that vessel, had slipped a *Nagra* recorder into the pocket of my overcoat. It contained the records of every deposit that had been made into *Erasmus'* Swiss account. Tallied up to about six million dollars. When I got recalled years later to Langley, I was able to match it up to the funds paid out to both *Erasmus* and *Osprey*. It also matched the funds withdrawn from the account after *Erasmus* was drowned. It is ironic."

"How so?" asked Diane.

"Because during our drive from Warsaw to East Berlin, *Osprey* had told me that he was most proud of the fact that he had never asked the Americans for a penny. What he did, he did to save his beloved Poland. It was clear that Jack Trellis had funneled payments intended for *Osprey* into *Erasmus'* account as well."

"How could Trellis be so corrupt?" asked Diane aloud, but within herself she realized it was entirely aligned to what she knew of his character.

Stanley then continued his explanation of his actions.

"When I got back to Warsaw, I made sure my Agnieszka was safe, and would remain so. I worked on a plan to buy her the Zgorzelec villa as a safe retreat. By then, Poland had driven out the communists, and Trellis had moved me into the Embassy as Deputy Head of Station, Warsaw. I was able to siphon off operational funds to buy the villa for Agnieszka. I kept this location from the agency, and specifically from Trellis. I needed somewhere my *Sarenka* could safely hide if Trellis should ever decide to hunt her. I had no idea I would, myself, use it as a safe harbor one day."

Diane remembered the villa that Stanley had used to elude her search team.

"That is why we couldn't find you. Trellis didn't know about the villa, but he knew her family was originally from there, so he posted his sniper on the border bridge, thinking you might try to cross there. This is all making so much sense, now." Diane could see all the missing pieces falling into place.

"During my next visit to Langley, when I managed to be alone with Trellis, I told him about the *Nagra* recorder *Erasmus* had delivered to me. Told him about the deposit details of the account, told him of what else was on the recorder."

"Which was?" asked Diane.

"Property addresses in Berlin. East Berlin. This really got his attention. I wondered why? Years later I found that after the reunification of Germany, when the rebuilding of East Berlin commenced, these properties were some of the first to be renovated. They were bought up by a business concern named the *Osiris Trust*."

"Incredible, Stanley. So, you are saying Trellis used the monies he stole from *Erasmus* to buy up dilapidated structures that his own spy had recommended?" asked Diane. "you are saying after killing *Erasmus*, he drained his Swiss account and invested that money in properties that would be torn down for the first wave of the rebuilding of East Berlin?"

Diane realized the return on that investment would have been enormous.

"More than that, *Erasmus* had likely set some sort of back door agreements in place while he was alive. Possibly, he and Trellis had hatched this scheme together. By the late 80's, everyone could see that, after the wall fell, East Berlin would soon undergo massive rebuilding. Trellis and *Erasmus* had figured out how to profit from it. *Erasmus* never saw, until it was too late, that it was just another motivation for Trellis to do away with him altogether."

"And you used this information from the *Nagra* to blackmail Trellis?" Diane was seeing it all now.

"No, not blackmail. I considered it leverage to keep my Agnieszka free from harm. I told Trellis his greed would all come out if any harm ever came to her. And that if he silenced me, a copy of his secrets was in the safe hands of a third party..."

"Jean Paul," realized Diane aloud.

"Yes, Jean Paul. And it worked. My *Sarenka* lived for another 21 years."

Then, it became crystalline clear to Diane what the evening in the cemetery had been all about.

"The music. The lilies. The stroke of midnight," Diane stated to the old man before her. "This is a ritual, Stanley? For Agnieszka?"

"I never got to say goodbye to her, Diane," he said, attempting to control his emotions. "This is not a ritual, as you say, but my requiem for her soul."

Diane's recollections were now interrupted by the urgency in Emory's voice.

"Come on, Diane, it is time to go. The driver is threatening to leave us here. He wants to know where he is to take us."

The driver spoke only German. Emory, having joined them, served as the interpreter.

"We have to go back to Berlin. What we need is in Berlin," said Diane urgently, having now remembered what Stanley had passed to her.

"Do we have a safe place to stay there?" asked Emory.

"No, no we don't" said Diane, realizing just how hard what was to come would be.

"It's OK. I have an old girlfriend who lives near the *Alexanderplatz*. We can trust her."

"Did she dump you?" asked Diane.

"Other way around. She adored me. She'll take us in. I am more worried about being spotted in Berlin. *Alexanderplatz* is pretty front and center."

"For what we are about to do, I want us to be seen. In fact, we will need it," said Diane starkly.

They then loaded into the car and headed for the *Mitte* district of Berlin.

Figure 9: Fernsehturm Television Tower and Alexanderplatz

(Photo Credit: Elizabeth Marie Trawinski)

22

BERLIN: THE STASI FILES

ater that night, the driver dropped them in Berlin's *Alexanderplatz*, under the beacon of the light of the massive television tower dominating the skyline. The tower was known as the *Fernsehturm* in German, and was the most visible entity of all Berlin, soaring over the Brandenburg Gate, the Reichstag, or any other elevated feature of the city. The *Fernsehturm* was the iconic visual reference point in this city since its completion by the *Ossi's* in 1969.

The three fugitives walked the short distance to the *Karl-Marx-Alee*, the boulevard where Emory's friend's apartment building stood. They did not wish for the driver to know the precise location to which they were headed, in case the agency somehow was able to track back to him.

The apartment building itself was massive, stretching for a long city block behind the tree-lined plaza along the *Karl-Marx-Alee*. The building was eight or nine stories high, exactly which Diane did not care to determine. Emory's girl lived on the fourth floor. Emory went up alone, with Diane and Sophie hiding in the darkness of the *Mitte* district's night.

Emory found Treva at home, spending another lonely night within her apartment. She was excited to see him, forgetting the way he had walked away from her almost exactly one year before. She pulled him eagerly into her modest dwelling, immediately raising her expectations.

It was when Emory explained he was traveling with two other

women, and they three needed a place to stay for a couple nights. While he did not expect this to stretch into weeks, he explained it possibly could.

Treva's only question was if he was romantically involved with either of his two travelling companions. He assured her he was not, and she allowed them to stay. Treva's fears were soothed when she saw them all together. Diane was too old to be a threat, and the younger Polish girl, while beautiful, moved stiffly around her Emory. She sensed she would have him for herself, at least for as long as they stayed.

Treva began to dictate terms in German. Emory would share her bed, she declared. Diane and Sophie could have the living room to share. Emory translated, no one protested.

Diane was relieved to see Treva had a desktop computer that she would need if her plan forward had the slightest chance of working.

"Emory," Diane asked aloud, "ask Treva if she has a friend who has a cell phone who would like to make some easy money."

Diane had already deduced that Treva spoke no English, as he had been playing the role of interpreter since they entered her home space.

"She says she has a cell phone you can use..." was Emory's translation of the young woman's response.

"No, tell her that is no good. It is already linked to this apartment. Tell her I will give both her and her friend two hundred Euro's if they can bring the cell phone here for me to use tonight," replied Diane.

Within an hour Treva's friend was at the door.

"Ask Treva not to let him inside," said Diane, responding to the knock. "He doesn't need to know how many of us there are, or what we look like."

"She," responded Emory. "Her friend is her girlfriend. Her closest friend. Treva says it is rude not to let her in."

"Here, here are the four hundred Euro's and another hundred. Ask them to go shopping or something. I need for them both to be gone for the next few hours."

The money and phone exchanged hands.

"Treva thinks we are running from the law," Emory relayed to Diane.

Diane was relieved to see Treva taking her sweater from a hook on the wall. She had decided to leave with her friend as requested.

"Tell Treva we are running, but not from the law. We are running from some very bad people, tell her Russian mafia. And, of course, thank her profusely for allowing us to stay here for the next few days."

Emory translated the message and an expression of angst tightened across her face. She kissed Emory goodbye, first on the cheek, and then on the lips, before slipping through the apartment door.

Soon after, Diane asked for Emory and Sophie to join her on the sofa and chair in the apartment's living room. Diane addressed her two companions, reaching out for their hands.

"I want to tell you how dire our situation is," she began. "Jack Trellis fears that Stanley passed information to me in that cemetery that is incriminating to him."

"Did he?" asked Emory. "Did Stanley tell you something incriminating Trellis?"

"Yes, he did. It came back to me earlier today. Even though the talk I had with Stanley is now clear, I still don't understand all that he told me."

"That is contradictory, no?" said Sophie, stumbling over the pronunciation of contradictory with her Polish accented tongue.

"Stanley said he watched Jack Trellis murder a man, an agent. That much is clear."

Diane was growing more and more concerned for the danger she had drawn them all into.

"Trellis will want to find the three of us and silence us. I want to make sure you both understand that. He is not interested in anything else but killing us all. And he has the resources of the CIA at his disposal."

The three of them looked at each other in silence.

"If either of you wants to walk, then now is the time. I have an idea that may get us out of this, but I cannot expect you both to

---

blindly join me. I think the odds that the three of us all get out of this alive are very slim, but I think I have a way I can protect you both."

Diane's eyes began to moisten. Her face was taut.

Sophie spoke next in a quiet, serious voice. "Diane, we are now whole. I think we stay whole, whether we live or die. Whatever we do, we do together."

Diane then turned her concerned gaze to Emory.

"I walked away once," he said, "but never again. We stay together. We stay whole."

Emory looked to Sophie, and they laughed at each other. A nervous laugh it was, but it brought joy to Diane's heart.

"Besides," Emory said, "you must think we were idiots if we hadn't figured this much out already. I was in fear for my life every time I left the apartment in Nuremberg. I figured it was just a matter of time before Trellis' sniper came calling for me."

"Carlyle," said Diane, "is gone. The Brits took him out in London. Devereaux relayed that much to me."

"So, why then did you and Sophie flee the Brit's protection?" he asked.

"Because once the CIA discovered the chalet on the Swiss mountainside where we hid, my experience said it was only a matter of time before they tracked us down. Even if MI6 moved us to other safe houses."

Diane said all this, knowing Emory's next question.

"OK, but now we are on the run, with limited funds, no secure safe houses, no protection. Where do we go next?" asked Emory.

"Nowhere," said Diane. "That is why I brought us back to Berlin. This is where we make our play."

"What's the plan, Diane?" asked Emory. "I'm in, just tell me the plan."

She directed her attention to him. "Emory, I need you to set up a steganography file. I need to communicate to a few trusted people what is going on. Make the key simple, so I can communicate it over the phone tonight."

"Piece of cake," he said.

"Good. We are going to expose Jack Trellis for the greedy bastard that he is."

Diane was determined, and the stiff spine of her voice conveyed that to her two young partners.

"You made this promise to *Pan Wisniewski*?" asked Sophie.

"No, my *Zosia*, I made Stanley no promises. He did not ask for my pledge of duty, but I am now sure he knew that I would be the one to carry on his mission. And I will, with the last breath of the life he saved for me."

In the Embassy in London, Jack Trellis had just been alerted to the fact that Diane and Sophie had been spotted by cameras in Nuremberg. There was no longer any sign of them remaining in Nuremberg, the team in the city had reported, however. It was clear the three were again on the run.

Trellis knew this meant they had rendezvoused with the Hauptmann fugitive, who had also just disappeared. She needed Emory Hauptmann, but why?

He was an expert on the *Stasi*. He was a fluent German language speaker. He had been stationed in Berlin long enough to know the city well enough to hide them there.

He called for his temporary adjutant.

"Tell Dominic Reeves to meet me in *the Blind* in Berlin tomorrow. Also, pass the word to Chartwell and Devereaux that I expect them to arrive there as soon as possible."

It was the only place Diane could be heading. She would not continue to run.

She wanted a confrontation. Jack Trellis would give her a showdown.

Diane left the apartment and walked along the *Karl-Marx-Alee*. Ahead of her in the night, the Berlin *Fernsehturm* pulsed high above the *Alexanderplatz*.

"Hello, Quindon Sprouse, please."

The female voice on the other end of the connection had been pleasantly British, presumably a house servant of some kind.

"Yes, this is Quindon Sprouse, who is calling please?"

The voice of an old friend ran through her, calming her every nerve. Subduing her every fear.

"Quindon, this is Diane. Diane Sterling."

"Yes, Diane. Of course. Well, my-my, you haven't rung me or stopped by the shop for an æon, it seems. What can I do for you, my dear?"

He did not know she was missing? The agency must have kept this all very secret. No public announcements about their capturing Stanley? At least, no announcement that she had been killed or injured during the attempted apprehension. Or perhaps he had just been oblivious to what had been published throughout England by *The Westminster Conservatoire*?

"I am fine, Quindon. I am sorry to call you so late at your home. I am afraid I am not in need of purchasing anything at the moment, but I will be stopping by the shop soon enough, and you can tempt me with your treasures as usual. Tonight, I just need some background on an Egyptian antiquity and thought you might be able to give me a little background."

Quindon Sprouse was an antiquities expert, as well as a connoisseur of *objects d'art*. He was a collectors' collector. He had made a fortune over the years from his shop in Chelsea, *The Speckled Grouse*. Diane had purchased much of what adorned her flat in Westminster from the man himself.

"Certainly, Diane. Perhaps, if we could delay this until tomorrow morning, when Devon is in the shop, his expertise on all things Egyptian is unsurpassed."

Diane could not wait. She knew it was likely that both the NSA in Fort Meade, and the Brits in Cheltenham's GCHQ "Doughnut" were listening in to this call. It would be a one-time deal.

"Yes, Quindon, that would be ideal, but I have an immediate purchase opportunity, and I just need background info."

"Can you describe the piece for me, my dear?" Sprouse asked.

"I am terribly sorry, but I can't, you know?" Diane responded.

"Yes, I understand," said Quindon, realizing that she used him from time to time for background material on a number of subjects related to collectibles.

"Father once taught me if you ever want to know the details of a subject, go to a collector. They pride themselves on knowing the most trivial details of those items they collect," she had once confessed to Quindon. He knew her line of work often demanded this level of detail, and so, from time to time, she utilized his expertise, but never before calling on him at his residence.

"Splendid, Diane, can you give me a starting point?" Quindon enjoyed these inquiries, and Diane had been an excellent client to him over the years as well.

"*Osiris*," she began, "what can you tell me of her?"

"First thing I can bring to your attention," began Sprouse "is that she is a he. *Osiris* was the Egyptian god and king who in the myth ruled Egypt, along with his wife Isis, and his brother Seth. *Osiris* was then murdered by Seth, who then became the ruler of Egypt. Seth had *Osiris'* body dismembered into fourteen pieces, all scattered throughout the world, which was at that time only known to be Egypt. Isis loved her husband, and travelled the kingdom collecting his remains. She was able to reconnect them, resurrecting him as the god of rebirth. After which, she conceived a son from *Osiris*. The son was the god Horus."

"OK. Rebirth makes sense," Diane said.

Quindon Sprouse continued, "Like Hades in the Greek myths, *Osiris* became the god of rebirth, but also the god of the underworld, that is the world of the dead, from which, by all definition, rebirth springs forth."

"Any ties to Berlin?" Diane asked, hoping not to lead the witness, but she was short on time.

"Berlin. No, not that I can think of. France, Napoleon, yes – they were bitten by the Egyptian bug after Napoleon's expedition to the Nile. Other than that Napoleon later conquered Berlin, I can think of no connection. Did you check for local businesses with the name 'Osiris'?" Sprouse asked.

"Yes, we considered that. A couple of enterprises that appeared to be unrelated. I did hear from an acquaintance of an *Osiris Development Fund* for the rebuilding of East Berlin, but I am having trouble finding any documentation on it."

"That certainly makes sense, though," added Quindon, "as East Berlin underwent a fantastic rebirth after the German Reunification. Damn Soviets wouldn't allow the East Germans to rebuild much of it. That which they did allow was in the uninspired Soviet style. You know, Diane, you may wish to consider the Greek translation of *Osiris*."

"Hades, you said?" recalling his comments a few seconds ago.

"Oh, no, Diane," chuckled Sprouse. "Not the Greek equivalent god. I mean the name given *Osiris* in the Greek alphabet after translation from the Egyptian hieroglyphs. The experts still debate this somewhat, but the generally accepted conversion is WSJR."

"I see, Quindon," said Diane. "WSJR, I will look into that. Thank you so very much."

"Diane, there is one last part of the myth you should know," said her friend.

"Yes, Quindon, please go on," encouraged Diane. She was tight on time and wished him to finish so that she could make her other calls.

"Horus is protected as a child from the god Seth by his mother, Isis," continued Quindon Sprouse. "Horus then grows to become mature and attacks Seth in retaliation of his father *Osiris*. During the skirmish, Seth puts out Horus' left eye. Horus eventually prevails, and Seth is slain. Horus goes on to rule and re-establish stability to the kingdom. He offers his detached left eye to his father *Osiris*, as a sacrifice. This is where the phrase *'the eye of Horus'* comes from. I don't know if all that detail is useful, or just the rumblings of the buggered old fool that I am. In any case, I am afraid that is all I have to offer you, my dear. Good luck, Diane."

Diane thanked Quindon again for his time, and then hung up. As she prepared for her next call, she thought to herself that there had already been enough sacrifice in this saga, and none other would be offered. At least on her side, but Jack Trellis, she realized, she could not control.

23

ZOSIA & EMORY

Jack Trellis sat in the darkened confines of the Berlin *Blind*, the ops center that was an annex attached to the American Embassy. Trellis briefly thought of the irony of the American Embassy, including the *Blind* in which he sat, being just to the south of the Brandenburg Gate. This location sits on what was once the East Berlin side of the wall. Not only had the West won the war with Communism, but it had, in its victorious, capitalistic gluttony, sucked up some of the prime real estate in what, not so long ago, had been the realm of the *Stasi*.

Dominic Reeves began to brief Trellis regarding the ongoing operation to locate Diane, Sophie, and Emory here in Berlin.

"NSA picked up Diane's voiceprint on a series of calls last night. We traced the calls back to a cell number registered to a German resident female, no known association with the German Intelligence Services. It appears our Diane is cracking under the pressure, making some rather fundamental mistakes. She's on the run, possibly running low on money, and having to care for the two kids, to boot."

"Dom, don't be so quick to dismiss our *Huntress*," Trellis snapped. "She didn't elude us this long and suddenly decide to show up in Berlin, of all locales, to make her first mistakes. She is up to something..."

"Who did she call?" asked Ellis Redmond, who Trellis had brought along from London.

"First call was to an antiquity dealer she has been known to frequent in Chelsea, one Quindon Sprouse," snapped Dom through his flabby, ashen cheeks. "We think she may be reaching out to him to forward funds to her. We are monitoring his business to assess if there are any outgoing shipments to Berlin."

"You have the call from Fort Meade or not?" barked Trellis.

"Yes, Sir, we have the call playback, but we thought they could have been using a pre-arranged code, something around the word *'Osiris'*. I doubt that she has taken a sudden interest in Egyptian mythology under her current situation."

"Dom, will you stop giving me your *f**king* conjecture and play the damn tape."

Dom played the audio through the overhead speakers. Trellis strained to remain emotionless as he heard Diane questioning Sprouse on the origin of the *"Osiris"* myth. Jack Trellis knew now for sure that Stanley had passed on to her his greatest secret.

The audio stopped. Ellison Redmond was the first to speak.

"I would say she thinks she is onto something. And as the DDO has stated, she is no novice. She knew this call would be picked up, that we would be listening to it. She is sending someone in this room a message, I believe."

"She thinks she is sending me a message," said Trellis coldly. While Trellis had shared many secrets with Ellison Redmond over the years, *the Osiris Fund* was not one to which his former adjutant was privy.

"Who else did she call?" asked Trellis sharply.

"She tried to reach Preston Amesbury, editor of *The Westminster Conservatoire*," said Reeves.

"I know who the *f**k* he is, Dom," exploded Trellis. "Play the audio."

Reeves cheeks had gone from ashen white to a brilliant red, contrasting with his whitened matte of coarse thick hair.

"There is no audio, Sir. Her call went to voicemail, then she hung up," said Reeves.

"Doesn't matter, Sir," added Ellison, "the Brits have Almesbury under close surveillance. We will know if she tries to reach him in any way."

"Final call was to Malcolm Devereaux. She asked him to come to Berlin. Needs to see him along the *Spreekanal* in the *Kupfergraben* district Friday night at 10:45 PM."

"Did he take the call?" asked Trellis.

"No, it went to his office after hours. Recorded on voicemail. He was already *en route* here with Chartwell by then. He picked it up when they got to Berlin," said Dom.

"Again, Sir, Diane is knowledgeable enough to know that call would have been intercepted by the NSA, and most likely by GCHQ as well," interjected Redmond.

Trellis looked at the two men, with an anger brewing inside him. "She knew exactly what she was doing. She knew we would have it soon enough. She asked for a meeting with Devereaux, but what she really wants is a meeting with me. Where are they now, Chartwell and Devereaux?" asked Trellis.

"Berlin Embassy, Sir, theirs. Apparently, Mr. Chartwell is very busy since he took over as the interim Chief of Service for MI6," answered Reeves. "They are due here, in the *Blind*, tonight, in just a little over an hour."

Trellis was again about to reprimand Dom for telling him details he already knew but didn't waste his breath. Trellis had made his play, and the result of which was the announced immediate retirement of the Chief of MI6.

While it was publicly announced as being due to health concerns, Trellis knew it was because of the fiasco, masterminded by Chartwell, that took Carlyle's life in London. However, Trellis was able to manipulate the details such that the CIA threw its full weight of recommendation for Chartwell to be named the successor. Indeed, the Service had done just that to appease the Americans, but at this point only in an interim capacity.

"Has Malcolm told us about this call?" asked Trellis.

"Short answer is no. Perhaps he is not aware you requested

a voiceprint scan for calls originating in Berlin? It is a rather bold gamble, Malcolm not making us aware of this, don't you think?" Redmond was watching his boss closely now, gauging the movement of his every facial muscle.

"I think we need to determine which side our Mr. Devereaux is playing for?" said Trellis. "Besides, his play is no more audacious than our tracking Diane here without notifying the German services. If Diane wants to have a rendezvous, then so be it. We'll give her one."

"Dom, do we have a bearing on where the calls originated from?" asked Redmond.

"Residential area, not far from the *Alexanderplatz*. We are watching it closely.

<hr />

An hour later, Trellis and Redmond had been joined by Chartwell and Devereaux. Dominic Reeves was no longer in the *Blind*.

"First, thank you both for joining us here in Berlin," started Trellis. "We are closing in on Diane and her team, and I think it best we do this as a joint operation."

"Interesting," said George Chartwell. "Why would you want MI6 along with you for the apprehension of a team of AWOL agents?"

It was Ellison Redmond who spoke next. "*Chief* Chartwell, I am sure that you have been quite successful to date in keeping your harboring of Diane over the past six months from your Service's leadership. Now that you are your Service's leadership, it would prove an inopportune time for that story to emerge."

Chartwell did not respond, but merely removed his spectacles and wiped them in the handkerchief he had taken from his pocket.

"What Ellison is trying to say, George," said Trellis, "is that since you are now, thanks to us, the *Interim Chief of Service*, and in consideration with our backing to be made permanent, well, now is not the time that you would want those deciding on this to know either that you personally hid Diane from us, or that you yourself ordered the killing of an American agent in London. So, as I said, we need your cooperation."

"You shall have it, John. So, you shall," said Chartwell, "providing no further harm comes to her."

Trellis looked at both Chartwell and Devereaux before moving his glance to Ellison Redmond.

"Well, now, George, how can harm come to a dead woman? Remember the DCI has already written her off as lost in action."

Now, Malcolm Devereaux interjected. "The point in fact is that Diane is neither dead nor lost …"

"Thanks to your mending her wounds," interrupted Trellis. "Mr. Devereaux, it appears you have a host of secrets regarding Diane. Including your symbiotic connections to Preston Almesbury. We know that you were the source of the articles published questioning if Stanley had been unnecessarily killed. As well as those questioning the disappearance of Diane Sterling. You fed this stream of crap to Almesbury to publish as disinformation. The American press picks it up and I get rewarded with a Senatorial inquiry into the matter. Which I need like a splinter in my ass right now!"

Trellis' voice increased in volume, exploding over the last several words.

"Well, that's a visualization I need never to draw on again," said Chartwell in a flat, succinct voice. "We will assist you, John, but as of yet, we don't have any information on Diane's whereabouts in Berlin. For all we know, she may not even be in the city."

"Care to bring your *Chief* up-to-date?" asked Redmond, looking across the room at Devereaux.

"Malcolm?" asked Chartwell, looking at his trusted subordinate.

"In point of fact, Sir, Diane had left a message on my office phone proposing a meet tomorrow night," Devereaux said, flushed with the embarrassment he had brought upon them both.

"Yes, right, I do recall you mentioning it," lied Chartwell. "How inconvenient of me to forget."

"You two are both full of shit," snarled Trellis. "Despite that, Mr. Devereaux will meet Diane as requested. Then, to keep things on an even keel, Devereaux will bring her to a meeting with the four of us. I will get what I need from her. You both (at this, he pointed at Chartwell and Devereaux) will be there to assure no harm comes to her. And Ellison will be there as my witness."

"And what exactly do you plan to do with her, John?" asked Chartwell.

"Well, what I will not do is pick up the Hauptmann and Czystowska kids until you signal me that you have Diane. Then, I am only going to scare the hell out of her, get any information that Stanley may have passed on to her, before putting her pretty little ass back on a plane to the States to answer for abandoning her station."

"Abandoning her station! You have an unlimited imagination. Your man nearly blew her head off. Then, you plan to charge her with abandoning her responsibilities? Incredible. I cannot standby and allow these levels of hubris and cowardice to go unchallenged," objected Devereaux.

"Oh, you will allow it, my dear Mister Devereaux. May I remind you that the official reports state that she was shot by Wisniewski, not by our security team. She returned fire, striking him in the leg, before our agency sniper took out Stanley. Diane fled, and we only now have found her."

Jack Trellis was calm, and in command of himself.

Devereaux was not. "I saw those wounds. That massive damage wasn't made by Stanley's 9mm, even at point blank range. You may think you can fool your superiors, but we all here in this room know what really happened in Pere Lachaise."

It was George Chartwell who spoke next, after giving Malcolm Devereaux a glance suggesting he lower his level of antagonism to the Americans.

"Come now, Malcolm. Let us not allow our emotions to bleed into this discussion. I am sure that even if Deputy Director Trellis' explanation was rather airtight, I would say that the only snag in the weaving would be that Diane knows none of this is true," said Chartwell.

"You'll have an incredibly hard time convincing her otherwise."

"That's my problem, now isn't it?" said Trellis somewhat defiantly. "Besides, after our agency PSYCHE team get through with her, who will be able to tell what she'll remember?"

"And should we interject and admit that we nursed her back to health, during which she told us a different truth," Chartwell now said, looking intently at Devereaux, "then the CIA will simply say we were interfering in their operation..."

Devereaux then picked up on the thread laid out by Chartwell.

"...and that would mean that the Interim Chief of Service had lied to the Service's leadership many times about concealing Diane. Then, the Interim Chief of Service is dropped from consideration as permanent Chief of Service. How nicely you have thought through this, Jack."

"Thank you, Malcolm." said Trellis, smiling at the recognition of his efforts in entrapping them both.

"I do have one last question for you, Jack. You certainly have no fondness in your heart for Preston Almesbury, given his critical publications of the CIA. Keeping that in mind, who exactly is the woman who goes by the name Collette Corbeau you have shadowing him day and night?"

"I don't know what the *f**k* you are talking about, Malcolm," said Trellis.

"Come, now, Jack. We're friends once again, remember. Allies. The special relationship, all that froth. You can tell us the truth, Jack," Devereaux continued.

"Two things I learned in my forty-plus years in this game, Malcolm. First, friends are a liability, so don't keep any. Second, the truth is a valueless commodity."

A silence came over the room. They all knew that the meeting was then over.

Jack Trellis stared at Devereaux and Chartwell. He knew he had them both exactly where he wanted them. He also knew that he would have them both eternally entrapped when he permanently silenced Diane in their presence.

Trellis then thought to himself, I will deal with Preston Almesbury when the time is right.

——————⊃《◉》⊂——————

Friday morning arrived. Emory Hauptmann was followed as he left Treva's apartment. He was followed by a joint British and American team which surveilled him as he walked to the *Alexanderplatz*, boarded a S-bahn subway train beginning a Surveillance Detection Run, or SDR. He made several stops, assuring himself he was not being followed, before proceeding to the *Stasi* HQ and Museum in the *Lichtenberg* district of Berlin.

He did not detect the joint surveillance team, who then followed him to his destination. He was observed inside the facility, accessing the public portion of the *Stasi* files.

An hour after Emory had left the apartment, Sophie departed as well. She made no attempt to hide her travels. She also walked to the *Alexanderplatz*, where she boarded a train to Berlin's massive, main train station, The *Hauptbahnof*. It was within this elegant glass postmodern structure that Sophie purchased a sightseeing ticket on one of the many cruise boats along the *Spree* river. It was a short walk to the loading zone in the *Spreebogenpark* across the river.

She was also followed, of course, by a second joint surveillance team although a single sidewalk agent could have just as easily followed her. Sophie was neither trained, nor naturally adept, in the art of counter-surveillance.

Sophie rode the river tour line along the *Spree* for an hour, then departed for an outdoor lunch along the open grassy grounds of the *Spreebogenpark*. This green space, an extension of the massive park known as the *Tiergarten*, once featured gently sloping hillsides which bowed gracefully to the banks of the *River Spree*. Today, its beauty was scarred with an over-utilization of post modern concrete walls, ramps and walkways. From where Sophie now stood, she was nearly in the shadow of the *Reichstag* building, just beyond which once ran the Berlin Wall.

Diane did not leave Treva's apartment that day. While she was sure the agency knew of her approximate location from her earlier calls, the apartment in which they had been sequestered for days now, was merely one of thousands within this Soviet-style apartment block. Within its walls, Diane sent a series of steganograhically en-coded photos over the internet to various individuals. She realized these very well might be her last communications ever sent.

For the rest of the afternoon, neither Emory or Sophie left their assigned posts. Emory continued to nose through the files of the *Stasi*, and Sophie continued to tour along the *River Spree*, inter-mixed with sitting along its open banks.

"Do we pick them up?" Redmond asked Trellis.

"Not until later tonight, just before we crash Devereaux and Diane's little meeting along the canal. Once Diane is in our grip, we move on those two."

Figure 10: Along the Spreekanal

(Photo Credit: Wikipedia Commons)

24

KUPFERGRABEN

That evening at sunset, Diane left Treva's apartment for her meeting with Devereaux. She was on edge as she walked the relatively short distance through the darkening streets of Berlin's *Mitte* district, ultimately taking her to the *Spreekanal* – the site of Trellis' taking of *Erasmus'* life, as well as his corruptive manipulation of Stanley's freedom.

She watched for anyone who might be a threat to her. The shadows crept longer as the late June sun had just dipped behind the city's skyline. Soon, the demons of the night would be upon her, of that much she was sure. She remembered Stanley, and what he had done for her, and she knew it was her responsibility – no, rather her duty – to face Jack Trellis tonight. For she knew, while she had left to meet Malcolm Devereaux, he would ultimately deliver her into the hands of Jack Trellis.

The *River Spree* meanders as it travels through Berlin. It snakes from East to West, even shedding its skin around the area known as Museum Island. The river itself flows boldly just to the east of this mass of land; its "skin" is the L-shaped *Spreekanal* encircling Museum Island to the west.

The island earned its name for the numerous museums that reside upon it. In fact, at its northwestern tip, the river and canal re-converge around one of Europe's great museums - the Bode Museum - to again form a single flow. Just beyond this point to the west is the famous, perhaps infamous, Reichstag building. To the east of this structure once ran the certainly infamous Berlin Wall.

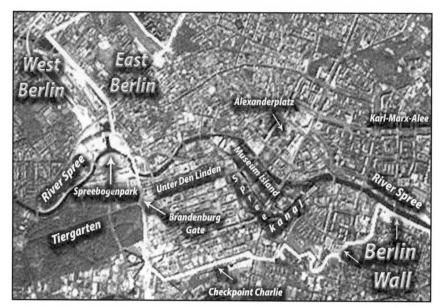

Figure 11: Map of Berlin

Image Credit - David Trawinski (made from en.wikipedia.org)

Along the northernmost end of the *Spreekanal*, is the area known as *Kupfergraben*. Here the avenue alongside the canal is named *Am Kupfergraben*, and the area has undergone substantial modernization since Berlin's reunification. Burgher houses, five and six stories high, now gleam in their mustard and bronze colored exteriors, as they overlook the canal gazing onto the Bode and Pergamon Museums across its waters.

Between these two museums runs a series of railways slicing across the norther tip of Museum Island. The bridge upon which they cross the *Spreekanal* is elevated high above the avenue *Am Kupfergraben*. Along this avenue, under this bridge, was the site where Diane had requested Devereaux to meet her. Only yards away, lay the boat launch in the canal, the site of Stanley's story, his secret revealed to her in the stillness of the first hour of Christmas in Paris' Pere Lachaise Cemetery.

Diane walked along the canal, her steps echoing off the street which was as empty as her future. Yet, she felt the comfort of Stanley walking astride herself. He would provide her the strength she needed to face Jack Trellis.

Diane soon heard a familiar voice call her name from under the rail bridge, just as a figure had emerged from the shadows behind a row of parking ticket machines.

"Diane, Darling, it is so good to see you again. We were terribly worried for you."

The voice was that of her charming *"Mad Mal"*. What Diane did not know, is that his welcome to her was electronically transmitted to waiting teams of MI6 and CIA agents across Berlin, declaring now that Diane Sterling had shown herself, they could move in on Sophie and Emory.

——————➤((◉))⬅——————

Sophie was totally immobile, as still as the concrete bench upon which she sat in the *Spreebogenpark* along the river. She looked at her watch, 10:45 PM. She had been here for several hours, watching the tourists and the river flow past her. The park was unusually alive this late Spring evening in mid-June, as the full cover of darkness was only now settling in. As Sophie rose to leave, her directions from Diane now fully satisfied, a woman approached her along the promenade. The woman spoke in an agitated German voice to Sophie, but the young Pole did not understand a word of what she said.

Sophie responded in English, "Please. I do not understand you."

The woman continued to rant in German at the young girl.

That is when a young man swiftly came in behind her and grabbed her arm. In Polish, he said to her, "Come with me, *pani*, as I have been asked by Diane to bring you to her."

A depth of fear embedded itself in Sophie. She knew Diane had not made such a request, but was concerned that they now must have apprehended her friend. As the man and woman took her by each arm, Sophie realized the ranting German woman was merely a distraction allowing the young man to approach unnoticed. The three figures then walked along the promenade. She recalled Diane having told her, "If you are collected up by the agency, do not resist. Stay silent. Do not answer their questions. Give them nothing."

The man and woman did not speak to each other. When they had cleared the other pedestrians, the woman who had railed at her in German now said into an unseen microphone in English, "Alpha team is en route with subject A."

Her pronunciation was crisp. Her accent was proper British.

As they followed the river, the promenade split in two. This promenade followed the river under a bridge, but from its inner edge split off a separate walk and stairs which climbed up the grassy hill to the bridge's roadway. which had itself just crossed the *Spree*.

Sophie's captors led her up the outdoor stairway. As they were midway up the steps, a black van pulled smoothly to the curb on the street above. Its side door then slid open like the jaws of a mechanical carnivore to which Sophie would soon be fed.

They proceeded to walk closer to the waiting van. Sophie feared for her safety but remembered that Diane had asked her to stay calm if she was apprehended.

As her two captors placed Sophie into the van, the scene around them became explosively charged with commotion. A black sedan had crossed the road's centerline and skidded dramatically as its front bumper crashed against the concrete curb in front of the van. A second sedan pulled up with less drama behind the van. Both sedans had now very effectively blocked the van in place, denying it any movement, and therefore no ability to escape into the evening's traffic.

Sophie watched the faces of the man and woman who had forcibly escorted her from the park. They had morphed from exhibiting the authoritative air of complete control, to an instantaneously startled look of confusion, quickly replaced yet again by recognition of their loss of situational command.

Men frenetically emerged from the dark sedans, fore and aft, with badges held high in front of them. Sophie could see them swarming, their guns drawn threateningly like insect's stingers. They converged on the van's driver, as well as Sophie's two escorts who still had not yet climbed into the van's open sliding door behind her.

Had the man and woman who had seized her thought of fleeing back into the park, they would only had been met by four additional agents with badges and weapons of their own who apparently had been trailing them. It was clear this take-down of her abductors had been meticulously planned.

Sophie next heard one of the badged agents yell out in heavily German-accented English, "You are all under arrest. We are agents of German Intelligence. You will all come with us. Immediately."

———⸻«◉»⸻———

Across town, Emory Hauptmann had long since departed the *Stasi* HQ in the *Lichtenberg* district. He sat in a café that was readying to close. He drank his beer, as a chubby gray-haired gentleman strolled casually up to his table.

"Hello, Dom," said Emory to his former boss. "I've been waiting for you."

"I'm sure you have, kid," came contemptuously out of his flabby cheeks as he sat himself in the empty chair opposite Emory. Dom's eyes, tired and old, watched the young man's hands closely. "Go ahead, Emory, finish your beer – it likely will be the last one you have for a very long time."

Emory drank deeply. After wiping his mouth with his forearm, he said, "With your two boys over there watching me all night, I almost didn't expect you to show yourself at all."

Dom's self-confidence suddenly drained from his face. He looked to the corner table in the café, where two young German men seemed to be speaking excitedly to each other as they uncharacteristically nursed their beers.

189

It was then that Emory, who had been sure these two were stalking him throughout the evening, realized that he had their professions correct, but their employer's confused.

At that point, an older man walked in from the street, and came directly over to the table where they sat. He laid his hand upon Dom's shoulder gently and spoke softly to them in very heavily German-accented English.

"*Guten Abend*, gentlemen. My name is Werner Gresham. I am with the *Bundesnachrichtendiest*. I am requesting you both join me on a little journey to our Berlin Headquarters for what I fear will be a lengthy discussion. We already have your British friends on their way from the *Spreebogenpark*."

Dom's otherwise red-flushed cheeks drained to an ashen gray, as he recognized the imminent humiliation of defeat. Both he and Emory knew that the BND, or German Intelligence, would be irate knowing that the CIA and British Intelligence were conducting joint operations on its soil, with neither their knowledge nor concurrence. Even if it was only in the act of apprehending two of their own wayward CIA agents.

Werner continued as his own two agents who had been situated in the corner, abandoned their station to come stand behind him.

"We can do this like gentlemen, or I can call in *der Berliner Polizei* should you prefer. Sirens, flashing lights, media — 'the whole ten yards' as you say in your country." Werner Gresham smiled at his use of the American phrase.

Dominic Reeves looked up at him, thinking through his apparently limited options.

"Whole *nine* yards," said Emory, enjoying the irony of the BND outflanking Trellis' team. "Comes from machine guns during the war. Their ammo belts were 27 feet long. The saying is, 'Give them the full nine yards...' That is where it comes from."

"Will you shut up!" barked Dom at Emory.

Werner Gresham ignored Dom's outburst.

"Very interesting, but my English is perhaps not as *goodt* as I think it to be. Now, shall I call out the local authorities?"

"Nein, Nein, Nein," said Dom, *"Wir gehen mit dir."*

Emory almost laughed aloud at Dom's butchered pronunciation, but contained himself to an impudent smile, which embarrassed Dom no less. He said in English to Werner, "Yes, as my old boss here tried to say, we will go with you."

"Darling, you are looking wonderfully well, given your forced flight," Devereaux said to Diane, having turned off his transmitter. He had come fully out of the shadows, and reached out to embrace her, but Diane took a step away.

"Where's Trellis?" The directness of her question surprised Devereaux.

"I don't know what you are on about," he said, his voice still in its semi-theatrical projection.

"I am taking him down tonight, Malcolm," she said. "I only ask that you not get in my way."

"Yes, darling, of course. I assumed as much. So much so, in fact, I have asked George Chartwell to join us to bear witness."

As Malcolm Devereaux said these words, a Mercedes Benz sedan came sedately around the corner. Its rear windows were heavily tinted, reflecting the street lights amid the darkening Berlin night. It kept Diane from identifying its passengers. Devereaux, grabbed her by her arm, and gently guided her toward the rear door as it opened. Diane instinctively resisted, until she felt a searing pain in her recently healed shoulder.

"Come now, Love, we will have a nice chat while we drive. Nothing more," he said, leading her into the back seat of the sedan.

Devereaux was careful not to further damage her shoulder, as he guided her somewhat more forcibly than needed into the back seat, directly behind the driver. The door slammed behind her, and Devereaux then climbed into the front passenger seat. The driver accelerated away with urgency.

"Malcolm, there is no need to be so brutish with Miss Sterling, now, is there?"

Diane adjusted her eyes to the interior, looking next to her at the spectacled George Chartwell.

"My apologies, Diane. So careless his generation can be. At times, I find, insufferably so. After all, the Crown just invested quite a tidy sum in healing that shoulder, didn't it?"

Chartwell was being as gentlemanly as he could, but Diane still sensed she was in danger. She felt alone now, as if Stanley had departed from her alongside the canal.

"Would you mind removing your shoes? Shall we call it professional courtesy? One never knows what tricky gadgets may be embedded in those things, now does one?"

Diane removed her shoes and handed them to Chartwell, who lowered his window and disposed of them into the night.

"I am quite sorry for all the precautions, but I will need to pat you down as well. Nothing personal, my dear. Simply professional protocol."

George Chartwell's hands wandered her torso, hips and legs in as respectfully a manner as he could undertake.

"Am I clean?" Diane asked, knowing the answer.

"Oh, yes, quite so," said Chartwell. "My apologies for the shoes, they were rather lovely. We will reimburse you, of course."

Diane thought of the absurdity of being abducted in the high English style.

"Where are you taking me?" demanded Diane.

"Oh, Diane," began Chartwell, "there are far too many eyes spying upon the *Kupfergraben* for the chat we need to have. Perhaps some place more remote would make the better venue?"

"Why aren't you taking me to your embassy?" snarled Diane.

"We don't require that level of formality, now do we, Dear? Far too much attention given to me these days, I am afraid. You haven't told her yet, have you, Malcolm?" asked Chartwell.

"I am sure she is completely unaware at this juncture," responded Devereaux.

"Well, Miss Sterling, you are now riding beside the Chief of Her Majesty's Secret Intelligence Service. Actually, I owe a great deal of it to you personally. After we took out the beast that your DDO so misguidedly released upon you and Mr. *Vish-NEV-ski*", your agency and mine came to somewhat of an understanding."

"I assumed as much, knowing how Trellis enjoys entrapping his enemies," said Diane, as she watched the streets of Berlin spill into its outer suburbs.

"Quite the contrary, my dear. It was I who entrapped him by tempting him to send his assassin into the streets of London. I hope you don't mind my having used you as bait. At least, the prospect of you, that is. Your Jack Trellis couldn't resist." Chartwell smiled a tight, knowing grin.

"Why not use me?" quipped Diane, "It seems everyone else has..."

Chartwell ignored the sarcastic comment.

"Then, after all we did for your recovery, you turned and abused us despite our generous hospitality. Poor Gerald here almost lost his partner of many years to that nearly fatal overdose of Fentanyl that you and your Sophie administered to him."

It was only then, that she recognized the driver as the paramilitary agent Jerry, who she had better known by the nickname *Jeckle*.

"Oh, don't concern yourself too much, my dear, as Hector was caught in time and is on leave making a full recovery," said Chartwell satirically, as he assumed Diane had never given the security agent a second thought.

Diane whispered, almost beneath her breath, but more to *Jeckle* than Chartwell, "I am sorry, we meant him no harm."

She looked away, thinking of how careless she and Sophie had been.

Jeckle had ramped the sedan onto the Autobahn. In the moonlit night, the suburbs outside her window slowly thinned before yielding to the German countryside.

"I'm rather sorry we can't share with you the same outcome for our dear Dr. Alec Rushe. After administering to you for so many months, he was unfortunately taken by the Cousins at the gates of destiny. I am afraid his skills are now forever lost to us all. Your agency tried to provide him one final deep cover, but we are rather adept at detecting that, now are we not?"

She looked at Chartwell in horror as he smirked at the turn of his own phrasing. A tear ran down Diane's face as she had become very close to the doctor in their months together in the chalet.

"There, there, my dear. I am sorry. I did not mean to burden you with that," said Chartwell. "I am afraid the rigors of my new position have absolutely made me thoroughly insensitive."

"He was a good man," she said before scoffing toward Devereaux, "The best of the lot of you."

"Yes, well, my dear, this business does demand that we take the rough with the smooth, now doesn't it?" said Chartwell. Diane thought him cold and uncaring for being so nonchalant over the loss of the good doctor.

They drove on for some time in silence, deeper into the countryside that had once been East Germany. The last road sign that she saw was for the city of *Frankfurt an der Oder*. Not the more famous, much larger city of Frankfurt, that lay to their west. She realized that they were traveling east, approaching the Oder River that separated Germany from Poland.

Jeckle had successively departed the highway and had driven cautiously along the barren country roads. He then searched for and found a marker, just after which turned down an unimproved set of tire ruts attempting to impersonate a road. The ride became rough, and Diane jostled against George Chartwell, who she had now come to vehemently despise.

The car stopped in a clearing that was nothing more than a gap in the tree line that ran along the river. Another sedan, already there, reflected their headlights as *Jeckle* pulled off into the tall grasses that grew in the open field before the trees. The headlights of their car now turned off, she could not make out the two figures in the darkness. Yet even without being able to see them, she knew they would surely be Jack Trellis and Ellison Redmond.

Devereaux exited from the passenger seat, circling the car, to pull Diane from its back seat. As he did so, *Jeckle* emerged from the driver's seat, carefully assessing the situation before him.

"What the *f**k* is he doing here?" objected Jack Trellis to *Jeckle's* presence. "We agreed to only us four, George."

"Yes, John, we agreed to only *we* four being here tonight," said Chartwell, correcting Trellis' butchery of the Queen's English. "However, given my now elevated position, I brought Gerald along for personal protection, shall we say."

Trellis thought, once again, George Chartwell to be a pompous ass.

"Bring her to me," demanded Trellis, as he motioned with his arm.

Jeckle had taken Diane from Malcolm Devereaux. He patted her down for a second time, more thoroughly, and without the concerns for her privacy that George Chartwell had displayed.

"No weapons, no wire," *Jeckle* said aloud.

She was pulled next by Ellison Redmond to the edge of the bluff that overlooked the river. Having thrust her the last several feet to its edge, Diane remained defiant keeping her back to Jack Trellis, who stood just behind her.

She faced out over the river. Through the darkness, Diane could hear the Oder's waters running swiftly. She could not yet see it as her sight was still becoming attuned to the pale dimness of the moonlit night. Her eyes slowly adjusted, and the width of the river came impressively into view. It was then that she first felt the kiss of a faint, late Spring breeze upon her cheek.

To the north of the bluff, she could make out a copse of trees which grew there. Just to the south, a great willow tree had rooted itself along the river. The drop of the bluff between them was modest, perhaps only seven or eight feet but it fell away into oblivion. Even in only the moonlight, the willow cast a shadow which thickened below her feet. She knew the river turned beneath her, but whether its shoulder was rock or sand, she could not tell.

It was then that the wind kicked up like a spirit. It danced through the great arc of the willow's limbs, which had been bowing in somber respect over the river's edge. Its leaves rustled in a beautifully reassuring whisper upon the wind. It was this whisper that told Diane that Stanley had rejoined her.

She thought to herself the moonlit view was almost beautiful, were it not likely to be the last vestige of countryside she might ever see. Stanley's whisper from the willow died with the wind. The silence reminded her that the life she had been given again by Stanley was now to be spent exposing the utter corruption that was Jack Trellis.

"Diane, it has been so *f**king* long," said Jack Trellis from behind her, "and we have been looking for you so very hard."

She slowly turned in her bare feet to face Trellis. Here toes tightened, grasping the earth, as if somehow it would provide the grip that would keep her grounded in the fury that was about to be released. Diane knew she might not outlive this night, but was steadfast that Trellis had to be taken down.

"I was only resting, Jack, regaining my strength for what was to come next," she said, staring hard into his eyes, delivering her threat. She then broke her stare from him to assess the situation just beyond.

The river now at her back, Diane could clearly see Trellis and behind him were Chartwell and Devereaux. Ellison Redmond had returned to a position just behind them both. *Jeckle* was the farthest out, but no further than twenty yards or so. Both cars were positioned behind them all, and both were now totally dark, so as not to draw any attention to the gathering in this field.

"We are going to have a very brief chat before we take you back to the Embassy," Trellis lied to Diane.

"You didn't bring me out this far for just a private discussion, now did you Jack? You brought me here to silence me."

"You have nothing of interest to say that would require that," he scoffed.

Trellis walked closer to her. Her naked heels were but inches from the bluff overlooking the river. She could not step away from the man who was now imposingly close in front of her.

"It wasn't all that much further upstream from here that your team botched the first hit on Stanley, was it Jack?" Diane needed to get him riled. For while she knew Trellis was a brilliant man, she also detected that if she could stoke his fury, within its raging flames burned the embers of his mistakes that would lead to his downfall.

Stanley had been attacked crossing the Neisse River, which flowed into the Oder, the two rivers defining the border between Germany and Poland.

He had escaped this assault, although just barely.

"Yeah, it was *f**ked up* by the team Dom had in place," Trellis said. "If I would have had time to get Carlyle in place on that tower, I likely would have never needed you, *Huntress*. But I didn't, so here we all are. Besides, your friend Stanley eventually got what he deserved."

"He who lives by the sword perishes by the sword, Jack?" she asked.

"Exactly," he responded. "Stanley believed in Biblical justice, didn't he?"

"Yet, I have raised no weapon against you, and you would have me slain?" she scoffed at him.

Diane looked over Trellis' shoulder to the darkened figures of Chartwell and Devereaux. Even without clearly seeing their faces, she instinctively knew they were anxious. Having delivered their offering to Trellis, they were clearly afraid of what they might be forced to witness.

Diane wondered how committed they were to their alignment to Jack Trellis.

"Look at me, you, I'm the one talking to you!" Trellis screamed at her from inches away.

She looked at him, directly but calmly. The breeze again kissed her face, and Stanley breathed strength into her from the rustle of the willow's leaves.

"I am listening, Jack," she said calmly, breathing deeply.

"We have your two comrades in custody, Diane, and if you don't cooperate with me, their futures look rather bleak."

Cooperate? She thought, *what does he want from me?*

Does he not know Emory and Sophie were in the hands of the German Intelligence by now? Or did the BND fail to act as she had requested?

She then thought to herself, *it doesn't matter. The BND either have them or not. I arranged it with them, but if they did not act, I cannot change that now. Sophie and Emory knew there was danger in my plan and accepted it without fear. I am the one who should be terrified. My life may end at any moment. Trellis could have me killed, here and now, but he still fears what I may know. More specifically, he fears what I have passed along to others.*

"What was the Hauptmann kid doing in the *Stasi* HQ?" demanded Trellis. "What was he digging for, Diane?"

She sensed the strain of tension in his voice. It was then that it came to her. He was afraid. Jack Trellis was fearful of losing all he had so corruptly obtained. Now was the time to stoke his fears.

"He only has you here to trap yourselves," she yelled over his shoulder to Chartwell and Devereaux. "Once you are complicit in my murder, he has leverage over you both, which he will wield over you like an assassin's dagger."

"Shut up!" he said, pulling a handgun from his waistband.

She froze at its sight. He aimed it at her. The moonlight gleamed along its metal exterior. 9mm semi-automatic, most likely with a magazine of fifteen to seventeen rounds, she thought.

"John, you promised no harm would come to her," objected Chartwell tensely.

Again, she thought of Stanley. It was she who had pulled a similar weapon on him in the cemetery. Yet, Stanley remained unafraid, as he knew he had nothing to fear from her. She certainly knew Trellis was very capable of harming her, and even of killing her, but not until he got the answers to his questions. This calmed her.

"He has done this before," she yelled again beyond Trellis to the Brits. "He murdered a *Stasi* agent along the *Kupfergraben* in front of Stanley Wis..."

Before she could finish the name, Jack Trellis had raised his right arm, then brought it down hard in a slashing movement upon her. He had hit her across her left eye with the grip of the handgun, splitting her skin at the edge of her eyebrow. The force of the impact had driven her to her knees, where she uncontrollably whimpered before him.

The river winds rose in protest. The tall grasses of the field swayed defiantly around them. They flailed wildly, suggesting if angered further, they would surely consume these men in revenge.

The willow again sang to her. Its leaves billowed wildly, its low morose moan rose over the river, then ascended into an enchanting bittersweet song, like that of a siren hidden beneath the river's watery depths.

Diane's hands had reflexively covered her face. Through her fingers, blood seeped with each wave of brutal radiating pain. Yet, the melancholy strains of the willow licked at her wounds like a wild animal. It was a salve, not to her physical trauma, but to the heightening fear deep within her. It again allowed her to collect herself.

Still kneeling before Trellis, she removed her hands from her throbbing face, both now covered with blood, showing itself black in the moonlight. She could then see that behind Trellis, Devereaux had his hand out, signaling to *Jeckle,* who had drawn his weapon, to stand down. The tension among the men was ratcheting, and with it the nerves of all tightened as they watched Diane and Trellis, not knowing what was to come next.

As her blood pooled into the dirt beneath her, Diane mustered the strength to raise herself to again look Trellis in the eye. The bleeding left side of her face throbbed in a continuous deep, inescapable pain. As Diane began to stand, she thought of Stanley, raising himself, despite the unbearable pain from the gunshot wound she herself had delivered to his leg, defying his excruciating injury only to stand to meet his certain death.

She raised herself. She lowered her hands from her bleeding

face. She looked Jack Trellis in the eye. She then raised her eyes, again looking beyond Trellis at Chartwell and Devereaux.

"What was Emory doing in the *Stasi* files?" Trellis screamed at her, his gun now repositioned to her midsection. She could feel him reining in the anger that was building within him. She knew it was time to stoke the embers of his fears once again.

"He had to keep Stanley quiet," she ignored Trellis and protested loudly anew beyond him to Chartwell and Devereaux, "because Stanley knew the secret of his corruption, of his insatiable greed!"

Jack Trellis raised his hand holding the gun again, but this time only bluffed a strike at her.

She flinched, but did not cower. The blood ran from just outside her eye, streamed across her face, and collected in tension around her chin. From there, a steady drip leaked in a staccato rhythm upon her clothes.

Yet, she again refused to cower.

"What was Emory Hauptmann doing in the *f**king Stasi* files?" screamed Trellis, his voice warbling on the edge of self-control.

Now, he was losing his restraint, she thought. Now is the time to strip him bare in front of the Brits. She returned her gaze to his eyes.

"You should be more concerned with what he was doing in the apartment for the several days before, Jack," she said loudly.

Diane wiped her face with her bare hand and flung the pooled blood at Jack Trellis accusingly. "You want to kill me, do it! But it's too late to silence me. The truth has already been released."

"What the *hell* are you talking about..." began Trellis. "Shut the f**k up."

"We found your *Osiris Fund*, Jack. It took some doing, because you had it reissued in a new name right after you emptied out *Erasmus'* Swiss account. Six million dollars, Jack. Four more from Poland that you later blamed on Stanley. Ten million dollars, Jack. What did you do with that ten million dollars?"

"I said shut the *f**k* up," Trellis roared, as he thrust the gun in the still bleeding face of Diane. The barrel of the handgun tremored with the rage that now was running throughout Jack Trellis.

"Let her talk, John," came a voice from behind Trellis. It was George Chartwell. "Put down the gun, John."

Malcolm Devereaux made a hand gesture to *Jeckle*, who now moved in order to have a clear line-of-fire at Trellis. The situation had become as incendiary as overdried grasses upon which they stood, awaiting just an isolated spark of lightning.

"The Weimar State Joint Reunification Fund" Diane continued. "The WSJR Fund, that was the name of the reissue, wasn't it? All its holdings were buying up critical buildings in what used to be East Berlin. You made a killing when that side of Berlin was rebuilt after the reunification, didn't you, Jack? Emory found the WSJR fund when he hacked your late father-in-law's financial holdings. WSJR was his biggest fund, by far, with astronomical returns, Jack. The funny thing is that fund did not show up in his portfolio until you took over as his power-of-attorney when he was ravaged with Alzheimer's. That's why the agency never picked up on it. They simply saw your wife's legitimate inheritance and they dug no further."

The nerves of Jack Trellis had now become taut, as the handgun he held inches from her banked wildly, as if a kite fighting the winds of a storm. She decided to continue.

"Then, we had Carter Norris check the Daedalus Destroyer Drone financials. Turns out, every drone sold included a line item valued at $123,000 for Weapon System Jamming Recovery software. WSJR software that actually did not exist. However, for each drone sold, these funds were ultimately routed into the WSJR Fund, and found their way through it into your personal account. So, kill me if you like, Jack, but you got some *'splaining* to do at Langley."

"You are *f**king* bluffing. You don't have shit!" screamed Trellis. His face showed the realization that the enigma of his deepest secrets had been unraveled by Diane and her kids and now were laid bare.

"Not only do I have all this information, but thanks to Emory, both Carter Norris and Preston Almesbury also have all the details," said Diane in a steely voice. "Devereaux showed me how. Simple steganography. Sent all the data embedded in images. Emory made it all happen, simply but effectively. You are finished, Jack."

"Well then, that makes two of us," snarled Jack Trellis. He then raised the gun to the bridge of her nose.

The gun's hard, metallic muzzle was pressed firmly into her soft, tender skin. Diane braced for what came next. Yet, she did not tremble. She stood proud.

The tension had become unbearable for George Chartwell.

"That's bloody well enough, John. I am positively adamant that we begin heading back to Berlin. You are remanded under my custody, now. I demand that you lower your weapon, or I shall be forced to act."

Jack Trellis ignored Chartwell, but knew he was a defeated man. Every secret he had kept hidden deep in the darkness had come to light. He knew that if it was true that his rival Carter Norris already possessed this level of detail, he was not only finished professionally, but would never again be a free man to enjoy the fruits of his "endeavors".

His rage seethed within him. Jack Trellis lowered his voice as he allowed it to spew its acrid vengeance.

"I am going to kill you now, and then watch as your Sophie and Emory are slowly beaten to death," he whispered to her.

Instead of terror flashing across her bloody, swollen face, Jack Trellis witnessed only a stiffened resolve.

"I don't think so, Jack," she said calmly. "By now, they are both in the custody of the BND, along with your CIA and MI6 teams to boot. Go ahead, have Redmond try to contact them..."

"Ellison, check on the collection teams," Trellis bellowed.

As Redmond did so, Diane continued.

"Since I controlled where Sophie and Emory would be, and I knew you would not pick them up until you had me in your grips," she said, "I anonymously alerted German Intelligence that the CIA and MI6 were jointly conducting ex-pat apprehensions and forced exfiltration activities within their territory. I was able to tell them where and when, even including photos of Sophie and Emory as well. You know how they detest not being made aware of these things, Jack. If you check with your teams, you will likely find they are being detained by the BND, as are Sophie and Emory. Which is fine with me. They are safe from you, you bastard."

The delivery of her words was that of an automatic weapon, pulsing round after round before Trellis could even return fire.

He was now seething. "I am going to enjoy killing you, Diane."

What ate at him the most? Was it that Diane had not groveled for her life before him? Perhaps it was the indignity of having been bested by a mere woman.

"You asked about the *Stasi* files, Jack?" Diane responded to his threat. She knew pressing him further might force a mistake on his part, or possible a simple reaction, the twitch of a finger, that might cost her life.

She decided to shame him further, to expose him in front of Chartwell.

"Emory was looking for confirmation that the *Stasi* had recovered *Erasmus'* body from the canal. Ironically, he never found it. No mention of the body, or the belt of gold. He called the apartment from the café, just before I left, asking for *Emmerich* - that was our coded message for his not having found a damn thing - came up empty. If he had asked for *Gunther*, it would have meant he struck gold - literally."

Trellis fumed, knowing if this was true, it provided German Intelligence, and even worse, the NSA, a call record tying Emory to the apartment, and thus, Diane.

She continued, "Could be these were some of the few records destroyed by the *Stasi* in their headquarters before the massing *Ossi* civilian crowds filled the streets and forced them to stop."

All of them knew the history. *The Stasi* had kept tremendously detailed records of their forty years of misadventure. They began destroying their records after the wall fell, but the German citizens mobbed outside the building, demanding they stop. Amazingly, the

Stasi stopped destroying their files, the crowd entered the building, securing the undamaged files for historical preservation.

Diane continued her assault upon Trellis.

"By my assessment, you never really planned that out, did you? You were supposed to give *Erasmus* that gold link belt as a thank you from our government in the *Tiergarten* when he delivered *Osprey*. Since the wall and the border crossings were down, you soon found yourself alone with Stanley and *Erasmus*, so you took advantage of the situation and murdered *Erasmus,* so you could abscond with the whole *Osiris Fund*. You told Stanley if he ever leaked any of this, you would have his Agnieszka killed. When you recalled him back to Langley, you then pinned the missing millions from Warsaw Station on him. When you forced him to retire, you thought you had completed your mission, all sewn up so nice and tidy. All your graft safely waiting for you yourself to retire."

Trellis' face was purpled by a combination of his humiliation and his rage. He still had not removed the handgun from the bridge of her nose.

"No answer from either team, Jack, either ours or the Brits," yelled Ellison. "They very well could have been compromised by the BND."

"The gun, Jack. You need to drop the gun immediately." The voice was Devereaux's now, "Jerry, on your guard."

Jeckle raised his weapon, taking aim on Trellis.

It was then that the tension of the situation forced its first critical error. Ellison Redmond returned his phone to his pocket just as Devereaux had commanded *Jeckle* to take aim to fire. He was repulsed that the Brit would even dare to take aim upon Jack Trellis. Ellison's hands were now only inches from his weapon, and he thought he could draw it unnoticed. Which he did. And he waited.

Diane continued to push Trellis further.

"You just never realized how that threat against Agnieszka ate at Stanley like a cancer, did you? When her plane went down under mysterious circumstances outside Katyń, he was sure you were behind it. Me, I don't think so, might have been pure chance, or perhaps it was the work of the Russians, who knows? I doubt you or the agency were in any way involved, but it lit the flame in Stanley. The flame that raged into the inferno that took Langston Powell's life. I would have brought Stanley in to answer for his actions, but you knew that, and you could not have him telling his tale to anyone. So, you used me to find Stanley, but sent Carlyle to quiet him forever. By then, I knew what you were up to. Stanley passed your secrets onto me. Carlyle was too late. You tried to have him kill us both in the cemetery, but you cocked it up again. Now you're going to pay for the rest of your life. Thanks to Emory's technical abilities, Carter Norris now has all of this to present to the DCI, and I even drafted and sent a tell-all article for Preston Almesbury to publish as well. So, you see Jack, I am no longer needed. Kill me Jack! Go ahead! Pull the trigger, it will make nothing disappear! You are finished, Jack!"

Diane then pushed her forehead forward, so that the barrel of his weapon pressed even harder upon her face.

"You *f**king* bitch," snapped Trellis, who was enraged, but managed to restrain himself from firing his weapon.

The British agent *Jeckle* had all along been searching for an opening to shoot to immobilize Trellis, but feared in his striking him, that Jack might reflexively trigger a round between Diane's eyes.

The tension strained like taut razor wire through that moonlit field; it stretched time itself. Like anything under sustained pressure, the long seconds gave way to an explosive instant.

In that instant, Ellison Redmond decided to protect his boss by pre-emptively firing upon *Jeckle*. Ellison had already drawn his weapon earlier, but had kept it concealed behind his hip. Now he raised it to fire upon the British agent.

Ellison's aim was made wild by his trembling nerves. Despite this he did manage to rapidly squeeze off a round from his weapon. Redmond's bullet struck *Jeckle* in the leg below his right hip. *Jeckle* fell to the ground yet maintained his grip on his own weapon. From the ground, he instinctively returned fire to Redmond. Ellison crumpled without a sound, before his dead weight dropped to the ground with a total loss of any controlled movement.

The guns' dual discharges echoed through the night. There were no residences or other properties nearby to react to hearing them. There were no screams. Only the hollowed echo of the rounds.

However, the noise of the shots and the thud of Redmond as he struck the ground caused Jack Trellis to react out of reflex, if only momentarily, looking over his right shoulder.

Diane seized the moment of his distraction. She moved her head sharply to her right as she brought both hands up onto the gun in Trellis' right hand. Trellis emptied two rounds in rapid succession harmlessly into the night air, but both exploding loudly only inches from her left ear. Her ears both ached instantly with a loud metallic ringing.

Diane still had both her hands on the gun and forced Trellis' arm high into the sky. His third shot rang out in a near vertical trajectory. She was stretched upright upon her bare toes, off balance, as she fought him to control the gun.

Jack Trellis then used his free left hand to drive hard into Diane's recently healed right shoulder. She was driven backward by the searing pain it produced. She felt her balance fail, releasing her into the drop of the bluff. She held onto the gun and Trellis' right hand as long as she could before the acceleration of her fall ripped her hands free from his. She had, in fact, held on long enough to pull Jack Trellis to his knees atop the bluff along its edge.

Diane fell into the darkness cast by the willow. She fell, seemingly in slow motion, not knowing if rock or sand awaited her below.

It was then that she landed into the wet grit of the sands that had lined the river's turn. Her heart was pumping violently, as she lay in a state of near shock, her face throbbing, her ears ringing so loudly she feared they themselves were bleeding. She quickly assessed that she had not been shot and had survived the fall. She knew no bones had been broken. She lay still, fearing what was to come next.

What came next was much like a dream. Off to her left, she could only see the image of the great willow above her, with the moonlight filtering through its rhythmically swaying leaves. She imagined it as Stanley standing over her once again, as he had in the cemetery. The ringing in her ear faded, the throbbing pain in her eye was forgotten. She entered a state of peace, within which she could hear, in her mind, the calming, tender music of Frédéric Chopin.

She knew that Stanley was gone and could not magically reappear to save her yet again. He had been taken, and in her mind, she felt that she was indeed his avenging widow. She had carried on his undertaking, exposing the sins that Jack Trellis had concealed in the darkness so stealthily, dragging them out into the bright light of accountability.

Listening to the music playing in her head, she realized that she was indeed the nocturne's widow. The tender music, which she always thought as mournful, she had since come to consider consoling. It brought upon her a great peace, and tonight prepared her to face her last ordeal.

Diane looked up to see Jack Trellis raising himself from his knees upon the edge of the bluff above her. The music continued to play within her mind's dreamlike state. She saw Trellis raise his weapon to take aim upon her. A muted fear returned within her. Not a conscious fear of thought, but the internalized terror that saturates sense and sinew uncontrollably under threat.

Yet, still she heard the peaceful nocturne play, its somber melody calmed her. Something told her to remain still.

Diane did not hear George Chartwell scream at Trellis, "Don't do it, John! It is over! Thoroughly over!"

She also could not hear Trellis growl in response, "It's not over, yet!"

Diane rested her head back in the wet sands at the water's edge. She closed her eyes and thought of Stanley, awaiting the sniper's round that he knew would grossly disfigure, and instantly kill him.

She opened her eyes to see the willow's leaves frolicking with the river's breath in gratitude...

"Lie still," said Stanley's gentle voice in her head, "it will soon be over."

What Diane had not realized was that Trellis was searching with the barrel of his gun. Just as Diane earlier could not see through the darkness cast by the willow blocking the moonlight, Trellis could not see her laying among the wet sands at the bottom of the bluff.

So long as she did not move, he could not be sure of his aim.

Trellis then steadied and fired his weapon into the darkness. The bullet missed her head by inches, throwing up an eruption of wet sand which she felt rain down upon the skin of her face. However, the flash of his muzzle provided adequate, if only instantaneous, light for him to correct his aim.

Jack Trellis saw her laying in the sands. He adjusted his aim. He began to squeeze the trigger.

Diane knew that he had another dozen rounds in his magazine. They would not all miss. In fact, she knew none would miss now that Trellis had adjusted his aim. She knew his fury was telling him to empty them all into the still figure laying directly beneath him.

Diane heard the weapon fire again. The nocturne's music left her. Her ears restarted their incessant ringing. Her body ached. It was already covered in her own blood from her once more throbbing left eye. The blood mixed with the sand, pooling in her eyes, and she felt nauseous.

The slurry of blood and sand in her eyes precluded her from seeing the muzzle flash. She knew she was close to losing consciousness. Instead, she willed herself, in the second that dragged like an hour, to open her eyes one last time. They burned like fire, yet despite this, she opened her eyes and saw.

She saw a darkness falling over her. The sky, the moon, the willow all were blotted out by it. A great blackness had befallen her.

Then, as quickly as it had come, the darkness passed, and she lay looking into the stars of the vast night sky. Beside her, she felt more than saw, or heard, the thud of that obscuring darkness, that was Jack Trellis' body impact the sand only a few feet away from her. She could hear his ragged, tormented screams of pain, as he had just taken a round in the shoulder from *Jeckle's* 9mm. The momentum had driven his body over the low precipice. Trellis' own weapon, which had threatened her only seconds before, had fired harmlessly above her, before it had flown loose from his menacing grip, and then splashed into the river a few feet behind her head.

Her last sight before yielding into unconsciousness was that of Malcolm Devereaux sliding down the sandy embankment towards her.

Ellison Redmond was dead. Shot through the heart by *Jeckle* at no more than nine yards. The British special operative had known it instantly from the lack of a scream, and the lifeless drop of the corpse.

The unexpected taking of Redmond's life had affected him. *Jeckle*, still laying on the ground, had turned to see Jack Trellis pushing Diane over the bluff. *Jeckle* then had squeezed off a round at Trellis, but Jack, having been forced to his knees by the grip of the falling Diane, had eluded the shot. When Trellis recovered, and raised to his feet, for some reason *Jeckle* uncharacteristically hesitated allowing Jack Trellis one more shot into the depths before him.

"Jerry, fire, damn you, man! Fire now!"

It was Devereaux's audible command that forced *Jeckle* to regain his composure. He aimed and hit Trellis square in the shoulder, just before the DDO squeezed off a second round. The impact of *Jeckle's* bullet slamming into Jack Trellis' shoulder blade twisted him wildly, pitching him from the bluff. Trellis' final shot was a fraction of a second late, and as a result was send wildly, harmlessly into the night.

Trellis' and *Jeckle's* gunshot wounds were serious, but manageable if addressed immediately. However, the group's distance was too far away from the British Embassy in Berlin to have their own medical team respond.

"Shall I call in the local response team, Sir?" Devereaux asked of

Chartwell. "The Germans won't particularly like finding a dead CIA agent and three wounded foreign intelligence agents."

George Chartwell understood that calling in the local medical responders would mean a response by the German Federal Police as well, which in turn meant a serious brouhaha was awaiting them with German Intelligence, the BND. This would most likely cost him his coveted position of becoming the permanent Chief of Service.

"I don't see where we have any real choice in the matter, Malcolm. It will infuriate the Germans when they discover this fracas, but we can't have these wounds wait forever, either, now can we?"

Chartwell removed his spectacles and patted his brow with his pocket handkerchief. Returning the glasses to his face, he added, "I do suppose they might as well receive the best treatment that can be afforded them. Thanks to Trellis' paranoia, 'the gig is up', as they say. Besides, the Germans most likely already have the teams sent to collect Diane's two wayward agents. Any of us, Malcolm, will count ourselves very fortunate indeed to retain any position at all with the Service after this fiasco. Nonetheless, yes, call in the locals, God help us all."

Devereaux then called for an emergency German medical team to be sent to the site, giving the GPS coordinates from his phone. The response was efficient, as all things are with the Germans, and arrived in minutes.

Diane's facial wound was found to be more serious than originally thought. Trellis' cold cocking her with the butt of his weapon was feared to have fractured the orbital socket of her left eye. She also had sustained a severe concussion during the fall. The medics were now expediting her to Berlin for more advanced medical care. Trellis and *Jeckle* were then taken along with her, all three being escorted by the German Federal *Bundespolizei*.

It was only then that Malcolm Devereaux and George Chartwell had given thought to their colleague and internet publisher, Preston Almesbury.

They feared the intent of the woman Collette Corbeau, with whom Preston had shared his life over the last several weeks. Was she there to exact Jack Trellis' revenge? Or had she already done so?

It was Devereaux who spoke next.

"If Jack Trellis was foolish enough to take coercive action on foreigners in Berlin without consulting the German Services, then who is to say he would not be desperate enough to make an attempt on our publisher of record, that is, to assassinate Preston Almesbury."

George Chartwell concurred.

"Yes, Malcolm, I think it is time to send in our team of brothers in MI5. I would certainly hate to have Almesbury come to foul play on some order that Trellis may have given before his gruesome little plan went so terribly awry."

⊸•◦(◉)◦•⊷

In London, Preston Almesbury was enjoying an evening with his intended mistress, Coco Corbeau. Incredibly, for weeks she had managed to avoid his advances. Tonight, he remained hopeful. This evening, they had just returned from a wonderful dinner and were enjoying a bottle of very fine Bordeaux from his cellar.

"I think this vintage displays an exceptional terroir," he said, swirling his glass, attempting to impress his companion from the American South. He had then steadied the glass, watching the rivulets of red wine form along its inside walls, and declared "Most certainly, it has great legs."

She had been glancing at her mobile phone. Apparently, a message of some importance had distracted her.

"Oh, I am so sorry, Sugar. The wine is perfect," began Coco, "but if you want to see some really fine legs, I suggest you join me in a relaxing bath upstairs."

Preston tried not to appear pathetic in his eagerness to agree.

"Well, Darling, I literally thought you'd never ask. I have been waiting for this moment for weeks," he said.

"So have I, Sugar," she purred. "You have no idea how I have been anticipating this."

"Oh, I do suppose the wait has sharpened my senses somewhat," he said.

"Oh, Preston, Sugar. You just have to be a little more assertive with me. It is unfashionable for a woman to throw herself upon a man where I come from."

Preston savored the ripeness of her voice as it melted away into the velvet matte of his expectant ecstasy.

They climbed the narrow stairs of his town house, entering his bedchambers for the first time.

As she drew the bath's waters, the steam danced erotically before it condensed onto the brown marble tiles lining the walls which surrounded the oversized white antique cast iron tub, complete with claw legs.

Preston and she had changed into their robes, and she took the liberty to turn down the linens in the adjoining bedroom. Coco brought forth a small pile of towels from the bedroom armoire where they were stored. She seemed to balance and place them with an almost unexpected reverence.

Preston arched his naked angular frame as he climbed over the wall of the tub before easing himself into its soothing waters. The aromatherapy of the salts that Coco had added eased his last remaining tensions. He drank from his glass of Bordeaux, its bouquet blending with, not fighting against, the therapeutic aroma of the bath.

"Come, darling, take off your robe and join me" he said, his eyes closed in total relaxation, "the water is splendid."

He anticipated her lovely form nestled against him tightly under the warm soothing waters.

"And I shall, Sugar, just give me a minute." Just before saying this, her mobile phone had emitted a sound that Preston had not heard it make in their many weeks together. It was reminiscent of the whoosh of a blade slicing through the air. Coco pressed the phones keypad buttons, as if acknowledging that she had read the text associated with it.

She knew from the sender that trouble was on the way and she must act fast.

She came into the bathroom, positioning her mobile phone upright on the marble vanity, propped it near vertically against the faucet's hot water handle.

The next thing that Preston was aware of was the high pitch of her wine glass shattering upon the tile floor of the bathroom.

"Good Lord, Darling! Are you hurt?" He began to raise himself out of the water.

"Preston, Honey, I am perfectly fine," she said as she came over to him. In reality, she had inadvertently sliced open a wound on her left hand.

She leaned over the tub, and rested her left hand on his shoulder, pressing him back down into the bath. In her right hand, she held the stem of the wine glass, its petals of jagged glass protruding threateningly around it. Preston ignored its menacing sharpness, focusing rather upon her wound.

"My God, Coco, your hand is positively jetting blood. I must call for medical assistance immediately."

Preston began to raise himself out of the tub, only to have the pressure of her left hand push him more firmly back into the bath. Her exertions had spread her trickling blood against Preston's neck and chest, tinting his bath in a rose blush.

"Sugar, Darlin', you need to stay right where you are. Lean back into the waters. There is something about me that you need to know," she said, "and I reckon you're not going to like it."

A look of concern washed over Preston's face. Coco continued to press firmly on his shoulder, pinning him against the tub's porcelained cast iron slope. He now stared at the sawtooth of fractured glass she held in her right hand, her elbow drawn back, he imagined, as if to thrust it into him.

For the first time, he came to fear this woman who he had so foolishly allowed into the deepest recesses of his privacy. He now laid naked before her, defenseless from any ill will she had so carefully hidden from him up to that point.

At that instant, a crash was heard below them, as an assault team breached the front door, and thundered recklessly through

---

213

the ground floor before ascending the stairs. Preston's fear gave way to terror, as he assumed he had been set up by Miss Coco Corbeau.

"Stay down, Preston" Coco said harshly to him. Her voice had flattened, losing the lilting syntax of America's South. She moved the shattered wineglass into her bleeding left hand and reaching into the pile of folded towels at the foot of the bath. Preston became terrorized to see her draw out the revolver she had positioned there.

She stood over him now, revolver in her right hand, her left hand clutching the jaded glass stem, bleeding profusely onto her white robe.

Preston heard the array of intruders climbing the hall staircase. He saw her raise her gun, covering the open doorway to the bedroom. In the vanity mirror, Preston could see three armed paramilitary figures appear in the bedroom door opening. The lead agent pointed his Heckler threateningly at her and took note of her bloodspattered robe.

"Ma'am, I am going to need you to release that weapon and back away from Mr. Almesbury straightaway." The voice was overbearing, and distinctively British. Behind him were two other agents, who began searching the bedroom for additional threats. Each bore compact submachine guns.

Coco Corbeau's face relaxed, its tension eased upon hearing the team's British commands. "Thank God, you guys are MI5," she said, "I have never been happier to see you."

Coco Corbeau lowered her revolver until it pointed at the floor.

"Are you wounded, Mister Almesbury?" asked the lead agent, spotting the blood upon his neck and chest.

"NO, I am in splendid health, thank you," he said harshly. "Please indulge me as to why I have Her Majesty's agents in my home, invading my privacy."

"We were instructed to forcibly protect you from this woman, Sir," explained the lead. His two fellow provocateurs now directly behind him, having satisfied themselves that the woman was the only threat on the premises. "Ma'am, I need you to drop both your weapons, immediately."

"Both weapons?" Corbeau's voice laughed, but now without its American Southern dialect. "Here, take my revolver. As for the other, it isn't a weapon, I merely dropped my damn wine glass."

She handed the revolver over to the lead agent. As she did so, her blood-stained robe opened, and briefly revealed her nakedness beneath it. She could see the agent's eyes wander from the hard threat of the weapon to the soft lines of her femininity. He took the pistol; she gathered her robe.

"Be careful," she teased, "there's a round in the chamber."

"I would never assume anything else, Ma'am," he said boldly.

"Who in bloody hell are you people?" demanded Preston, still naked himself beneath the frothed waters of his bath.

"As the lady said, Sir, MI5 Special Services. Here to protect you, Sir."

"From what, may I ask, exactly, having too exciting an evening at home?" ripped Preston.

"Our information suggested that the madam here was working as a potential assassin for the CIA," the agent said with an authoritative air of credibility.

Preston Almesbury then looked at Coco Corbeau accusingly, remembering her pressing him strongly against the bath, the jagged glass stem threateningly close.

"Coco, how could you?" asked Preston incredibly.

"Oh Preston, if I were an assassin you would not be asking questions right now. And watch who are you calling a Madam, hot shot." She directed at the lead MI5 agent. "In any case, that makes two of us assigned to protect Mr. Almesbury. If you'll check, my credentials in my purse on the bed, you'll see I am a licensed investigator, working on behalf of the United States Senate. You can confirm my credentials through Mr. Paul Renard, lead investigator to US Senator Malinski. I was sent to assure Mr. Almesbury remained secure. We feared there might be rogue elements of the CIA sent to assassinate him. By the way, that cell phone over there is transmitting all this as we speak directly to the offices of Mr. Renard. So please remember to remain professional. You can start by lowering that Heckler."

A second agent moved into the bathroom, removing the battery from the phone. Despite this, the lead agent lowered his sub-machine gun.

"Why then did you have Mr. Almesbury at knifepoint in the bath?" asked the lead British voice.

"To be completely transparent with you," she said while she again gathered her ever gaping robe, "I received a flash notification that a CIA hit squad might be on its way, so I thought the best place for Mr. Almesbury was surrounded by cast iron. I conned him to get into the bath."

She flashed a seductive smile while she gathered her robe tightly, highlighting the bait with which she had lured Preston into the bath.

"I am going to have to detain you both for your own safety tonight,' said the lead agent. "Mr. Almesbury, do you need assistance getting out of the bath, Sir."

"No, I certainly do not. I am not a bloody invalid. Just give me a shred of decency, will you?" *I promise not to attack you with the sharpened edge of a bar of soap*, he thought, but did not say.

"Ma'am, please come into the bedroom and allow Austin to patch up that nasty cut on your hand. He is a premiere medic, I assure you."

"Why certainly," Coco said, returning to her Southern accent. "Preston, Sugar, I am so sorry for all this. Please watch out for those broken shards of glass on the bathroom floor. After all we've been through, I couldn't bear to have you slice open an artery and bleed out, now could I?"

"Coco, Darling, don't you think you've made a big enough fool out of me for one evening?" he scoffed at her.

"Oh, it's been weeks now, Sugar..." she said, correcting him as she walked out to the bedroom, leaving Preston hiding in the bath. He no longer desired her to see his nakedness. What once was enflamed desire had now become only a cold indignity.

At this point, two things became very apparent to Preston Almesbury. First that he was under no immediate threat from either the MI5 team or his mysterious American companion. Second, he would never encounter the sweetest bliss of Coco Corbeau.

25

AFTER-ACTION

Several weeks had passed. Diane found herself back at Langley. The left side of her face was mostly healed, but from certain angles one could see it was still somewhat swollen beneath the heavier than usual foundation she applied. The threat of losing her eye had passed, but the scars of the assault would never leave her.

She had just left the DCI's office. He had personally invited her to return to Langley, so they could meet once again in his seventh-floor office. He began by apologizing profusely for the hell that she had been through. He went on to tell her that the information she had gathered on Jack Trellis was the foundation of a devastating corruption case that was even then being prepared with the assistance of Paul Renard. The DCI assured her that Trellis would also be brought up on charges of murder and attempted murder for the authorization of actions taken against Stanley Wisniewski and Diane, herself.

Trellis remained in custody, and the DCI assured her that it was his personal intent that Jack Trellis would never see the light of freedom for the rest of his natural life.

Diane, in turn, assured him that it was not she, herself, but the team of four, that had uncovered the greed that consumed Jack Trellis.

The DCI looked at her, clearly showing his confusion at the number she referenced...

"Agent Czystowska and agent Hauptmann are still in Europe. I understand they had been reinstated with back pay. Who else did you consider so crucial in all this?"

Diane paused before offering her response.

"Stanley Wisniewski, of course," she stated, knowing the name of a murderer and fugitive would not be welcome in this office. "Without him, we would never have suspected DDO Trellis, who would soon be retiring to enjoy his ill-gotten gains."

She sensed the DCI was now struggling for a response that would not incense her.

"Well, I wish this could have all come to light in a very different manner," he offered. "Now let me get to the other reason, beside the agency's apology, that I invited you here today."

Diane listened, fearing what was to come.

"I would like to place your name in consideration to take over as Deputy Director of Operations, reporting directly to me, of course."

She looked at the man carefully. She respected him. He had always been more than professional with her when she had been called to brief him in the past. His reputation was impeccable. Her mind considered these facts, but it was her heart that answered him.

"It pains me to say, Sir, that I absolutely cannot consider applying for that prestigious posting."

The DCI was stunned.

"You are certainly as qualified as anyone I have ever known to assume that position. Certainly, you are better qualified than any man within the agency today. With your experience, I am sure you would keep an eye focused to cleaning up any residual abuse within the agency of which you might became aware. Diane, this would be the apex of an already stellar career. I ask you to please reconsider your response."

She had lowered her head as he spoke, then raised herself to look deep into the man's eyes.

"I am honored by your confidence in my abilities, Sir. However, I can no longer work for the agency that tried to kill me. Not once, but twice."

"That was not the agency, Diane, that was the warped mind of Jack Trellis."

A pause left unspoken between them indicated that Diane made no such distinction.

"Are you telling me that you cannot work for the agency in the role of DDO?" asked the Director.

"In any capacity, Sir. I have come to Langley at your request, but also with the full intention to tender my resignation," Diane responded.

"I can only hope there is some way in which I can change your mind, Diane..."

"You cannot, Sir. I have had many months to consider this, ever since the attack of last Christmas. I am proud of my many years with the agency, of my professional accomplishments, but the lesson I have learned from this episode is that there are aspects to life other than career only."

"Diane, you are making a tremendous mistake. Don't let your emotions ruin what you have accomplished."

"What I have learned from all this, is that a life lived without emotion is a wasted life."

She was paraphrasing some of the last words Stanley had spoken to her in the graveyard in Paris.

He had said to her, "A life that is lived with purpose is never wasted. I fear only for those who have wasted their talents and their passions, for these are God's gifts."

She knew that she had lived a life, up to that point, suppressing her emotions, and these were, she now thought, the greatest of God's gifts. For now, she felt pain, remorse, guilt and love. Love for the man she had so recently hunted. Love for the man who sacrificed himself for her. Not so that she could merely continue living, but more so that she would live a deeper, more meaningful life.

The DCI spoke next. "What will you do, Diane? You are a talented investigator, please don't waste your abilities."

"To the contrary, Sir. Now that my personal financial resources are no longer frozen by the agency..."

"Again, Trellis's abuse of his power..." interrupted the DCI.

Diane paused, then continued "... I plan to open my own firm in the private sector, Sterling Investigations International. I intend to offer Sophie Czystowska and Emory Hauptmann to join me in getting it off the ground. Perhaps we can do some good through that enterprise."

"Diane, if I can't change your mind, then Godspeed to you. However, should you change your mind in the future, know that you always have a home here to come back to."

"Thank you, Sir," she said, extending her hand, which the DCI took warmly in both of his. They shook farewell, and Diane departed the office.

Over the next several days, Diane was officially debriefed on the details of the operation to find Stanley Wisniewski, and the subsequent events of her care under British Intelligence. Before being "read out" of her many project clearances and "need-to-know" status, she was informed by her contacts within the agency that George Chartwell was now sure not to be named the permanent Chief of Service for MI6.

He must have realized that night that allowing Jack Trellis to entrap him into witnessing Diane's impending murder along the banks of the Oder would have been a fate far worse than the disgrace he would ultimately suffer by stopping Trellis that night.

At least he had tasted the power of the position, signing his initial in the green ink of tradition. Now, having tasted the sweetness of obtaining his ambition, George Chartwell would only have it sour upon his palette.

Diane wondered about Malcolm Devereaux. Would he retire to his wife Pet's inherited estate, *Millhaven*, in the Cotswolds? No, Diane always knew Malcolm to be a survivor, and she was sure he would survive this fiasco as well.

Over the next several days, Diane processed out of Langley. She was slightly terrorized at the idea of starting anew, her having had this as her only real job since graduating from Princeton. Yet, another side of her was energized by the challenge of going out upon her own, to build from nothing something meaningful and lasting with nothing else than her abilities. No longer would she merely analyze the actions of others or be called upon to hunt the trails of the condemned. She would determine her own path forward.

On her last day, leaving the Langley facility for the final time, the sun's rays cut brightly through the lobby of the complex. As Diane passed the iconic seal of the CIA embedded in the marbled floor, she paused.

She reflected on her good friend and mentor, Stanley Wisniewski. She then told herself that this was how she would always remember him. Not as the fugitive that she had hunted. Not as the man who gave his own life to save hers. She would always have Stanley, her friend and mentor, with her.

She remembered, early in her career, during the days of preparing for Project INDIGO, Stanley reciting the story his own father had shared with him as a child.

He told of the Polish squadrons that flew with the RAF during the Battle of Britain. Driven from their native country by the Nazi's, they had become among the fiercest of all flyers engaged against the *Luftwaffe* over the English Channel. They would close in on the German aircraft at near point-blank range before tearing them asunder with their guns.

At the time, Diane had thought the story was the understandable exaggeration of the pride of a Polish World War II survivor. That was, until she accessed the archives and personally went over the statistics. Not only did she find the overall story to be true, it was understated. For the Polish 303 "Kościuszko" squadron had the highest number of kills of any air squadron of those engaged in this historic battle.

However, the most impressive part of the story was not that. It was the banner under which they flew. It had been sewn, at great peril, by the women still entrapped within their vanquished home-land and smuggled out to their brave young men facing yet a sec-ond onslaught of the feared *Luftwaffe*.

Yet, it gave those pilots great resolve. For the banner under which they flew, in the exiled defense of their homeland, bore, in the native Polish tongue, the simple but most inspirational motto:

"Miłość żąda ofiary"

which translates to

"Love Demands Sacrifice"

AUTHOR'S NOTE

There are, in our times, great treasons that have been undertaken against the state. In my last book, I tangentially examined the betrayals of Aldrich Ames of the CIA and Robert Hanssen of the FBI, by dealing secrets to the Soviet and Russian states.

In "*War of The Nocturne's Widow*" I examine the reverse case. My fictional character "*Osprey*" is a Polish spy within the General Staff of the Polish leadership.

While *Osprey* is fictional, his character is based upon the real-life CIA asset codenamed *Gull*, who was indeed a Colonel on the Polish Army's General Staff. His name was Ryszard Kukliński, and he spied for the CIA from August 1972 through the initial days of November 1981, exiting just before the establishment of Martial Law in Poland.

As *Osprey* is fictional, I have shifted his dates of CIA service, as well as the details of his extraction from Poland to fit the timeline of my tale. However, the spy Ryszard Kukliński that served the American CIA, like *Osprey*, did so for virtually no payment.

His family and he were exfiltrated in November of 1981, as the Soviet and Polish Governments were closing in on a mole within the Polish Army who had delivered the plans for martial law to the West. Kukliński, his wife, and their two sons were boxed in Diplomatic crates and driven for over eight hours across Poland and into East Berlin, before crossing over into West Berlin.

Kukliński had delivered some 40,000 pages of highly classified materials. His efforts have been credited with easing the possibility of nuclear war in Europe during this period and beyond, as he continued to serve in an advisory role to the CIA and US military.

In Poland his role is, to this day, contentious. He was viewed as a traitor and sentenced to death in absentia by the communist government. His sentence was eventually overturned after Poland once again became a free republic in 1990. However, his role is still a source of controversy – was Ryszard Kukliński a traitor or patriot?

One can only look to his motivation. From his knowledge of Soviet war planning, of which he had tremendous access, he knew that his country of Poland would become a nuclear wasteland in an exchange between the NATO and Warsaw Pact forces.

Kukliński died in 2004 near Tampa, Florida. He had become an American citizen. Before dying, he did have the opportunity to return to a restored free Poland, where he was both warmly received and heavily criticized.

Today, Ryszard Kukliński's body lies in a military graveyard in Warsaw. It is often both decorated with flowers and defaced in graffiti.

I view this man as a hero to the world, and specifically to the Polish state. I think it is only fitting that he arrived in the United States after his exfiltration from Poland on November 11, 1981.

This day is celebrated in the United States as Veteran's Day, and in Poland as Independence Day. The latter marks the resurrection of the free state of Poland on the eleventh hour of the eleventh day of the eleventh month of 1918, after its shamefully having been wiped from Europe's map for over 123 years.

On the rememberance of this day of independence, Ryszard Kukliński started his new life in America. How very appropriate. How so very wonderfully appropriate!